J. B. Priestley

Sir Michael and Sir George

A Tale of
COMSA and DISCUS
and the New Elizabethans

GREAT ✦ NORTHERN

First published in Great Britain by
William Heinemann Ltd 1964

This edition published 2020 by:
Great Northern Books
PO Box 1380, Bradford, West Yorkshire, BD5 5FB
www.greatnorthernbooks.co.uk

ISBN: 978-1-912101-43-6

Design by David Burrill

CIP Data
A catalogue for this book is available from the British Library

For more information contact
the J. B. Priestley Society at jbpriestleysociety.com

J. B. Priestley was born in Bradford in 1894. He was educated locally and later worked as a junior clerk in a wool office. After serving in the army throughout the First World War he went to Trinity Hall, Cambridge before setting up in London as a critic and renowned essayist. He won great acclaim and success with his novel *The Good Companions*, 1929. This and his next novel *Angel Pavement*, 1930, earned him an international reputation. Other notable novels include *Bright Day*, *Lost Empires* and *The Image Men*.

In 1932 he began a new career as a dramatist with *Dangerous Corner*, and went on to write many other well-known plays such as *Time and the Conways*, *Johnson Over Jordan*, *Laburnum Grove*, *An Inspector Calls*, *When We Are Married*, *Eden End*, *The Linden Tree* and *A Severed Head* which he wrote with Iris Murdoch. His plays have been translated and performed all over the world and many have been filmed.

In the 1930s Priestley became increasingly concerned about social justice. *English Journey*, published in 1934, was a seminal account of his travels through England. During the Second World War his regular Sunday night radio *Postscripts* attracted audiences of up to 14 million. Priestley shored up confidence and presented a vision of a better world to come.

In 1958 he became a founder member of The Campaign for Nuclear Disarmament and later in life represented the UK at two UNESCO conferences.

Among his other important books are *Literature and Western Man*, a survey of Western literature over the past 500 years, his memoir *Margin Released*, and *Journey Down a Rainbow* which he wrote with his third wife, the archaeologist Jacquetta Hawkes. J. B. Priestley refused both a knighthood and a peerage but accepted the Order of Merit in 1977. He died in 1984. His ashes were buried near Hubberholme Church in the Yorkshire Dales.

Introduction

When we were wondering which other of my father's novels we should suggest to our publishers, Great Northern Books, I recalled a conversation with my late stepmother, my father's third wife, Jacquetta Hawkes. I had asked her which of his novels were her particular favourites. She quickly responded by naming the two 'comic' novels, *Low Notes on a High Level* and *Sir Michael and Sir George*. This memory encouraged me to suggest both books and have a closer look at the dates involved, though it is sometimes hard to guess the time for the actual writing of a book from the publication date.

J.B. and Jacquetta first met in 1947. She was a Civil Servant, Principal at the Ministry of Education, and secretary to the British delegation to UNESCO, while my father had been selected as a delegate representing Literature, Drama and the Arts. But he never stopped writing. Nor, in the event, did she. In October 1946, his best-known play, *An Inspector Calls,* finally opened in London, and in August 1947 so did *The Linden Tree*, prior to the UNESCO gatherings in France and Mexico. Jacquetta's best-known book, *A Land*, was published in 1951, while his charming short essays in *Delight* had come out in 1949. In 1952 they visited Japan together, and afterwards New York, then combined to write the platform play, *Dragon's Mouth*, and toured with the cast around the UK. They then co-wrote *The White Countess*, but that play was a failure. In 1953 they each divorced their respective spouses and were married in July. In 1954 J.B. published *Low Notes on a High Level*, while Jacquetta published *Man on Earth*. Then in 1955 they collaborated on *Journey Down a Rainbow*, an exchange of travel letters about the southern States. And in 1959 they moved to Kissing Tree House near Stratford on Avon, which remained their home till my father's death in 1984. *Sir Michael &*

Sir George was published in 1964, and one wonders how many of the details about goings-on in the two rival cultural organisations derived from Jacquetta's own experience as a senior civil servant.

Tom Priestley is one of Britain's most highly acclaimed film editors. He won a BAFTA in 1967 for his work on the now cult classic Morgan: A Suitable Case for Treatment *and was Oscar nominated in 1972 for* Deliverance *directed by John Boorman. He has worked on numerous prize-winning films with many talented film-makers including Karel Reisz, Lindsay Anderson, Bryan Forbes, Michael Radford, Jack Clayton, Blake Edwards and Roman Polanski. He now spends his time more in the world, lecturing on film editing and promoting his father's life and work. He is both President of The Bradford Playhouse and The J. B. Priestley Society.*

Sir Michael and Sir George

A Tale of
COMSA and DISCUS
and the New Elizabethans

J. B. Priestley

Author's Warning

This is the sort of novel in which it would have been temptingly easy to introduce portraits or caricatures of living persons. I have been at some pains to avoid doing anything of the kind. The characters who move in and out and around COMSA and DISCUS are as fictitious as they are, all creatures of my invention. Coincidence may have too long an arm to be always successfully warded off; but I can state emphatically that, from Sir Michael and Sir George down through the cast of characters, I have never had in mind any person of my acquaintance—or of yours, dear reader.

J.B.P.

1

SIR GEORGE STARED for a moment or two at his tall windows overlooking Russell Square. Out there the April afternoon was fussing away with its rain and glitter. With a reluctance he hoped he did not reveal, for he believed in courtesy and still fought hard beneath its shot-torn velvet standard, Sir George attended again to his American visitor. 'I'm sorry, Mr Bacon. You were saying—?'

Mr Franklin Bacon was in Europe on a grant from the Lincoln Applebaum Foundation, to write a treatise on state assistance to the arts. He was a tall wide young man, carelessly put together, and with a face so apparently innocent of experience that it might just have been unpacked—factory-fresh. His voice suggested a very remote fog-signal, and was difficult to listen to with any interest.

'I was just saying, Sir George, sir, that I don't rightly understand the difference between this Department of Information and Cultural Services of yours—'

'We call it DISCUS, Mr Bacon. Saves time.'

'Surely. Well, I still don't rightly understand the difference between your department, DISCUS, and this National Commission for Scholarship and the Arts—'

'COMSA It's known as, Mr Bacon.'

'Yes, sir, that's what I've been told. Well, sir, as I was saying—'

But Sir George cut neatly through the fog-signals. 'By the way, have you by any chance seen my opposite number at COMSA—Sir Michael Stratherrick?'

'No, sir. So far I've failed to contact Sir Michael Stratherrick.'

This reply annoyed Sir George, and for two good reasons. First, it proved that COMSA and its director had been tried first, therefore given the preference. Secondly, it made plain the fact that the artful Stratherrick knew how to dodge these tedious fellows. Or that his staff knew how to protect him. Which was more than Sir George could say about his DISCUS people, who had somehow left him wide open to this Bacon. A stiff memo, perhaps: *The Secretary-General hopes it will be clearly understood—*

11

'Let me explain about DISCUS and COMSA,' Sir George heard himself saying. 'They don't entirely overlap. We here at DISCUS are responsible for certain important information services with which COMSA has nothing to do. On the other hand, it's only fair to say that there are some minor matters of scholarship that are—er—COMSA's pigeon, not ours. But as far as the arts are concerned—yes, I know; that's precisely what you're investigating: you told me—the two organisations have very similar functions.'

'How come?' Mr Bacon's eyebrows nearly reached the edge of his crew-cut.

'You mean, we can't need two separate organisations. You're quite right, Mr Bacon. Anything COMSA does for the arts can be done better—I won't tell you why, but there are good reasons—by us here in DISCUS. It's an absurd situation, of course. What happened is a long story, and I won't bore you with it now. But—'

Sir George paused here, lowering both his voice and his head. On these occasions he could do little with his face, which was large, still handsome in all its features, but now melting and running a little, as if one of the nobler Roman emperors had been modelled too quickly in some softish, pinkish substance. It was a face that could express surprise, non-comprehension, indignation, complacency, and a modified enthusiasm, but nothing conspiratorial. So at these times his voice had to do all the work, and now it was almost ventriloquial.

'Between ourselves, Mr Bacon, the whole thing dates back to a time—only two or three years ago, actually—when the Lord President of the Council and the Minister of Education weren't on speaking terms. And while the Minister was setting up this department, DISCUS, the Lord President—not the present one, his predecessor—insisted upon creating COMSA, unnecessary then and absurdly redundant now. A great deal has been said, of course—anybody badly in need of a joke never forgets us—and sooner or later one of us will have to take over the other. It's said the P.M. amuses himself resisting any pressure to decide between us. So there we are, Mr. Bacon.' Sir George gave this a full warm tone, as if making an unusually generous admission.

'And what would you say, Sir George, sir, were your precise responsibilities and dooties?' Mr Bacon had brought out a notebook, shiny and handsome, probably a present from the Lincoln Applebaum Foundation. 'Not personal but those belonging to your department.'

As if Mr. Bacon had hit some bull's-eye that set him going, Sir George began nodding rapidly. 'I'm glad you asked that. Very glad indeed. Because this is what I'm going to do, Mr Bacon. I'm going to hand you over to Miss Walsingham, who's in charge of our public relations. Has the whole thing at her fingertips. Ask her anything you like.' He frowned at the inter-com. 'Secretary-General here. Ask Miss Walsingham to come along to my room.'

Mr Bacon flicked over the pages of his notebook, like a conductor trying to catch up with the orchestra. 'I read a piece in *Time* magazine where it said that COMSA, from the point of view of the strictly contempor*airy* arts, was way ahead of you people here in DISCUS.'

Sir George replied from a chilly height. 'I've no idea what—er— *Time* magazine would call strictly contemporary arts. We have certain standards here. Naturally we don't encourage mere charlatans, mountebanks. But you ask Miss Walsingham. She knows all about that kind of thing.'

'What kind of thing?' Mr Bacon appeared to be genuinely bewildered; and Sir George, not for the first time, thought how difficult it was to achieve real communication with so many Americans, just because they used the same words but gave them different meanings. Gabbling some rubbish about what Miss Walsingham would be able to explain, he listened anxiously for any sound of her approach. At last—'Ah—good! Here she is.'

It was not often that Sir George welcomed June Walsingham with such enthusiasm. Not that he disliked her. And indeed her work as P.R.O. for DISCUS was excellent. But she puzzled him. She was a handsome blonde, rather larger and more dazzling than life, as if she had just stepped out of a poster or an old-fashioned musical-comedy. She carried around with her, as a planet does its atmosphere, a suggestion of something alien to the interests and purposes of DISCUS, an air of raffish femininity, traces of a world of double-gins-and-tonics at all hours, of Beluga caviare and mounds of smoked salmon off tax, of drunken and lecherous conferences in five-star hotels, of aircraft chartered to take winter sports parties to distant film premieres. And yet, when fact was preferred to fancy, there she was, on a modest salary and a tiny expense account more carefully checked than most prescriptions, one of the most loyal, dutiful and successful members of the DISCUS staff. Not a civil servant of course, as Sir George himself had been now for nearly thirty years;

she had come to them from some vague sort of woman's journalism, exclamation-mark columns about bargains in evening bags and holidays in Spain; but Sir George realised, while he was explaining why he had sent for her, that really he knew nothing about her that was worth knowing.

Now she flashed and sparkled away at him, then coruscated at Mr Bacon, who stood grinning beside her, also more than life-size, even if half-finished, so that they looked as if they were waiting for the cue to begin a waltz duet. They went out happily together, the talk already beginning. Sir George felt nothing but relief. He didn't like Americans; he didn't like young men writing treatises; he didn't like questions; so he was damned glad to be rid of this Bacon chap. And it mustn't happen again. He rang for his secretary, Joan Drayton.

'I don't know how that chap Bacon, the American, managed to barge in here,' he began.

'It was rather difficult, Sir George. I know exactly what happened—'

'Never mind.' He handed her some letters he had signed. 'Only it mustn't happen again, Joan. Can't see him—in any circumstances. Incidentally, our friend Sir Michael dodged him successfully. He *would*. Miss Walsingham has this chap in hand now—'

'Yes, I saw that.' Mrs Drayton's eyes, her best feature—umber in melancholy and boredom, but gold-dusted by any excitement—now gleamed with amusement.

'I was thinking—and it may be because her work has been so satisfactory up to now that I've taken her for granted—that I know very little about Miss Walsingham—'

'June? Oh—Sir George—don't you *know* about her—?'

What Sir George did know—the flash of the eye and the tone of voice telling him—was that he was now threatened by some sexual saga, and he hurriedly waved it away. Too many members of his DISCUS staff appeared to have very complicated and often squalid private lives. Joan Drayton herself, a widow, had been foolish enough to fall in love with an actor, Wally Somebody-or-other, married and with two children, who could neither leave his wife nor live with her steadily. Everybody in DISCUS knew when Wally was back with Joan or had gone home again. When he was living with her, generally when he was not in work, the early rising (to cope with housekeeping) and late retiring, the midnight gin sessions with Wally's theatrical chums, barred from visiting him at home, the cooking and mending and sitting up waiting for love, the familiar but still-to-be-dreaded awakening of Wally's conscience ('I'm no good to either of you'), leading to scenes that Wally, a bad actor, always overplayed, these wore her out, ravaging her dark once-handsome looks. But as soon as he had gone again ('It's no use, girl. They're paying me thirty a week, so the least I can do is to go back to Dorothy and the kids'), she looked even worse, umber-eyed and utterly desolate, until Wally began telephoning again. It seemed to Sir George a dreadful way to live; and he could not understand how a woman like Joan Drayton, sensible and efficient, could ever have allowed herself to be trapped by her sexual feelings into riding endlessly on this sad switchback. Moreover, Wally, to whom she had once introduced him, seemed to have nothing in his favour, being a seedy blotched fellow, quite impossible. Yet, so strange, so unaccountable and perverse are women, that when Sir George told his wife all about the wretched dragging affair, Alison refused to join him in condemning it, saying rather sulkily 'Well, it may be what she wants. And anyhow it's *something*.' A preposterous observation.

Having so hastily banned the June Walsingham saga, and not wishing Joan Drayton to feel snubbed (and, probably because of Wally, she was an eager snubbee) as well as disappointed, Sir George smiled at her. 'I can tell that it's all very complicated and personal, and I'd really rather not know.'

'Yes, Sir George, but remember, you did say—'

'Yes, yes, yes, that I knew very little about Miss Walsingham. Well, now I prefer not to know any more. Much better. It's an odd thing—I don't know whether it's ever occurred to you, Joan—that there's COMSA, a rickety organisation, with a director, anything but a sound type, brought out of a museum and various shifty odd jobs—and yet it has some extremely decent dependable fellows on its staff— Jim Marlowe, Dudley Chapman, Edgar Hawkins, for example—all thoroughly sound. Then here *we* are—a government department, with the Treasury behind us, not kept going by grants and various cadgings from trusts and foundations—and though of course the work is well done here, and I'd be the last to complain about my DISCUS staff, the fact remains that the peculiar touch-and-go fellows that half a dozen permanent secretaries haven't known what to do with, are all here—not with COMSA. Is that a mere coincidence, I wonder—and if not, how has it been worked?'

'I don't know, Sir George.'

'No, no—didn't expect you to know. Rhetorical question.'

'But what you've just said reminds me,' said Mrs Drayton happily, her face suddenly alight. 'I meant to tell you earlier but you were with that American. Timmy's back.'

'Timmy's back? I don't understand what you mean, Joan.' He stared at her out of an enormous not-understanding face, an impressive production even if part of a very limited repertoire.

'Tim Kemp,' said Mrs Drayton, firmly but still happily, still alight, 'has returned to us.'

'Kemp? Good God! Are you sure?'

'Yes, he came to see me, hoping to see you. We had a little talk.' She smiled at the recollection of it. 'He's so sweet, Timmy.'

'I don't know what you women mean by your *sweet,* and sometimes I think you don't. I hope nobody else here thinks he's sweet—'

'Everybody does. Everybody adores him.'

Sir George's resources for expressing an angry despair were not large. He pressed his lips together so that his mouth disappeared, then he inhaled and exhaled through his nostrils sharply, sounding like an impatient locomotive. 'Well, *I* don't adore him. And I thought I'd seen the last of him. Good God!—it's monstrous. Look what happened. Education, not knowing what to do with him—after all, he's been a Principal for years and if he'd kept sober and in his right mind he'd have been an assistant secretary long ago—so, I say, not knowing what to do with him, they have him seconded to me. After a few months, by pulling every string possible, I have him transferred to COMSA. Then Stratherrick, by some extraordinary hocus-pocus, always a mystery to me, is able to return him to Education. They try to send him here again, but I put my foot down. Then, I heard, he was given sick leave—'

'Yes, he was telling me about that. He went to Ireland—'

'And now he's here again, you say. Absolutely preposterous!' He returned to a head-of-department formality now. 'I'll see Mr Kemp as soon as possible.'

After she had gone, Sir George stared with gloomy incredulity at a very long letter, which demanded DISCUS support for a tour of religious plays in verse through the mining towns of Yorkshire and Durham. He made a note to enquire very sharply why Hugo Heywood, in charge of the Drama Section, should have seen fit to send up such an appeal. It was one thing to believe, as Heywood did, that poetry alone could redeem the Theatre, and quite another thing to imagine that Yorkshire and Durham miners were anxious to enjoy religious plays in verse, performed by two half-mad actresses in their seventies and six youngsters little better than amateurs. There were times now when Sir George, in spite of his optimism, his sound liberal views, his belief in a gradual but sure progress, began to feel that the world was slipping out of its mind. This seemed to be one of the times. And the arrival of Tim Kemp did nothing to restore any sense of order and sanity.

He was a small chubby man in his fifties, with large round eyes, a midsummer sky blue, like a child's, and the kind of grey hair, wispy but tufty, that so many crackpots seem to have. He was clean enough but disgracefully shabby, not at all like one of the Her Majesty's civil servants, holding the rank of Principal, but suggesting perhaps the itinerant proprietor of some obscure herbal remedy. Sir George could see nothing sweet and adorable about him. All that the sick leave spent in Ireland had done for Kemp, apparently, was to make him look even smaller, shabbier, odder, perhaps adding a hint of leprechaun.

'I must tell you, Mr Kemp,' Sir George found himself saying, 'that I simply don't understand this at all.'

Kemp had now sat down, and had lit a stumpy pipe, bubbling and malodorous. Ignoring Sir George's remark, and as usual speaking rather slowly and with a precision that only gave point and edge to his more outrageous statements, he began: 'I ought to have seen you this morning, I know. But the house next door to where I'm living did turn out to be a brothel after all, and this morning—an odd time to choose, don't you think?—the police raided it. There was some confusion, almost panic, in which we were involved in a neighbourly way. I don't know if you're familiar with the Holland Park neighbourhood these days—'

'No, Mr Kemp, and I suggest we don't discuss it. What I want to know is—what are you doing here?'

'Didn't the Ministry—George Dunne, actually—write to you? No? I'm sorry. He will be writing, of course. All in order, I assure you.'

'Are you certain you weren't being transferred back to COMSA?' Sir George looked at him hopefully.

'Positive. It was mentioned, as a possibility, but I made it clear that I'd much prefer to be back again with DISCUS. I find your people here much pleasanter to work with. And, though this may surprise you, I don't care for Stratherrick—a Highland charlatan, a cynical Celtic rogue.'

This came so close to Sir George's own private opinion that now he modified the severity of his manner. 'Well, I'll have to look into this transfer business—have it out with Dunne. I don't say we can't find room for you here, Kemp—'

'And who else here has been with COMSA?'

'Nobody, to my knowledge.'

Kemp's smile, for which he removed his pipe, went curling out and up. 'I could be useful.'

Sir George knew what he meant but felt that it was beneath his dignity to meet Kemp on this low conspiratorial level. 'But—look here—I have to ask this, Kemp—are you still drinking?'

'I am—yes. Gin. Rarely drink anything else. I don't get drunk, if that is what's worrying you, my dear Secretary-General. All I've ever been accused of—quite wrongly, in my opinion—is a certain irresponsibility—suddenly laughing at meetings, for instance—'

Sir George frowned. 'But that's gin, isn't it?'

'The gin helps there, certainly. But isn't there something to be said for it, even from the point of view of DISCUS? Isn't it of some value, especially in a department of this kind, to have some expression of opinion from a man, not unintelligent nor insensitive, who needs a great deal of gin to keep himself going in this world? To be able to appeal, at certain moments, to the gin-drinker's judgment— um? Even if you think it bad to drink as much as I do—oh wicked, wicked!—remember Shakespeare's wise Duke of Vienna.' Here Kemp leant forward, widening his eyes so that they were a blaze of blue. *'And let the Devil Be sometime honour'd for his burning throne.* Always makes my hair stand on end, that line in *Measure For Measure*—but of course I think we have to interpret it as meaning—'

'Not this afternoon,' Sir George cut in grumpily. 'We haven't to do anything about *Measure For Measure* this afternoon, Kemp. The real question is—now that you're here, what are we going to do with you?'

Kemp looked at him reproachfully, the blue all faded. 'You think it as bad as that, do you? It isn't, y'know. I'm an intuitive man—unlike you, I imagine—and I have a feeling that I might prove to be of great help to you.'

'Well, let's hope so,' said Sir George, annoyed now because he could not help feeling ashamed of himself. 'Have you told Neil Jonson you're back with us? Yes? Very well. I'll talk to him and to our section heads. And that's all, I think.'

Twenty minutes later, the last traces of Kemp's visit—the sweetish reek of gin, the rank tobacco, some influence, destructive to good sense, emanating from the man's essence—having vanished, Sir George found his original suspicions returning. 'I don't understand this,' he told Mrs Drayton. 'If the Ministry didn't want him—and that I *can* understand—then why wasn't he sent back to COMSA, where he was last before he went back to the Ministry?'

'But he prefers to be with DISCUS.' She spoke lovingly, still under the Kemp spell. 'He told me.'

'He told me too. But then he'd say anything. Quite irresponsible. No, I don't understand it, don't like it. But I won't talk to the Ministry. I'll have it out with the man I believe to be at the bottom of this Kemp business. Joan, ring COMSA—say I want to speak on an urgent matter to Sir Michael Stratherrick.'

But COMSA replied that Sir Michael was out of the office that afternoon.

'It's always the same.' Sir George knew he was shouting, but didn't care. 'Every confounded time I try to talk to him, he's out for the afternoon. What on earth does the fellow do with his afternoons?'

2

AT THE VERY moment Sir George was asking that question in Russell Square, Sir Michael, in Hampstead, was sitting on Sir George's bed, his tie in one hand and a cigarette in the other, wondering if a whisky-and-soda would be worth the trouble of going down to the dining room for it. On the other twin bed, Alison, wife to Sir George, was lying naked beneath a bedspread, its pink several shades lighter than her face, flushed from the act of love. She was a handsome woman, generously designed, who could assume a formidable manner in company, where most men imagined her to be sexually cold, when in fact she was sensual and ardent. This was one reason why Sir Michael was here; he liked his affairs to be spiced with such contrasts and contradictions, to pluck fruit where most men only saw a fortress in a desert.

Loitering like this, tie in hand, he realised he was not being very clever. He had escaped from her embrace, no more than her body's gratitude, her wits not working yet, by muttering something about COMSA and an engagement, and he had begun dressing with a fair show of briskness; but now here he was, unable to keep up the pretence, inviting the kind of comment that could cut and wound a man when he was feeling drained out, empty and melancholy, vulnerable. They were all the same, except the real sillies; feeling vulnerable themselves, let down, insecure, because no protestations of devotion, no emotional and spiritual guarantees, followed the excitement, which, now they no longer needed it, began to seem a cheating male trick, they lashed out angrily—but not blindly, being guided by intuition to the gaps between joints in a man's self-esteem. Well, once again, he was asking for it.

'I must be mad,' she began.

'My dear Alison, we're both mad.' A light drawing-room comedy tone. 'Would you like a drink?'

'No. Yes—as you obviously want one. And tie your tie and put your coat on before you go down. There's nobody here of course, but somebody might see you through a window.'

20

He found himself creeping down, and then, annoyed with himself, he moved with weight and dignity, as George Drake himself probably did all the time here, even when his wife had just refused his uncertain advances. But though Sir Michael had put on his coat and his tie, he had not put on his shoes, and he soon discovered that it is rash to move with weight and dignity without shoes. After removing the loose carpet tack, he went hopping and cursing into the dining room, a sullen little browny-greeny place, haunted by all the unsatisfactory dinner parties it had known. The Lowland Scotchness, the graduate of St. Andrews in Alison, came out in this dining room, Sir Michael reflected at the sideboard as he gave himself a good three-fingers of George's whisky.

It was no help in the bedroom. 'Quite mad,' said Alison, cueing herself, clearly in the same mood. 'I look at you and I can't imagine why I ever thought you were worth it.'

'I've never pretended to be worth it—whatever that means.'

She ignored this. She had worked out a speech while he was fetching the whisky, and it made no allowance for interruptions. 'Really you're just another Highland fraud. I admit you're very attractive at first. But even that isn't really you. Some 18th Century ancestor, some dark and romantic and ruined Jacobite, left you that face, that ravaged expression, just as he might have left, for you to inherit, a snuffbox or a silver drinking cup. We women wonder what's behind it, and we have to go to bed with you a few times before we admit to ourselves that there's nothing behind it, except the desire to have a few women in the afternoons, without accepting any further responsibility. And, though I don't say you're bad at it, probably that desire has more vanity than honest sex in it.'

'You may be right.' He was still using a light tone. 'Some vanity, no doubt. Some mischief too. And something that isn't quite either— very old, deep-rooted, probably—an urge to take the enemy's women.'

'Really? Are we all married to your enemies?'

'This is the capital of the English. But this plural of yours seems to be getting bigger and bigger—*we women*—as if there were scores of you—'

'There may be, for all I know.' She looked hard at him; she had hottish brown eyes, and it was on these, ignoring her manner and rather large firm features, that he had taken his initial gamble. 'I can

21

name three—I've had confidences from two of them, and the third's better than a guess. We ought to organise ourselves—the *Michael Stratherrick Afternoon Association*. Except that you wouldn't be worth it. Because we all soon begin to see—and that isn't just *our* vanity—that you don't love us because really you're incapable of love.'

'I think you're right. It isn't you, it's me. I never arrive at the crystallising process—you remember Stendhal. It's never worked with me, not even when I was young and silly, and now it never will.' He remembered saying that, a fool stiff with *hubris* challenging the luscious but implacable goddess; remembered it on very different afternoons, not long afterwards. 'So you're too good for me, all of you, yourself most of all, my dear Alison.'

'I wish I'd a tape recorder,' she cried, 'so that I could play that back at you. You couldn't avoid catching the patronising tone, the underlying contempt. And perhaps you're right. What idiots we are, to risk so much for so little! Not that we haven't a sense of mischief too. All the husbands I know or guess to be involved, the English you raid in the afternoons when they're out doing what you ought to be doing—working, perhaps they're all a bit solemn, too complacent. But better men than you, Michael.'

'Better at some things—certainly,' he murmured, not looking at her.

'Poor George is worth ten of you. That's something I could really hate you for—if I thought you came here chiefly to get at George!'

For the first time he protested vigorously. 'Don't entertain any such notion, Alison. I imagine that George dislikes me on every possible ground he can have for disliking another man. And because he never spends much time examining his mind, questioning his motives, because he immediately ties up anything he feels strongly to some abstraction in capital letters, like a flag to a flagpole, he can really enjoy himself disliking me. I'm not an Anglo-Saxon but a Celt, I'm an obviously unsound type, I'm running a rival department without being a civil servant, I have a better staff than he has, I understand and sympathise with artists and he doesn't, I'm a cad about women— and so on and so on. All of which, my dear Alison, I accept cheerfully. I've not the least desire to *get at him,* that is, outside DISCUS and COMSA. As the head of one I resent him as the head of the other, simply because he's doing the wrong job and represents, to my mind, a stupid policy. But, in point of fact, I rather like him personally.'

'He's much better at his job than you think he is, Michael.' The edge had gone from her voice. 'You underrate him just because you're quicker and cleverer and have fewer scruples. You're like all the quick clever foreigners who for ages have been underrating English officials of George's type, only to regret it afterwards—'

'That was before your time, my dear Alison. And the money and the Navy did it really, not the officials. Now, with neither ace to play—'

'Never mind about that. George has qualities that you're ready to ignore because you don't understand them. And if it's a fight-to-a-finish between DISCUS and COMSA—'

'And I'm afraid it *is*, you know—'

'Then he'll probably beat you. And I hope he does.'

'I must go.' He put on his shoes, then stood over her. 'Well, Alison my dear—'

'Don't say it. We haven't had a lovely afternoon. What we did was damned silly, in the circumstances, and it left you sad and me angry. And it's the last time—I really mean it.'

Sir Michael did not own a car. It was an easy walk in all but the worst weather from his flat in Knightsbridge to COMSA's headquarters in Princes Place, Mayfair, near Shepherd Market. Why bother with all the parking nonsense? Why try to get out of London by car, as a multitude of imbecilek did every fine Saturday and Sunday, when there were still trains that did it better? So now he found a taxi on Haverstock Hill that took him to Mayfair, across several miles of a London that seemed to him without character and meaning, a huge melancholy jumble, America without its zest and drive, Europe without civilisation and gaiety, a city that kept its bomb sites as if they were the graveyard of its older self, its character and meaning.

'I'm sorry about this, Dudley,' he said to Chapman, who was waiting for his return, and said it with all the charm he could muster. 'It's not good enough, I know. I keep forgetting that you fellows are family men, with homes you're eager to get back to. Not like me, a bachelor with nothing but a dreary flat. I won't deceive you—not that I could, I imagine—and it's simply that I hate trying to work in the afternoon, always have done since I was up at Oxford, so that I'm ready to get back to work just when you fellows, very sensibly, are hoping to knock off. Well, let's go through this lot quickly. I'll keep anything that I ought to think over.'

At the end of not too long a session, Dudley Chapman, a chunky chap, conscientious but entirely without ambition or imagination, suddenly grinned. This was noticeable because he had one of those solid meaty faces, as solemn as a piece of fillet steak set aside for a Guildhall banquet.

'What, Dudley? Something I've missed here?'

'No, Sir Michael.' The director of COMSA was informal with his staff but had contrived to discourage any informality from them to him. 'It's something I've just remembered. While you were out, Dunne at the Ministry of Education rang up to tell me he'd sent Tim Kemp back to DISCUS today.'

'Good work! Anyhow, I wouldn't have had him here again. If there's any drinking to be done for COMSA, I'll do it. Besides, little Kemp disliked me — God knows why, because I must have been more tolerant than most of his chiefs have been. Anything else now?'

'One thing — yes, Sir Michael. Now that Miss Tudor's gone, we need another shorthand typist. We're entitled to advertise for one, of course, or I might ask Dunne — we're good friends —'

A smile entirely malicious illuminated Sir Michael's dark long face, his sea-green glance. 'Dudley, do this for me. First, ask Dunne how many people Drake has at DISCUS. If, as I suspect, he has more than we have, then ask Dunne as a favour to insist upon DISCUS releasing a shorthand typist to us. Can you do that?'

'I can do it, and I think Dunne might play. But is there any point in it?'

'Frankly, no. Pure devilment. Don't tell Dunne that, however friendly you are. Tell him I feel we're working at a disadvantage, with a smaller staff than DISCUS has, and that I was about to make a formal complaint to the Lord President, telling him that the Ministry of Higher Education is not honouring the agreement he came to with the Minister. Or anything better that occurs to you. But what I'm up to — and I ought to be ashamed of myself — is rattling poor George Drake, already shaken, I imagine, by the return of Kemp. Just devilment, Dudley, but humour me in this, humour me, my dear fellow.'

And Sir Michael waved a hand, as light, as easy, as careless as his tone of voice. So might one of his ancestors, moved by an unconscious urge to self-destruction, have agreed to do battle. Even from civil servants in the Administrative grade, to which Dudley Chapman belonged, no gift of prophecy is demanded—if Tim Kemp had it, he had drunk himself into possession of it—and so Chapman stood there smiling, incapable of devilment himself but ready to admire it in a director outside the service. There was nothing, not even the tiniest throb of intuitive feeling, to tell Chapman that Sir Michael was beckoning to his doom, bringing down on himself with that careless wave of the hand much bewilderment and humiliation, even despair and anguish.

'I think,' said Sir Michael, still, smiling, 'that we're entitled to amuse ourselves a little at Sir George Drake's expense.'

3

IF HE HAD had any luck with his staff at DISCUS, Sir George would have enjoyed the weekly meeting, as in the past he had enjoyed similar departmental meetings, even though he himself had not chaired them. With a few decent keen chaps and a sensible agenda, a meeting could be reassuring, even cosy. But not at DISCUS, not with these types.

There was Gerald Spenser (Visual Arts), who had a very long nose and a very long neck and very little between them, though what he had there he could use unwearyingly, talking on and on and on. He had a contempt for any kind of art that Sir George could appreciate, and reserved his very small stock of admiration for things that looked like parts of machinery and pictures of the human form and face apparently half-eaten by maggots. Nicola Pembroke, a fine-looking fierce brunette, really a nice woman and the prop and happy slave of an invalid husband, a musical scholar, looked as if she ought to be fiddling away in a gipsy band, but in fact never enjoyed anything but early polyphonic music and the tuneless contemporary stuff. Hugo Heywood, in appearance a romantic actor gone not to seed but to lard, was sufficiently amiable but his one firm conviction, that only poetry could save the Theatre, had so far done little either for his DISCUS drama section or for the Theatre. Neil Jonson, responsible for finance and general administration and Sir George's second-in-command, was capable of superb efficiency, but having missed promotion at the Treasury because of some sudden rebellious whim, and having been then seconded at his request to DISCUS, now he could not resist favouring any form of rebellion, anything that the Establishment would dislike, as if behind his splendid *persona* as a sound official—and nobody in DISCUS, not even Sir George himself, looked the part better than Neil—another Trotsky was plotting and orating. And now to these four, a permanent fuse for any explosives they might contribute, Tim Kemp had been added, and there he was, smiling round his stumpy pipe, a Holland Park version of a Zen master. Sir George glanced across the table at him, wished he could utter the despair that might remove the almost Oriental grin from that face, then forced himself to look again at the agenda.

'Where are we? Oh yes—*Five*. Spike Andrewes concert.' He frowned at the name. 'This is your item, Nicola.'

'You remember him, Spike Andrewes, don't you?'

Sir George did. 'He was the composer chap who forced his way in here—and made a thorough nuisance of himself. Couldn't stand the man. But why is he bothering us again? Better explain the whole thing, Nicola.'

Mrs Pembroke jabbed hard at the ashtray with her cigarette, as if she had suddenly decided to give up smoking, closed her eyes for a moment, then opened them wide, and began: 'He's written a *Space Symphony*, for full orchestra—very full—two singers and chorus, a very ambitious work—takes an hour and a quarter. Both the L.P.O. and the L.S.O. are ready to do it, either at the Festival Hall or the Albert, but of course they want a guarantee. Quite right, with a new work on that scale. He applied to us and to COMSA, and we both turned him down. Now he's persuaded the B.B.C. to provide half the guarantee if we'll put up the other half—two hundred pounds. It's very important to him now because the B.B.C. will record the work during the concert. So now he's come back at us—and I've had hours of him. I happen to know that he's already tried COMSA again, and again they've turned him down. I may say that my husband's read the score—and says it's a difficult work, not altogether satisfactory but interesting and worth doing. Now that the B.B.C.'s in, I think we ought to risk two hundred. Remember, it's only a guarantee against loss. If the concert goes well, it might not cost us a penny.'

'Thank you, Nicola,' said Sir George. 'Before asking other people for their opinion, I must add that in my view we cannot usefully discuss this application unless we assume that it will cost DISCUS two hundred pounds.'

'Quite so,' said Hugo Heywood. 'We'll lose two hundred. Whichever orchestra does it will probably drop something, and so be round all the sooner asking us for more. And all for one performance, with nothing following on, no sustained creative work. I'm against it.'

'I agree,' said Spenser, laconic for once.

'And I don't, Mr Chairman.' This was Neil Jonson. 'It enables us to show up against COMSA's refusal. And even if the whole guarantee is lost, we'll have spent it obtaining some favourable publicity for the department, what with the B.B.C., the musical press, and all the people involved in the performance. I'm in favour, Mr Chairman.'

Now Sir George looked enquiringly at Kemp. He in turn looked at Nicola Pembroke. 'Do you like this man Spike Andrewes, Nicola?'

'I can't bear him. But that proves nothing. Probably I'd have hated Beethoven.'

'Beethoven blessed the English and their Philharmonic Society just before he died,' said Kemp. 'Who blesses anybody now? Who deserves to be blessed? The Philharmonic Society sent Beethoven a hundred pounds, in advance of his benefit concert. Equal to at least fifteen hundred pounds now. Why do we imagine—'

'Mr Kemp,' said Sir George, not disguising his impatience, 'if you've anything to say about this grant, this guarantee—'

'Oh yes. I'm for it.'

'So far, three in favour, two against. I'm against it too.' Sir George looked round sharply. 'And for once I must exercise my privilege. We refuse this further application by Mr Andrewes.'

'Sir George,' said Nicola Pembroke, who seemed unhappy about the decision, 'would you mind very much writing to him yourself— top level stuff?'

He lifted his eyebrows and his tone was rather lofty. 'It oughtn't to be necessary—I can't believe anybody called Spike Andrewes is exactly on that level—but I will, to oblige you. Make a note, Mrs Drayton—write to Andrewes. Now then—*Six*. Ned Greene show?'

Gerald Spenser, who had been slumped down, now raised himself, his length of neck and nose suggesting some fabulous animal. In the shadowy place between nose and neck his almost invisible lips, which might have been made of pale indiarubber, twisted and writhed, hissed and spat. 'This is really rather important, I think. Ned Greene's been living in France for the last ten years. He's shortly having a small one-man show, his first for years and years, at the Baro Gallery. Lucien Baro assures me—and I've always found him reliable—that it'll be a sensation. There won't be a painting there under two thousand pounds. Baro says he could sell them all at these prices without having the show, but he wants it for the sake of the Gallery. I'm not excited about Ned Greene's work myself. It's too obviously a compromise between representational and abstract painting—like Villon or de Stael—but all done with tremendous energy, confidence, blazes of colour—so it's easy to understand why everybody who collects without too much discrimination is after him. Now Greene's coming over to look at this show at the Baro — and — this is the point — Lucien Baro has agreed to let me know when he arrives and to bring us together. This is tremendously important because Greene's a very difficult fellow, very elusive, hates publicity and ordinary social life, all rather in the Turner anonymous-low-life tradition. Now comes the really important, tremendous point —' He stopped for breath.

'Good!' said Neil Jonson, who did not like Spenser.

'The idea is — that as soon as Greene arrives we talk him into allowing us to do a DISCUS show of his work. Baro says Greene will probably agree to this. It gives the ordinary public a chance of seeing pictures of his now shut away in private collections. And DISCUS gives him a big show to himself just at the right moment. COMSA don't get a look in. Baro had a row with their visual arts man, Cecil Tarlton. Baro also says that Greene dislikes Michael Stratherrick — it all dates back to the time when Stratherrick was still at the V. and A. So it's all ours. Nice idea, don't you think?'

Sir George led the chorus of approval. He commanded Spenser and his section to begin planning the Ned Greene show. 'And while I'll make sure you're given full credit for all this, Gerald,' he continued, 'as soon as Baro tells us that Greene's arrived and where we can find him, I should like to talk to him myself about the exhibition, to put the idea to him on the highest DISCUS level. I think it's sufficiently important, isn't it?'

The meeting agreed that it was. But then Kemp had to say something, much to Sir George's annoyance. 'You're going to see Ned Greene yourself, are you, Secretary-General?'

Sir George was stiff with him. 'That's my intention, Mr Kemp. Have you any objection?' The irony was obvious, and the meeting showed no sign of enjoying it.

Kemp looked innocent and faraway, a contemplative on some Chinese mountain. 'It's not for me to object, of course. But I don't advise this interview with Ned Greene. And I used to know him fairly well, before he settled in France. You might find this talk with him — rather difficult.'

'Really? Are there any good reasons why, when you used to know him fairly well, I would find it difficult to approach him with what is after all a very flattering suggestion?' Not an easy question to bring out, in that form, but Sir George even gave it a challenging ring.

Kemp's face crinkled a little, his eyes narrowing, their blue darkening. 'They seem good reasons to me. But of course I could be wrong. Still, knowing Greene, I don't advise it.'

Sir George hesitated a moment, then watched his finger moving down the agenda paper. Four items later he found himself able to strike back at Kemp for that unnecessary intervention, that half-insolent warning. 'The Bodley-Cobham Scheme,' he announced, with a gigantic air of weariness, as if refusing for the thousandth time to give a hand lifting a dead elephant off the table. 'Any developments there, Neil?'

'No, Mr Chairman. We've had one or two telephone messages from Lady Bodley-Cobham, but I really haven't had the time—nor, I'll admit, the inclination—to see her again. It would be quite useless if J did. As I've said before, she's taken a violent dislike to me. I don't think we ought to let her go completely, if only because she'll then turn to COMSA, if she hasn't done so already. Perhaps one of the section assistants ought to take her over. Not a girl, though. She hates girls.'

'All right, Neil. Take her out of your file. But it seems a pity not to treat with her on this level.' Sir George looked round the table, then smiled, not without malice, at Kemp. 'As this Bodley-Cobham affair is since your last spell of duty here, Mr Kemp, I'd better explain— briefly. Lady Bodley-Cobham is a very rich old widow—eccentric, probably socially though not legally out of her mind—who wants to do something generous for the arts. Her favourite scheme, on which we've already wasted an appalling amount of time and paper, is the conversion of an enormous mansion she owns into a place where creative artists can live and work. But so far whatever she proposes is quite unreasonable, and whenever we offer her a practicable scheme, she rejects it at once. Now you're the only one here not responsible for a section of the department, suppose you take over the Bodley-Cobham Scheme—um?'

'Certainly, Sir George. Why not?' Kemp was still smiling broadly as he turned to Neil Jonson. 'You'll let me have all the material, will you, Neil?'

'I will, Tim. And I warn you it'll nearly fill that cubby-hole of yours.'

'And *I* warn you, Timmy,' said Nicola Pembroke, 'that the old girl's round the bend. I went to see her once—never again!'

'Thank you, Nicola dear,' said Kemp. 'But I don't mind the round-the-benders these days. It's the people generally supposed to be sane who frighten me.'

'Next item,' Sir George announced. 'Oh—by the way—why isn't Miss Walsingham here?'

After a moment, during which all the rest looked blank, Kemp said: 'She went to her dentist. He rang unexpectedly to say he could give her an appointment. I know because I happened to be talking to her in her office when she took the call.'

'Indeed! She ought to have sent a message, explaining her absence from this meeting.'

'She did—through me. My fault,' said Kemp, not looking nor sounding sorry. 'I forgot to deliver it.'

Sir George gave him an angry look, and then went grinding and worrying through what remained of the agenda. Fortunately, for he might easily have lost his temper now, the meeting ended without his having to exchange another word with Kemp, who puffed away at his horrible little pipe, fixed his blue gaze on nothing, and obviously made not even a pretence of listening to what was being said. A fellow useless in himself, Sir George decided angrily, and a bad influence on other members of the staff.

The meeting took the morning with it, and ten minutes after it was over, and after firing some notes at Joan Drayton, Sir George marched gloomily, a Roman general back from the Teutonic tribes, to his club for lunch. The thought of Kemp worried him. Then, when he had driven Kemp away, the thought of Alison, his wife, worried him. With the contrariness and perverseness of woman, moved by tides of feeling and eddies of caprice below a sensible man's view and understanding, Alison, who at one time had defended Stratherrick, dismissed the rivalry between DISCUS and COMSA as if it were a boys' game, told him he took himself and everything else too seriously, now for no reason that he could discover had swung to the opposite extreme. Morning and night now she was telling him that he had too much respect for Stratherrick, a second-rate phoney who spent most of his time (she had been told) chasing women, that it was time he swept COMSA out of the way of DISCUS, that he was too easy and indulgent and not fully exercising his gift of command. Her reproaches had not been without their effect on him during this morning's meeting: for example, his sharp decisions to dismiss finally the appeal of that wretched composer chap, Andrewes, to talk to Ned Greene himself, to dump the whole Bodley-Cobham mess on to Kemp; and if Alison were in a listening mood, he would sketch the meeting for her at dinner. Nevertheless, he had to admit, all was not well; some shadow, impossible to trace and to recognise, remained at the back of his mind; and it was a bewildered and rather unhappy Sir George who arrived at the club and accepted a small dry sherry from Wilkinson, an Assistant Secretary at Fuel and Power.

4

SIR MICHAEL was bored. He detested meetings, only holding them because all the senior members of his COMSA staff were the kind of people who liked meetings. The poor devils still failed to understand that London was not a city in which official discourse round a table settled anything important; power in London went to work behind winks and hints and nudges, murmurs in the corners of club smoke-rooms, a few sleepy remarks over the second cup of after-luncheon coffee. Here they were, the innocents, dead keen down to the last item on the agenda: Dudley Chapman, with his square Sunday-joint face; Jim Marlowe, finance, glaring at every wretched grant they made as if they were providing funds to manufacture some gigantic useless rocket; Cecil Tariton, sniffing delicately round the visual arts; Jeff Byrd, conscientious, reliable, sensible, and for ever defeated by his incapacity to understand the Theatre people with whom he had to deal; Edith Frobisher, all Greek profile and solemn silliness; and Edgar Hawkins, who looked like a well-hammered retired lightweight, was recognised as something of an authority on early Chinese pottery, and, though unceasing and unsparing in his efforts, was about as well adapted to running public relations as anybody's deaf maiden aunt. Sitting a little to one side and behind Sir Michael, waiting to catch his lightest word to her, was his secretary, Miss Tilney, deliberately chosen—Sir Michael felt he knew himself by now—for her lack of any possible sexual attraction: she was squat and thick and looked rather like a hastily shaved Ibsen. As usual he could hear her breathing raspily over her notebook. It never occurred to him that he would have made a much wiser choice if he had taken as secretary any young woman, however well-favoured, who was engaged or satisfactorily married or at least had her affections firmly fixed elsewhere. Miss Tilney might be squat, thick, Ibsenish, but she had a heart, and there burned in it a terrible passion for Sir Michael Stratherrick.

'Edith dear,' said Sir Michael, smiling at Miss Frobisher, 'not only will we turn down this Spike Andrewes once again, but this time, I suggest, we must do it quite offensively, so that we never hear from him again.'

'Director, I know he's a nuisance. Nobody knows that better than I do. And of course we've told him twice already we can't do anything for him. But I don't really feel we ought to be unpleasant.' And Miss Frobisher, whose severely classical features did not permit any nose-wrinkling or mouth-pursing, bent her head to the right as a token of appeal.

'You mean you don't want to be unpleasant, Edith. Very well. I'll do it for you. Remind me, Miss Tilney, to write Mr Spike Andrewes a brief but thoroughly nasty letter. Now, what's next? *Lithographs for Sunderland?* What are you up to now, Cecil?'

Much further down the agenda, Sir Michael, clearing in one bound an old quicksand of an item concerning students from Pakistan, pointed an accusing forefinger at Dudley Chapman, and cried: 'You must have put this one in, Dudley. *Bodley-Cobham Scheme?* I never heard of it. What does it mean?'

'I decided to make a few enquiries before troubling you with it, Sir Michael,' said Chapman. 'It offers us a chance to take something away from DISCUS, who seem to have fallen down badly over it. Our friend, Neil Jonson, I gather from the letter we've had from Lady Bodley-Cobham.' He held up the letter, as if to prove he had not just invented Lady Bodley-Cobham. 'It's rather long and not easy to disentangle, so perhaps you'd like me to give you the gist of it.'

'The gist, please, Dudley. You might even make it the gist of the gist.' Sir Michael sank down into his chair, looking darker, nobler, more ravaged than ever, the last Jacobite in exile.

'Lady Bodley-Cobham, I've gathered, is very rich — she's the widow of the shipping man — and well into her seventies. She's a recluse and rather eccentric. But she wants to talk to us about a scheme she has for turning her largest house, which she never uses nowadays, into a kind of great hostel for creative artists. She realises that this would cost a lot of money, but she's prepared to put up a very considerable sum, once her scheme is officially accepted. She's been dickering with DISCUS for well over a year now, and she's turning to us because DISCUS always send Neil Jonson to see her and she can't take him any longer.'

'Drake doesn't tackle her himself then?'

'No, he's never seen her — she lives in Berkshire and never comes to London—and this has helped to put her off DISCUS. By the way, the mansion intended for creative artists is up in Derbyshire, and appears to be a vast place. We needn't bother about that yet, but I do feel strongly, Director, that one of us ought to see her, especially as she seems to be almost through with DISCUS. One final point—we mustn't send a girl. She refuses to discuss her scheme with any girls. Men only for Lady Bodley-Cobham.'

'I feel, as I trust you all do, that COMSA must come to the rescue of this scheme, no matter how hare-brained it may be at the moment.' Sir Michael looked round, receiving glances and murmurs of approval. 'After all, Berkshire's no distance. The whole thing would only take half a day. And it would be rather a lark for COMSA to snatch the scheme, after DISCUS had spent a year or so trying to hatch it out. I think one of us must descend upon this Lady Bodley-Cobham.'

'Sir Michael, you ought to go,' said Miss Frobisher. 'Highest level from the beginning. I'm sure that's where DISCUS went wrong.'

'You know, I think I will. Leave that letter, Dudley, please. It may offer me a few clues to the old lady. Well, let's get on.'

It was when Chapman was handing over the letter, half an hour later, the meeting at an end, that he mentioned the shorthand typist. 'You remember, last week, suggesting we should take one from DISCUS, working it through Dunne at the Ministry?'

'I must admit I'd forgotten,' said Sir Michael, 'but now I remember—it was the decision of an idle and mischievous moment, probably belonging to the devil. I almost hope nothing has come of it. Has it?'

'They're sending a girl next week. She's only just come to DISCUS from the Ministry pool. They wouldn't be transferring her to us, I think, with so little fuss if their Secretary-General knew anything about it, but my guess is that they haven't told Sir George. It was Tim Kemp who telephoned me yesterday, saying that the girl would be along next week.'

'Kemp? If he's looking after this transfer, what we'll get next week is some sort of young female monster. However, that's your affair, Dudley. But send her back if she's useless. We won't have little Kemp laughing at us in every saloon bar from *The Plough* to Euston Station. And now I'll brood over this letter from old Lady Thing-What's-it.'

At this very time, and roughly between *The Plough* and Euston Station, Kemp was discussing the shorthand typist, soon to leave

DISCUS for COMSA, with Nicola Pembroke. 'She worked for me two days last week,' Nicola was saying. 'She's a very pretty child, as you've probably noticed, Timmy. You do notice girls, don't you?'

'Certainly I do. A man who doesn't notice and appreciate pretty girls is halfway to the cemetery. But it's possible to arrive at a stage—and I've arrived at it—when you can appreciate them without wanting them. But go on about young Shirley.'

'She's quite pleasant in a suburbanish sort of way—but not very quick, not very bright. We can certainly spare her, though there are one or two of the others, especially that smelly one, I'd rather send to COMSA.' She watched him shake his head. 'Timmy, my darling, you're up to something. I can see it in your beautiful blue eye. Why must this girl go—and no other?'

'She's having lunch with me,' said Kemp. He was very clever at not answering questions in this way.

'Lunch? You don't have lunch, do you?'

'I have a sandwich in the pub, and I shall buy the girl a filling slab of pie and a heap of salad. I'll then explain to her about COMSA.'

'Explain what? I don't see the point of all this, Timmy.'

'No, there probably isn't any, really,' said Kemp vaguely. 'But I thought I might explain one or two things she might be glad to know—'

A light flashed from the sepia and ebony depths of Nicola's great eyes. 'I can see you're not going to tell me a thing now, you wretch. But will you promise to tell me sometime? If you won't, I'll go straight to Neil Jonson and say I object to your sending Shirley Essex to COMSA. Now promise, Timmy.'

He promised. An hour later, with a half-eaten sandwich and two double gins in a tumbler on his side of the small round table, he was watching Miss Shirley Essex systematically and efficiently dealing with veal-and-ham pie, salad, roll-and-butter, and grapefruit juice. Clearly she was a healthy girl with a healthy appetite. What she said and the way she said it suggested nothing but the North London suburb where her twenty-two years had been spent. A blind man would have been unable to distinguish her from ten thousand other shorthand typists packing into the Northern Line of the Underground twice a day. But her appearance was astonishing; and Nicola Pembroke's casual reference to her looks, Kemp reflected, did not begin to do them justice. Some freak inheritance, some biological alchemy, had been at work in that North London bungalow when Mr and Mrs Essex produced Shirley. She was one of those rare young women who suggest to the eyes of sensitive men an *anima* figure, a soul image; her hair, an old dark gold, thick and soft, smoothly parted above her brow and richly coiled in the nape of her neck, and her long eyes, a trifle slanted and a soft brown not without an occasional glimmer of green, belonged to some princess of a lost race, awaiting discovery among cyclopean ruins in the jungle, to some troll king's daughter, some nereid floating towards a drowned sailor, some sylph guarded by geni in an Arabian tower. The manner of her talk might come from the secondary school and the shorthand-typing courses, its matter from the women's weeklies and the television programmes; but if a man disregarded his ears and let his eyes signal to his imagination, her glance came out of mythology. And Kemp, seeing her freshly as she chomped away at pie and salad against the background of the pub, congratulated himself on his first quick decision, his intuitive perception that here, in this naiad of the typists' pool, was a long-range weapon for the war between DISCUS and COMSA, an exquisite inter-departmental missile.

'You see, Miss Essex,' he said, continuing in what seemed to him either an extreme fatherly manner or sheer imbecility, 'it really is quite respectable, isn't it?' She had had some doubts about the pub.

'Quite all right at lunch time like this,' said Miss Essex, 'though I expect it might be a bit much at night. And the pie's a lot fresher than it is where I usually go. Thanks very much, Mr Kemp. Did you want to talk to me about something? You said you did.'

'I do, my dear. About COMSA. I was there at one time. I'm the only one at DISCUS who can tell you about COMSA. You'd like to know something about the people there, wouldn't you? Of course you would, my dear. Well, they're a dull lot, not as interesting as our DISCUS staff. With one exception—but a very very important exception.' He broke off. 'Would you like some more of that grapefruit stuff? No? Well, if you'll excuse me, I'll just get myself a touch more gin.'

She had finished eating when he returned. No, she would not smoke. All she wanted was some account from him of this very very important exception of a person at COMSA.

'Ah—yes, of course,' said Kemp. 'That's what I was talking about, wasn't I? Yes, indeed. The Director—Sir Michael Stratherrick. Know anything about him, Miss Essex?'

'One of the girls I worked with at the Ministry said he was very good-looking—a bit like Gregory Peck.'

Kemp swallowed half his gin. 'Sir Michael,' he began gravely, 'is one of the handsomest men I know. Tall, very dark, romantic, melancholy, and yet, I always felt, if he were looking at the right person—and I was never the right person, I must admit that, Miss Essex—with a warmth, a glow, kindling there. Yes, unmarried. He has pursued many women, and many women have pursued him, as you can imagine. Not essentially a bad man, though he's often been called a bad man, a wicked fellow. But I would say, in spite of his gay reckless ways, his influence and position as head of COMSA, at heart a lonely and unhappy man.' He finished his gin, observed his glass in surprise as he set it down, then looked rather sternly at Miss Essex. 'What I asked myself over and over again, when I was with COMSA, was this—could a woman's love—or, better still, the love of a simple warmhearted girl, very different from the sophisticated women of fashion who have been his playthings—where am I?'

'Where are you?' Miss Essex, who had been listening with the sharpest attention, was flustered by this sudden question. 'I don't know what it's called, Mr Kemp—you just brought me here without telling me—'

'No, no, I know I'm here. I'd forgotten how the sentence began. But the point is this. I can't help wondering if what he needs is to love and be loved.'

'I wouldn't be surprised,' said Miss Essex, foolish enough, yet looking like some damsel for whose sake the Holy Grail had been missed. 'I don't know any men like that, but I'm always reading about them. They're transformed by love, Mr Kemp.'

'Very well put, Miss Essex. There's one other thing, though.' He regarded her almost sternly. 'Whoever this woman, this girl, might be, she would have to keep him at arm's length until he'd proved the depth of his love. Another easy conquest, another plaything, would only leave him lonelier and unhappier than ever, more cynical—'

'More blarzy,' cried Miss Essex, a wild rose on fire.

'It would have to be marriage—or nothing.' Kemp stared at her for a moment, then changed his tone. 'Well, my dear, that's all I have to say about COMSA, because really it's all Sir Michael. Now if you feel you ought to be getting back to work, then don't let me keep you here. Unfortunately I'll have to stay on. I see one or two men I ought to have a word with, across there at the bar. Most obliging of you, my dear, to keep me company!'

'A pleasure, I'm sure. And thanks ever so much for the lovely lunch and the nice talk, Mr Kemp.' And off the naiad tripped. Kemp watched her go, so much brightness leaving the air, and suddenly felt sorry. Not sorry for her of course, and not sorry for himself, a complaint from which he was unfashionably free. For the first time since they had known each other, he was feeling sorry for Sir Michael Stratherrick.

5

THEN CAME THE Mountgarret Camden morning, which might easily have created a fellow-feeling between the heads of COMSA and DISCUS, both being equally involved in the disaster; but what actually happened was that each resented the presence of the other more than he resented anything else. After that morning the rivalry between COMSA and DISCUS could no longer be called 'healthy'—one of the Prime Minister's many bright coinages. It became embittered, neurotic, reckless, reaching out towards the final catastrophe.

Joan Drayton brought the message to Sir George. She was all eagerness and smiles, Wally having returned the previous day. The message, delivered by hand, was from Mountgarret Camden who begged Sir George Drake to see him that morning, precisely at eleven-thirty, at Gizzards Hotel.

'Isn't it exciting?' cried Mrs Drayton, who permitted herself these liberties during the early days of Wally-being-back.

'I don't know, Joan.' Sir George, knowing about Wally, never snubbed her for taking these liberties, but he refused on principle to show any trace of excitement or even unusual interest. 'Ask Mrs Pembroke to come along, will you? She may know what it's all about.'

But Nicola Pembroke did not know. 'All I do know, Sir George, is that you must go, of course.'

Sir George himself had felt that from the first but preferred not to say so. 'Oh—do you think so, Nicola? If it's a musical matter, he could have asked for you, couldn't he? And it's all a bit peremptory, isn't it?'

'Yes, but he's an old man, a great man, a *great old man.*' Her fine eyes blazed away at him. 'I wouldn't care—and I know my husband feels the same—if I never heard any work of his again. We've *had* Mountgarret Camden—like Strauss and Sibelius and Elgar. But he's a *giant*, Sir George. It's absolutely fabulous that there he is—staying at Gizzards Hotel—and wants to talk to you. He hardly ever comes to London now—but there he is, and of course you simply *have* to go.'

'You don't think you'd do instead?'

'Not if he says he wants you. I couldn't face him. And it might be something marvellous he wants to do with DISCUS.'

'Well of course I have that in mind,' said Sir George, still trying to sound grudging. 'I'll go along then. Thank you, Nicola.' He rang up Alison, who was still on at him to challenge and defeat the wretched Sir Michael and COMSA; and he made the mistake, the foolish mistake as it afterwards turned out to be, of pretending that this talk with old Mountgarret Camden was the first move in a new and more vigorous campaign. His wife, for once, was enthusiastic. She loved the music of Mountgarret Camden, and venerated the magnificent old man. 'Now don't do or say anything silly, George. Just remember what it means. Why—it's like being sent for by Brahms. Do, for goodness sake, darling, try to *realise*—' And he spent most of the time it took him to reach Gizzards, trying to realise, and then, he felt, realising.

Meanwhile, in Princes Place, Mayfair, Sir Michael had had some talk with his public relations man, Edgar Hawkins. 'Old Mountgarret Camden, no less,' cried Sir Michael, making no attempt to disguise his elation. 'And he sends me an urgent summons to meet him at Gizzards at eleven-thirty. I'll have to go in a few minutes. Haven't been in Gizzards for years and years. Thought it had disappeared in the war. Gizzards—my God! Had a most peculiar night there once, just after I came down from Oxford.'

'A girl?' Hawkins, unmarried, had a rather donnish taste for not too rankly libidinous anecdotes. It was one reason why he enjoyed working with Sir Michael, who openly represented a self that Hawkins had buried.

'She was sitting at the next table in the dining room, and she was being thoroughly ticked off by her husband and his father, a horrible pair. Suddenly, in the middle of it, she looked at me—and winked. Well, that was just the beginning of a most peculiar night. But back to the rat race, Edgar. And take all your mind off those old Chinese pots. Mountgarret Camden, now that he's reached eighty, is news. Probably when he was doing his best work, they wouldn't toss him a paragraph. It's survival that counts in the London Press. News, Edgar, news!'

'I'm quite aware of that, naturally.' Hawkins took himself seriously as a public relations man, and had often been discovered staring gloomily at the popular dailies. 'If he has any musical scheme he wants to discuss with you, I can guarantee it will receive immediate publicity.'

'What's the time? I must go. Very well, Edgar, obviously we're ahead of DISCUS here, so be ready to splash us in the public prints.'

'You'll come straight back, Director? It may be very necessary.'

'I will—and that's a promise.'

Only somebody like Mountgarret Camden, old and famous and not caring a damn, would stay at Gizzards, Sir Michael thought as he asked for him there. It was a place of narrow twisting corridors, where a fierce red-and-blue Turkey carpet was held down by giant stair rods, and brass hotwater cans and unbelievable shoes waited outside doors. The paint everywhere was still the dullest and most hopeless of all browns. The same waiters, now crippled with arthritis and blue with heart disease, staggered under loads of gigantic white-metal dishcovers. Wild young girls from the Irish bogs, roughly costumed as chambermaids, went clattering and chattering from room to room. The lift, trembling with senile rage, took Sir Michael to the third floor.

There, turning the first blind corner, he walked slap into George Drake. The two knights stared at each other in astonishment that soon changed to disgust. 'Mountgarret Camden?' said Sir Michael.

'Yes. Did he ask you to see him at half-past eleven?'

'He did, George. I don't know why. And now, to be perfectly frank, I don't like the look of it.'

'Neither do I,' said Sir George gloomily. 'Well—let's find his room. I've looked that way.'

The sitting room, when they did find it, contained a great deal of mahogany and ultramarine plushy stuff, Mountgarret Camden wrapped in a very old dressing gown, and the composer who had given them both so much trouble—Spike Andrewes. Mountgarret Camden greeted them briefly, then turned to Andrewes, who, to the combined relief of Sir Michael and Sir George, was about to take his leave.

'You have my promise, Mr Andrewes,' said Mountgarret Camden, 'both for the guarantee and my attendance at the concert. I hate making promises because I always keep them. And remember, try to get an extra rehearsal—it's the horns in the *adagio* that are going to need it.'

Andrewes having gone, the old man returned with massive deliberation to the sofa that he appeared almost to fill, and then gazed sombrely at the two knights facing him—or, rather, looking up at him, for they were both sitting in low armchairs. Both had been feeling annoyed, first at finding each other there, then at the sight of the egregious Andrewes, who had had time to give them a belligerent stare; and each of them had told himself, while Mountgarret Camden had taken Andrewes to the door, that having obeyed this peremptory summons he did not propose to stand any nonsense from the old man, for all his years and prestige. But now as he looked from one to the other of them, their resolution began to waver. Old Mountgarret Camden was undoubtedly a most formidable figure. Even under the weight of his years, which seemed to have driven his great head down into his shoulders, he looked enormous. But there was more in it than that. No doubt his fame had something to do with it, the fact that this man's name and works had been known to them ever since they were children; but in addition there was something in his bearing and manner that made him seem one of the last survivors of a giant race, still existing in an atmosphere unknown to all the people they met every day, people who needed something—and were ready to do a deal to obtain it—to prove their individuality to themselves, to make another move towards the Top. This huge old man still seemed to live in a pre-Top era, to breathe an air that London could no longer afford to manufacture. And Sir Michael realised, as he felt himself shrinking, that his earlier thought, when he had first arrived at Gizzards and had half-contemptuously wondered why the old man still stayed here, was only too true: Mountgarret Camden did not care a damn, not only for what so many people thought about Gizzards but also for nearly everything that Sir Michael or Sir George considered to be important.

'I'm not a rich man, gentlemen,' said Mountgarret Camden. He had a deep rumbling voice in which some burr of the countryside still remained. 'Not at all. But I've promised that young man, Andrewes, to find two hundred pounds for the guarantee he needs. I've looked through the score of his work—and feel doubtful about it, though of course my musical ideas may be out-of-date. He's not the kind of young man I take to—too sorry for himself, too shrill, too neurotic, like his music. But he has to have his chance. He applied to your organisations, he tells me, not once but several times, for a little help. Not only did you refuse to give it to him but both of you, personally— he showed me your letters—were condescending and then offensive.

Why? That's all I want to know from you—*Why?*' He opened his sunken old eyes to glare at them; the effect was terrifying, as if they were catching a glimpse of some furnace not really in this world.

It was Sir George who replied, using his best official tone and manner. 'Dr Mountgarret Camden, I can assure you that Mr Andrewes' application was given very careful consideration, and the decision not to award a grant was only made—'

But that was all he was allowed to say; Sir Michael was thankful that he had not tried to reply. What stopped Sir George was at first simply a kind of roar from the old man in which no words could be discovered. But the words soon came. 'Why do these pitiful little organisations of yours exist at all? To return a tiny fraction of the money filched by the state from the community to the arts, after all these pompous blockheads have spent as much as they can on manufacturing bombs and rockets and aircraft they'll never use, building roads so that imbeciles can travel at ninety miles an hour, and all the rest of their nonsense. To keep alive a little culture in this paradise of secondrate business men, bureaucrats, and idiot hobbledehoys. What?'

'Certainly,' said Sir Michael, compelled by the old man's fiery gaze. 'That's what we're trying to do.'

'Very well—keep on trying. And if thinking you're somebody helps you, then keep on thinking you're somebody. But don't talk and write to a fellow like Andrewes, however irritating he may be, as if you were somebody and he was nobody. He's Bach, Mozart, Beethoven, Brahms. He's *Music*—by God! If the pair of you lived another hundred years you still wouldn't be able to appreciate what hopes, fears, delights, miseries, a composer knows, what lives and burns and blazes in him, what torments him, what depths and heights he reaches, the effort he has to make, the feeling he has to sustain. You sit there—dictating and signing your damned silly letters—knowing nothing. A chimpanzee could be trained to do it. And remember this, both of you. You've behaved badly to Andrewes, and I've had to come to his rescue. I'm doing it quietly, and nobody need know. But if it ever happens again, I warn you, I'll blow it all wide open, for everybody to know—my oath I will. And that's all. Good-morning, gentlemen!' And without another glance at them, the old monster picked up a large orchestral score and buried his great head in it.

Sir Michael and Sir George, on their way to the lift, then in the lift, then crossing the dark and smelly hall towards the bright promise of the air, never exchanged a single word. No fellow-feeling had been created between them. Sir Michael and COMSA had been humiliated in the presence of Sir George and DISCUS. Sir George and DISCUS had been made to look small and foolish in the sight of Sir Michael and COMSA. Whatever resentment Mountgarret Camden had aroused in them was now directed by each man to the other and the organisation he represented. Confound COMSA! To hell with DISCUS! Each felt that the morning's disaster, after such high hopes, was really the other's fault.

No sooner had Sir George reached his room than Nicola Pembroke came charging in. (It was undoubtedly a mistaken policy to promote women above the executive grades and routine work) 'What news? What news? Something marvellous?'

'No. The old man was annoyed because he thought we'd treated that fellow Andrewes badly. Especially with Stratherrick and COMSA. He was very rough with Stratherrick—serve him right too. And that's all, Nicola. I'm rather pressed this morning. Ask Joan to come in as you go out.'

She did, and then pulled a comic sour face and nodded it at the Secretary-General's door. Joan pulled a similar face and nodded it in agreement. Then they both felt better.

Over at COMSA, Sir Michael found Edgar Hawkins, his cheek-bones almost luminous with triumph, waiting for him in the entrance hall. 'Director, everything's laid on. A press conference here at two-thirty.'

'Then you've just time to cancel it before lunch. And tell everybody I'll be out for the rest of the day.' Sir Michael wheeled round and as he hurried out he bumped into some fool of a girl. Muttering an apology he had time to notice that her hair was a curious shade of old dark gold. At the club, exchanging stories and witty comment with two men he had always disliked, he had three whiskies before going in to lunch.

6

AT DISCUS COFFEE time, next morning, Tim Kemp wandered into Nicola Pembroke's office.

'Tim darling,' she cried at once, 'please go away. You'll *unsettle* me. And I must — I must — concentrate. Music got poor Sir G. into that mess yesterday, and now somehow or other — by some great coup — I must pull him out of it — '

'Nonsense, my dear!' Tim, settling down, looked at her over his bubbling pipe. 'Besides, I've news. Hot from COMSA.'

She stopped whatever she was not really doing anyhow. 'How do you know what's happening there?'

'You're forgetting I used to toil there — '

'Darling, of course I'm not. But you know very well they hated you. So why — '

'Only heads of departments disliked me,' said Tim mildly. He was a master of cutting-in without raising his voice. 'I was quite popular on lower levels. I have in fact a secretarial fifth column over there in COMSA. My chief contact — I'm calling her that for atmosphere — rings me here as her Uncle Walter. Usually just before eleven. I get all the news, though of course some of it I have to unscramble at this end.'

'You're really a wicked little man, Tim. I don't know why I dote on you. Or do I? Anyhow, what *is* the news?'

'Sir Michael took it even worse than Sir George, my dear. More pride of course. Thunderclouds and rockets this morning over there at Princes Place. It's thought that the Director is also suffering from a particularly bad hangover — '

'But how can she tell you that over the phone?'

'We have a simple code. Anything she tells Uncle Walter about her little dog Mistra refers of course to Michael Stratherrick.'

Nicola looked dubious. 'I never know if you're making things up, Tim. And don't tell me that that girl you planted on them, Shirley Essex, is in on this.'

'Certainly not. She wouldn't know how to begin. She's there for quite a different purpose. The point I was trying to make, my dear Nicola, is that things here are merely a pretty grey compared with the deep black at COMSA. So stop pretending to be desperate.'

'That's all very well, but we'll have to do *something* that might please old Mountgarret Camden. Perhaps help the L.S.O. to fake up some kind of *Tribute Festival* concert — God save us!' She shuffled a lot of papers around on her desk, though she ought to have known that Tim, an old hand, would not be impressed. 'There's a man here called Denerk, who's done a lot of full orchestral transcriptions of Bach organ works — you know, like Stokowsky — ugh!'

'I'm against you, woman. I like 'em.'

'Tim, you can't. They're so *vulgar*.'

'I like a bit of vulgarity in my music,' said Tim. 'And a full modern orchestra makes such a wonderful noise.'

'But to do that to Bach! You've only to mention it to start poor Arthur wincing and shuddering.'

Tim was not impressed. Arthur was the invalid husband, and Tim's opinion, impossible to mention to Nicola, was that Arthur had winced and shuddered himself into the invalidism that had captured Nicola's unwearying devotion. But she might have a secret lover at that, some randy fiddler, originally from Odessa or Bucharest, who now kept flying over from New York or Los Angeles. 'Arthur can please himself. But I still like Bach tarted up.'

'I'll bet you've never been near a concert for years and years, you old fraud '

'I haven't — no. But two girls who live above me have a really splendid gramophone, and sometimes they invite me up to listen. I don't know exactly what they do for a living,' he continued thoughtfully, 'but I've sometimes thought they may be call girls.'

'Tim, I don't believe you.'

'Why not? We're all riffraff of one sort and another where I live now — a most enjoyable neighbourhood. Everybody keeping out with the Joneses. There's a man in the basement who's writing an enormous book proving that we're turning into machines. Don't see much of him because he's away every night — washing up at one of the big hotels —'

'I'm not listening,' she told him. 'I have *work* to do even if you haven't. So go away, just go away, Tim.'

Drifting along the corridor, he ran into Gerald Spenser, who hustled him into the Visual Arts department and never stopped talking for the next five minutes. Spenser's assistant, Miss Whitgift, was a little fat woman whose enormous spectacles, above a sharp nose, made her look like an angry owl. What with her owlishness and Spenser's length of neck and nose and his tortured pale lips, the pair of them reminded Tim Kemp of Hieronymous Bosch.

'I take it you agree, don't you, Kemp? You must agree.'

'I don't know.'

In his astonishment, Spenser seemed to elongate himself by about a foot. 'You don't know. But you must know. Surely I made myself clear.'

'I wasn't listening.'

The Bosch Hell types exchanged looks. 'Well, I must say,' Miss Whitgift began, but didn't. 'I'll be trotting along then, Gerald.' And off she went, rather like an indignant toy.

'Who winds her up?'

'You really are a bit much, Kemp, you really are. I wouldn't have bothered at all, but you said at the meeting you knew Ned Greene.'

'Years ago. Were you talking about Ned?'

Spenser began rotating his head. A horrible sight. 'I took objection to the way in which you suggested at the meeting that Sir George oughtn't to talk to Greene about the exhibition. Of course I'd be delighted to do it myself—indeed as it was entirely my idea that we should organise a Greene show, I was hoping to talk to him myself—but naturally the Secretary-General of DISCUS would carry more weight.' There was a lot more of it. Tim took out the mouthpiece of his pipe and began blowing down it.

Spenser broke off his official gabble to make a protest. 'Look—I wish you wouldn't do that, Kemp. Making a frightful mess and stink.'

'Pity. Now Ned Greene,' said Tim dreamily. 'Unless he's completely different—and hardly anybody ever is—he and our Sir George wouldn't get on at all. That's what I was trying to say at the meeting.'

'You think that I—'

'Worse, if anything. You'd want to talk about art. Ned Greene doesn't talk about art, except perhaps when he's with another painter whose work he likes. He'd shout you down in two minutes and then tell you to bugger off.'

Spenser closed his eyes. 'That type, is he? Well, Sir George wouldn't want to talk about art. You ought to know that, Kemp.'

'I do.'

'Then why warn Sir George against him?'

'When he's not painting, Ned is chiefly interested in drink and women and a general rowdy-dowdy. He'll probably want to meet our good Sir George at midnight in some Soho basement.'

Spenser's eyes were open now and full of suspicion. 'You wouldn't, by any chance, be arriving in a roundabout way at the idea that it's you who ought to talk to him, would you, Kemp?'

'Certainly not. Wouldn't take this on if I were ordered to. Try one of our more luscious women—Nicola Pembroke or June Walsingham—'

'Mrs Pembroke and Miss Walsingham have nothing to do with Visual Arts—'

'They have, though not in the departmental sense. But don't send your Miss Whitgift—'

'I shall leave the matter now as it stands,' said Spenser. 'Sir George insisted upon seeing Greene himself. I shall plan the exhibition, see Baro and ask him to let us know when Greene arrives and where he can be found, and leave it at that. About what happens afterwards,' he added with passion, shaking and screaming, 'I couldn't care less.'

After lunch—a ham sandwich and four large gins—Tim spent an hour in the cubby-hole they had given him, cleaning three pipes and then drawing strange faces, some of them really frightening. Joan Drayton rang down to say that Sir George wanted to see him.

He did not go straight through to the Secretary-General's room. 'How's Wally?' he asked Joan, keeping his voice down.

'Oh—Tim, dear—it's rather awful,' she whispered. 'Poor Wally can't decide what to do about a part in a new TV series. They want him to play a barman. The characters in this series will be always going to this bar. And Wally thinks if it goes on and on, he may be permanently type-cast as a barman. What do you think, Tim?'

'I think he ought to risk it, Joan.'

'Well, so do I—for *his* sake, I mean. Not for mine. As soon as they start paying him fifty pounds a week, he'll feel he ought to go back to that woman and his children—you know—'

'I know. But then the series mightn't last—or the characters might stop going into Wally's bar—and then you'll have him back. And he won't be able to say—that is, if you tell him to take the part—that you stood in his way, Joan.'

'I'll ring him up while you're talking to Sir George,' she hissed. 'So give me ten minutes at least, Tim dear.'

Sir George was wearing his melancholy late-Roman face, brooding over vanished legions. 'Kemp, it's about this Lady Bodley-Cobham business. I trust you remember you agreed to take it over from Neil Jonson, who promised to hand over to you all the material we have on her scheme?'

Tim nodded and smiled; he was brisk and businesslike now, not dreamy; he made a point of never appearing to be what Sir George expected him to be. 'I have it. I've read it. Actually at a sitting. Enjoyed every word. I'm looking forward to meeting this woman.'

Sir George stared at him. 'You surprise me, Kemp. However, we've had a message to say she won't be available until the middle of next week. Wednesday, at the earliest.'

'Then I shall go and see her on Wednesday. If possible, in the morning.' Tim rubbed his hands.

'Hasn't Jonson explained about her?'

'Certainly. She's an old harridan. She never stops talking. She's generally half-plastered. She disgusts Neil.'

'Well?'

'She won't disgust me. I know several old women like that. The point is, you must drink with them. If you're not half-plastered too, there can't be any real communication.'

'Possibly. But you can't start drinking with her in the morning— surely?'

'Certainly I can. May begin the night before. Not with her of course, but independently.'

Sir George looked very dubious. 'Don't forget you'll be there representing DISCUS—'

Tim held up a hand that seemed to have two charred finger tips, from his pipe. 'I'm a DISCUS man—on a DISCUS errand. I shan't forget that, Secretary-General.' He was about to end on that fine note, but then he remembered that Joan needed more time for her telephone call. 'Moreover, there's something I know that you may not know.' He paused, both for dramatic effect and further time-passing. 'Something that will give my visit a certain *urgency*.' Another pause.

'Well, what is it, what is it?'

'COMSA's on to Lady Thing.'

'I don't believe it. She's insisted upon negotiating with us.'

'Now she's trying COMSA.'

'How on earth do you know that?'

Tim explained again about his pipeline into COMSA.

Sir George was horrified. 'Look here, Kemp, I really can't tolerate this sort of thing. It's simply not playing the game.' He waited for some protest but none came. 'Besides, I can't believe that kind of girl would know anything.'

'They know everything,' said Tim.

'Nonsense! I'm not talking now about a responsible woman like Mrs Drayton—but the ordinary secretaries—'

'They know everything.'

This produced Sir George's indignant-shouting face, the purple one. 'Who says so?'

'I do. Everything.'

'Don't keep repeating *everything* like that—most irritating. Are you asking me to believe that the girls here not only know all that's happening but may be ringing up some fellow at COMSA—'

'No, no. No, no. To begin with, there's no such fellow at COMSA. Michael Stratherrick wouldn't have any scruples of course, but he's too grand to work on that level. The other thing is that though the girls know everything, they're not really interested.'

Sir George was horrified again. 'Of course they are. Must be. Stands to reason.'

'But they don't. I mean, stand to reason. They're interested in people. As I used to be with COMSA, we're all friends. And they'll tell a friend anything they think he'd like to know.'

'What about their loyalty to COMSA?'

'Doesn't exist. People for them, not bunches of initials. Same here of course—'

'I've always prided myself upon having a most loyal staff,' Sir George began heavily.

'Certainly,' said Tim, clearly waiting for more.

'Some men are able to command loyalty. Others can't. I'll be surprised if Stratherrick can. He's obviously conceited, self-centred, neurotic.'

'He is indeed.'

'Sound administration demands certain qualities—'

'It does, it does.'

Sir George waited a moment or two, first looking at his desk and then out of the window. 'Well, Kemp, if COMSA is now in touch with

Lady Bodley-Cobham, what do you gather is happening there?'

'Sir Michael's going to see her himself. Top level work.'

'He can't know anything about the woman. You haven't been told when he's going, I take it?'

'Not yet. But unless he's keeping this visit a dead secret, I'll know soon. And, barring accidents, I'll be there next Wednesday morning.' He gave Sir George a slow wide grin, then wiped it off and stood up. 'Nothing more for me, I imagine, Secretary-General? Good! By the way, if you write to Lady Thing, you could tell her I was with COMSA but am now happily back with DISCUS again.'

'I had that in mind, Kemp, thank you.' Sir George's tone was dry, ironical, really a reproof.

Once outside, Tim bent over Joan Drayton's desk. 'Did you get Wally?'

Looking unhappy, Joan nodded. 'He's a bit tight already. And he's been offered a stage part he wants to play—the door-keeper of a Moroccan brothel at the Arts. All avant-garde symbolism. This means he won't go back to that woman of course, because he won't have any money and she won't let him sit up half the night, drinking her gin and whisky and arguing with the director and the other four people in the cast. But it's horribly wearing for me, and it's always worse when it's avant-garde symbolism, I don't know why.'

'They spend the evening not communicating, Joan,' he told her, 'so then afterwards they have to communicate like mad. Ah—that's Sir George, isn't it?' There had been a buzz.

'Yes. How is he now?'

'So-so. Only so-so.' He had left the desk and was nearly at the door. 'He'll be dictating about me to Lady Bodley-Cobham—'

'My God—that woman again!'

'Not to worry.'

But what was the use, he asked himself in the corridor, of saying that to poor Joan—or to Sir George—or for that matter to nearly everybody else. They wanted to worry.

7

'No, CECIL, NOT a penny,' said Sir Michael. 'Not even a hope of a penny. And I don't care if they never have a show.'

'They were on *Monitor*, Director. Didn't you see them?'

'Certainly not. I spend all week mucking around with Contemporary Arts. I don't have to have them hashed up for me on Sunday nights.' Sir Michael looked down again at Cecil Tarlton's memo. *'The Atomistic Group.* One of 'em only paints *Rhythmical Space*—whatever that means; another draws portraits only from X-ray photographs—'

'Because he worked in a hospital—'

'He should keep on working in a hospital. The third one—the sculptor, my God!—won't use anything but pressed spare parts of cars. No, Cecil, tell 'em to try DISCUS.'

'They already have.'

'What? They can't even fool that ass What's-his-name—Spenser, and yet you want to push 'em on to me, Tarlton? What are you trying to do to me? What are you up to, man?'

'I feel I have a responsibility, as head of COMSA's Visual Arts—'

'Not that speech, Tarlton. I don't like it even when I have to make it myself. Well, anything else?'

'I understand that Ned Greene, who's been living in France for the last few years, is coming over for a big one-man show at the Baro Gallery.'

'I know, I know, I know. I also used to know Ned Greene. A good painter, but we're keeping well away from him—'

The unhappy Tarlton mumbled something about DISCUS.

Sir Michael's dark and ravaged face was illuminated by a wicked smile. 'Wonderful! Now if you should run into Spenser, tell him he ought to persuade George Drake to take on Ned Greene. But of course don't tell him I said so. You work that nicely, Cedi, and I'll even forgive you *The Atomistic Group.* But not a penny of course. Now ask Miss Tilney to come in, as you go through.'

Not for the first time, Cecil Tarlton wondered if he would not be happier at DISCUS, working with a chief who did not even pretend to know anything about the Visual Arts. Better still perhaps running some cosy Municipal Gallery, though of course Mona would loathe it. Not that she really liked his COMSA job. And he wondered, again not for the first time, why Mona, within the space of one month, a year ago, had lost her enthusiasm for Sir Michael and had then taken to such a sharp dislike of him that now there could be no question of inviting him to dinner. 'I just can't bear the thought of him here,' Mona had said. A curious way of putting it.

'Miss Tilney,' said Sir Michael, after he had signed the letters she had taken in, 'I've just remembered something. Didn't we steal a typist from DISCUS? She's here, isn't she? Good! Then I'd like to see her.'

'Her name's Essex, Shirley Essex,' said Miss Tilney. Then she hesitated.

'Very well. Shirley Essex is the one I want.'

'Yes, Sir Michael. But I think you ought to know that Miss Bury has already asked her about DISCUS — she told me only yesterday — and this girl really doesn't know anything worth knowing. She was there only a short time, and Miss Bury says she isn't very bright.'

For some reason impossible to discover, Sir Michael found himself disliking both Miss Tilney and her friend Miss Bury. 'I've never thought Miss Bury very bright, if it comes to that. And I don't think you are at your brightest, Miss Tilney, when you assume that my only motive for talking to this girl is some sort of low-level curiosity about DISCUS. I may want to ask her if she's happy here. I may want to ask her how her father is. After all, she's now a member of my staff here, and so far I haven't exchanged a word with her or to my knowledge even set eyes on her.'

'I thought you must have noticed her, Sir Michael.'

'Why?'

'She's very attractive. Miss Bury says — '.

'No, not Miss Bury again.'

'But a very *ordinary* sort of girl. Typists' pool level. I suppose if she'd been clever, DISCUS would never have let us have her.'

'Possibly not, though that's assuming that DISCUS is clever, which it isn't. Does she happen to know which of them arranged for her to come here? Neil Jonson — um?'

'No, it wasn't Mr Jonson,' said Miss Tilney rather slowly and in a level tone. 'She says it was Tim Kemp. He's the only one of them she really knows. He took her out to lunch once. To a pub of course.'

Turning to look up at her, now he spoke as slowly as she had done. 'Knowing Kemp as I do, Miss Tilney—and you remember how dearly he loved me—I don't like the look of this little arrangement. Either the girl must be a complete fool, even by DISCUS standards, or she's not only bright but very bright—too bright for you and Miss Bury—'

'I'm sorry, Sir Michael, but that's quite absurd. I'll admit it's odd that Tim Kemp should have been responsible for her coming here—though of course by this time he may be really completely irresponsible—but the girl herself, I'm sure, is rather naive, rather stupid—a typical suburban secondary-school product. But probably a thoroughly nice child.'

'A good headmistress was lost to England when you decided to turn secretary, Miss Tilney.' He gave her one of those smiles that turned her heart over. He rationed them to two a day; three if they worked late.

'Do you still want me to send for her?'

Before he replied—and he lit a cigarette to give himself time—he suddenly felt that he was about to make a choice of the gravest importance. This was ridiculous of course; he had asked for the girl only because he was bored and did not want to tackle any real work; a mere whim was now monstrously enlarging itself and claiming all manner of undertones and overtones, which even Miss Tilney, a rational and insensitive woman, seemed to be catching. Prowling and grumbling in the basement of his own mind, he knew, was an intuitive, who often sulked and refused to come upstairs and whisper a warning (the Mountgarret Camden fiasco was his fault), but then at other times came hurrying up as if he had heard a fire alarm. This appeared to be one of those times, so everything now was out of all sensible proportion. 'Yes, yes—why not? I'll have a word with the girl.'

His tone was irritable. Miss Tilney did not say anything but she made, by way of reply, her mysterious little noise—not a sniff, not a grunt, not a cough, but borrowing something from each—that always indicated disapproval. As she went out, her wide back, clothed in a cardigan the colour of faded milk chocolate, somehow suggested this disapproval.

Sir Michael tried to be busy with reports on three provincial repertory theatres that Jeff Byrd had left on his desk. They would, he knew, be conscientious reports, containing all the relevant facts; and that is all they would be, Jeff having no real feeling for the Theatre. Sir Michael felt that this was just what he himself did have, on a very fastidious high level of course; but though he could go for nothing and take one of his women along, he hated playgoing. Jeff Byrd, on the other hand, was like a schoolboy who had arrived at permanent Christmas 'hols'; he could sit in a theatre every night; he would see anything anywhere, from too many Dames and Knights at the Haymarket to the Darlington Railwaymen doing *The Rose Without A Thorn;* the poor devil, after years at the Fisheries Board, was stage-struck.

Still moving in an aura of disapproval, Miss Tilney ushered in Shirley Essex, a vague figure apparently wearing a dusty pink blouse and a dark skirt. She was vague because Sir Michael did not really look at her. He asked her to sit down and then pretended to be busy with something on his desk. When he did look up he found she had taken a chair, one of a number used only at meetings, about thirty feet away. 'No, no, Miss Essex, we don't want to shout at each other. Sit here.' He indicated the armchair, not too low and fat, close to his desk and in a good light.

'I thought,' he continued, still not really looking at her, 'there are one or two things I ought to explain. Especially as you came to us from DISCUS. A certain situation exists that I want everybody working with me to understand. You'd like to know about this, wouldn't you, Miss Essex?'

'Yes, I would, Sir Michael. Thanks very much. Though I do know a bit about it.'

'You do? Tell me.' He saw now that she was obviously a very pretty girl.

'Well—I mean—you're sort of—competing, Sir Michael, aren't you?'

She was not a very pretty girl. His imagination rose to deny any such banal notion. It told him that she was beautiful and more terrible than an army with banners. Out of the typists' pool had risen a face, flawless and mysterious, for which cities had been sacked and provinces ruined. It smiled at him out of mythology. It announced at once and with appalling certainty that for years he had been wasting his time, attention, energy, on creatures of bone and lard and scented rags. It wiped away nearly three decades of shabby experience. He felt for a moment that he had not left school, that he knew nothing but only imagined everything, that what the poets had told him was true. Lines out of Yeats's huge mad infatuation came knocking at his memory.

'You're quite right of course,' he told her hurriedly, after a pause to settle his mind. 'We are sort of competing. There's a place only for one organisation of this kind. There never should have been two. It was a mistake. Our functions aren't completely identical, but they're so close that sooner or later either DISCUS or COMSA must go.' Now he risked looking at her again. He tried a smile. She smiled back at him, but not in this world, perhaps under the unfading apple blossom of Avalon or down from the walls of Troy or somewhere. His throat felt parched, so, muttering an excuse, he hurried across to the drink cupboard, poured himself an inch or so of white malt whisky, which he hoped might have a medicinal look, and downed it in one fiery gulp. He thought he saw then in her long mysterious eyes a hint of reproach, but ignored it to begin talking more hurriedly than before.

'The real difference between us can best be understood if you consider the difference, the essential difference, between the Secretary-General of DISCUS, Sir George Drake, and myself. Did you meet Sir George? No? A pity. Well, he's a civil servant and always has been, and I am not, never have been, never will be. He's an administrator. I'm a connoisseur. He has no background in the arts. I have. Strictly speaking, he doesn't know what he's doing. I do. On the other hand, as it happens, I have here at COMSA by far the better administrative staff, which is as it should be. The taste, the discrimination, the civilised enthusiasm, should be at the top, as they are here, Miss Essex. At least that is what I believe, and I hope you'll soon come to believe it too.'

He smiled at her again, but then he realised that while she was still looking at him with a kind of grave concern, rather as if she were a nurse and he a patient, she had not really been listening to him. Feeling foolish, he continued: 'Well, that's how it stands between us. And even if you didn't meet Sir George, you must have had some dealings with his department heads. Didn't you?'

'I didn't much, Sir Michael. It was mostly copying. But I did meet Mrs Pembroke, who does music and was quite nice. And Mr Kemp, who took me to lunch. I don't know what he does—nobody seems to know—but they all like him. He *is* rather sweet, although he does drink too much.'

'He used to be here. He may have been rather sweet then—I wouldn't know—but we found him a nuisance. Sorry, if he's a friend of yours—'

'Oh—no, nothing like that. I only saw him that one time—for lunch—'

'Why lunch? He wasn't—making a pass—?'

She ought to have laughed, but she didn't. She looked solemn and shook her head. 'It wasn't like that at all. I'm sure even if he does drink too much, Mr Kemp would never behave like that. He knew I was coming here to COMSA. He'd been here himself, so he wanted to tell me something about COMSA—'

'And about me?'

'Well of course he mentioned you, Sir Michael. He could hardly not do, could he?'

'And what did he say about me?'

She hesitated and betrayed certain signs of confusion. His legs wanted to run round the desk; his arms ached to take her into them; it was appalling. 'Well, he said most of them here were dull—not like DISCUS—but you weren't—you were very clever, he said. But not happy, he said.'

'Happy? Happy? What a way to talk, even with all that gin! Who *is* happy? Are you happy, Miss Essex?'

'Well, I sort of go up and down.'

'Of course. Like the rest of us.' Miss Tilney, whom he had suspected of eavesdropping before, probably hadn't missed a word of this. He would have to put an end to it. 'I hope you'll go up, not down, here at COMSA, Miss Essex.' He stood up and so did she.

'Thanks ever so much for seeing me, Sir Michael.'

Her legs were superb. Oh—to be passing a hand over them! 'By the way, Miss Essex—' and this brought him round the desk—'how is your shorthand?'

'It used to be all right. But I haven't taken much dictation lately. All copying.'

'Much duller, I imagine.'

'Yes, it is—ever so much.'

'We must see if we can't make use of your shorthand.' He smiled and put a hand on her shoulder. Two things happened, both extraordinary. First he felt her quiver, which of course was an effect he had often encountered before, but never at this early stage. Then, quite calmly, as if there had never been a quiver, she reached up and removed his hand.

'Will that be all, Sir Michael?'

Would that be all? God's truth! But before he could say anything, Miss Tilney had the door open. 'Mr Nutt is here.'

'Mr Nutt?'

'Of the University of Bedford. You arranged to see him at half-past four.'

'Did I? Oh—well—thank you, Miss Essex.'

Gone, gone, gone! Where all that brightness was, Nutt of Bedford University, an implacable bore even on paper and over the telephone, was now here in his horrible person.

'You'd like some tea, wouldn't you, Sir Michael?' said Miss Tilney. She was happy, he felt, now that Shirley Essex had vanished.

'Certainly not, Miss Tilney.' His tone dismissed her. He looked at Nutt, a suety man with the kind of mouth that ventriloquists' dolls have. 'I'm trying to stop this tea nonsense. All England floats on a tepid tide of the stuff. Have some whisky?'

As he helped himself he heard Nutt going on and on explaining why he never allowed himself to drink whisky at any time of day or night. An occasional glass of sherry perhaps, though not just now, thanks very much. The taste of the white malt reminded him of the golden glances across the desk. Trying to forget them, he glared across at Nutt. Only a man from the University of Bedford would be wearing a tie like that.

'And very naturally,' Nutt was saying, 'we felt that we couldn't award our first Creative Arts Fellowship without some guidance— whether or not it would involve a definite recommendation from you—but some guidance from you at COMSA—possibly a short list, which was what, I think, Dr Meltby also had in mind—though he's allowed me a certain latitude—I think I can fairly say that. I spoke this morning to Dr Meltby—'

'Who's he?'

'Dr Meltby? He's our Vice-Chancellor, Sir Michael. Surely it was he who first wrote—'

'Yes, yes, yes, I remember now. We have a short list for you. Somewhere here, I think. Yes, here it is.' He passed it over to Nutt, who immediately looked as if he had been given the draft of a peace treaty at the end of a long war.

'All genuine Creative Artists, I see,' said Nutt. 'Young men too. A poet, a dramatist, a novelist, a painter, a composer—a splendid choice. And what an equally splendid opportunity for one of these five! Nothing like it when we were young, Sir Michael—um?'

Sir Michael glared at him and said nothing. But Nutt was still looking at the list.

'He will spend three terms with us,' Nutt continued, 'with rooms in the Robbins Wing, not quite finished yet but getting on, getting on, with a splendid view overlooking what will eventually be, when the bulldozers have finished and the flooded area has been properly drained, our playing fields. He will enjoy all common-room facilities. Apart from giving a few talks to the students, he will be free to proceed with his Creative Work. Dr Meltby has stated it quite clearly—'

'I know he has,' said Sir Michael, a masterful cutter-in when feeling desperate.

'A remarkable man, don't you think? A splendid choice for us at Bedford—um?'

'Yes.' Sir Michael was now working hard on his own problem—how to get rid of Miss Tilney for a day or two so that he could bring the bewitching Essex girl up here? Tricky, but not insoluble.

Nutt went droning on and on about Dr Meltby and Bedford. Then he suddenly stopped, so that Sir Michael felt he had to attend to him, and he said archly: 'Now, Sir Michael, I just can't help wondering—though I must admit Dr Meltby did give me a hint when we talked this morning—if I pressed you, all between these four walls of course—you might not have—in the very greatest confidence, naturally—a teeny little personal preference for one of these five.'

'No, I haven't.' In fact, he knew nothing about any of them, and he was glad he didn't. Some poor devil would soon be on his way to the Robbins Wing. Dr Meltby and Nutt, and those drenched turnip fields. 'But I have an idea, Mr Nutt. You need some help here. You shall have it.' He rang for Miss Tilney. 'We can't have your first Creative Arts Fellowship going wrong, can we? We're hard-pressed here, as usual, but I can't refuse you, Mr Nutt.'

Mr Nutt closed his eyes, set his ventriloquist's doll lips into a smile, and began nodding, all in a highly gratified fashion.

'Now, Miss Tilney,' Sir Michael began, sternly, 'Mr Nutt and I need your help. We have five candidates for the Bedford Fellowship. Which is the right one? I can't consult my department heads because each of them will favour his or her choice. I need an unbiased opinion. Somebody will have to find out about these fellows and then visit Bedford University. I can't do it—I wish I could—I'm too heavily committed. Miss Tilney, *you'll* have to do it. Field work at last for you.'

'Oh—but—Sir Michael—'

'I know, I know. You feel you can't be spared here. Quite right. But this is an emergency. I'll have to manage as best I can.'

'Perhaps Miss Bury could take over up here—'

'Leave that to me, Miss Tilney. The important thing now, with Mr Nutt here, is for you and him to decide on a plan of action—prompt action too. Mr Nutt has the list. Now off you go. I'll speak to Marlowe about your expenses, Miss Tilney. And don't bother about me. This is top priority.'

'Splendid—really splendid!' cried Nutt. 'Dr Meltby will be delighted, I'm sure. A first-class move, Sir Michael.'

'You've offered us your trust. It's the least we can do. Well, Miss Tilney?'

Her heavy Ibsen face was scarlet; she was shaking a little; she seemed unable to move; she was in fact bewilderingly divided between her innocent pride in being selected for this task and her intuitive suspicion that Sir Michael was now hurrying her out of his way. Had they been alone, her suspicion would have won; but here was Mr Nutt, still beaming but clearly a little puzzled. 'Very well, Sir Michael. We can talk in my room, Mr Nutt.'

An hour later, after the pair of them, now very thick, had looked in to say goodbye to him, Sir Michael, who had been dozing over one of the new French novels full of furniture and objects and nothing happening, heard a timid knock on his door. It was Miss Tilney's friend, Miss Bury, in charge of the typists and all copying and duplication. She was a very thin, very anxious woman, who always gave Sir Michael the impression that the COMSA building was surrounded by some brutal army of occupation. He did not realise that she was terrified of him.

'Miss Tilney suggested you might like me to take over for her in the morning.'

But he was ready for this. 'I would of course, Miss Bury, but it can't be done. I was about to ring down and explain. Now you see these memos—from Dr Frobisher, Mr Tarlton, Mr Byrd—and so on. Here, catch hold. I want you to go round in the morning, and ask each of them, from me, if he or she has anything to add. Then, whether in their present form or suitably enlarged, they must be copied and then duplicated—by you personally, please, Miss Bury. This is a new scheme, to make sure every department knows what every other department has in mind. It's time we were more methodical here,' he added sternly.

'I'm sure you're right, Sir Michael,' the poor woman faltered, knowing only too well she was addressing the only really unmethodical person in the building. 'And of course if you think I should, I'll attend to it myself.'

'You must, Miss Bury, you must.'

'But you'll have to have *somebody* up here—'

Sir Michael stopped her with his hand. He still looked stern but his tone was confidential. 'I had a word or two this afternoon with a Miss Essex, who came to us from DISCUS. Ask her to report to me here in the morning.'

'Miss Essex? I think you'd find several of the girls—' He stopped her again. 'Of course—more experienced. But they didn't come to us from DISCUS. *She did.*' He dropped almost to a whisper. 'Miss Bury, that may not seem important to you. But it is to me. *Very important indeed.*'

'Oh—yes—I see—of course—then I'll tell her—'

He was louder and casual now. 'She's not still here, by any chance, is she?'

'Oh—no, Sir Michael. They've all gone home now.'

'Quite right. I'm apt to forget you've all homes to go to—not like me. A bad habit of mine. Now off you go, Miss Bury. Goodnight!'

His imagination, which had not left him in peace since he first stared at that girl, now went to work on him with more vigour and enthusiasm, as if it were already one in the morning. He could not recall her face; he had only a vague sad picture of a brightness, a deep gold comet, rushing away to some suburb that did not deserve it—and why hadn't he asked the girl where she lived?—and leaving the COMSA building, Princes Place, Mayfair, the whole West End, to a new darkness, a thicker fog of boredom. And what did he do now with his evening? He was supposed to be dining with Clarice Esborn, an intelligent novelist who wrote women's magazine pieces under another name and was always hoping he would do more for her than start her clutching and moaning again on his bed or hers. An old standby, almost a friend, and a handsome woman, but always desperately too hungry—for the food she did not allow herself to eat, for praise and fame, for love, for the big breakthrough that never came. He liked Clarice, who was tender with his ego, and she would carry him through this long and darkening evening. But could he take her now?

'Clarice darling, I tried to ring you earlier—'

'I was having a facial. And I've bought two Dover soles—'

'I simply can't make it tonight, Clarice. It'll have to be some other time.' He had to cut through the wailing protest. 'I know, I know. I'm desperately sorry, darling, but it's COMSA business and I simply can't cut it. No, not even later, I'm afraid. My dear, I'm just as sorry as you are—sorrier.'

He really did like poor Clarice—she was closer to him in type and outlook than those afternoon wives, like Alison Drake, who began reproaching themselves and him as soon as they had pulled a sheet over their nakedness—and now he saw her sitting up there in that Maida Vale flat, with her facial-and-Dover-Sole evening wrecked all round her, weeping in self-pity or already desperately ringing up some old standby of hers—'Darling, I know it's ridiculously short notice . . .' Perhaps he oughtn't to have done it. And what the hell was he to do now with his own evening? A typist, not half his age, probably stupid, possibly engaged to some young guffawing moron! He had never even noticed if she wore an engagement ring. In fact he knew nothing about her. But then he remembered something. Tim Kemp came into this. It was a thought that trailed a mysterious shadow behind it but for the moment he preferred to ignore this: Kemp could tell him something about her. He rang DISCUS.

No reply. Only quarter-to-six but the whole lot of them over there had hared off. Pretty bloody typical.

8

IT WAS THE WEEKLY meeting again at DISCUS. Sir George looked around in despair. He had made his announcement, carefully choosing the right moment, the right tone of voice, but it was as if he had tossed them a bomb that had merely exploded into whistles, riddles and paper hats. Apparently nobody cared—except Joan Drayton, and she, having had the news from him much earlier, was only reacting again out of loyalty. Spenser and Hugo Heywood were actually beginning to talk together about something else. Kemp, probably far from sober, was smiling. Nicola Pembroke was examining a string of those large beads she was fond of wearing. Neil Jonson seemed to be scribbling notes on his agenda sheet.

'Now will you all kindly listen to me?' Sir George rapped on the table. Now they were all quiet and looking at him. 'I don't believe you can have heard what I said. And I'm not attempting to discuss a mere rumour now. I had it direct from the Ministry.' He looked around and then held up a finger. 'There's going to be *a Question in the House.'* This time there was no chattering, no bead-examining, no note-scribbling, though Kemp, drunk perhaps, was still smiling. 'It was bound to happen, of course. I'm not saying it's altogether a surprise. But there it is—*a Question in the House.'*

June Walsingham, who had been peering at a small diary, now caught his eye. As usual she looked as if she were about to make some quite improper proposal: relays of giant gins-and-tonics followed by strip poker, that sort of thing. 'Well, Sir George,' she cried cheerfully, 'that should be good for some publicity. What should be my cue?'

'You should ask your Fleet Street friends to spare us, Miss Walsingham.' Sir George shook his head at her. 'When you've been in the government service as long as I have, you'll realise that questions in the House generally try to bring a department into disrepute. You know that, Neil.' He was appealing to the only other civil servant present.

But Neil Jonson, as Sir George should have remembered, was now a rogue civil servant, a permanent rebel. 'It's not the questions

I mind,' he said gloomily, 'but the idiotic Establishment answers. When's this happening, Mr Chairman?'

'Not settled yet. But quite soon. I don't know if COMSA are equally involved—'

'They are,' said Tim Kemp, still smiling.

'I won't ask how you know, Kemp,' Sir George told him. 'But I'd like to think that it's because of COMSA you've been looking—er—so amused these last few minutes.'

'Certainly. They're having a meeting. Probably at this very moment. Stratherrick didn't want one, but Dudley Chapman and Jim Marlowe have forced his hand. Yes, Sir George, I find this amusing. And it'll be more amusing soon, I can promise you.'

June Walsingham now stared across at him. 'How do you know all this?'

'He knows, June, don't worry,' said Nicola Pembroke, giggling a little.

Sir George quietened her with a frown. 'I've no doubt, if the Question in the House has wide terms of reference, we can make a better showing than COMSA. But that's not enough. I have here a full list of all your possible projects, but I must confess I'm not impressed and I don't think the Ministry will be. It's thin—very thin.'

'I did what I could to tart it all up,' said Hugo Heywood, 'but the Theatre's having a lean time.'

Several other voices now claimed lean times too.

'I *have* heard a rumour,' said Heywood, widening and then rolling his eyes, 'that I'm anxious to follow up. But it's too early for anything to be said about it here, Secretary-General.' Now he narrowed his eyes and looked like a middle-aged repertory actor playing a South American conspirator.

After the other lean-timers had made some apologetic remarks, to which Sir George listened in deepening gloom, June Walsingham, who had the presence and voice to do it, commanded the meeting's attention. 'If you want to know what I think,' she began, 'I'll tell you. We're not approaching this Question thing from the right angle. You're not giving me anything I can use. All itsy-bitsy stuff, none of it worth a paragraph. We ought to concentrate on one big dramatic thing that might hit the news the very day this Question is being asked. I may not have been a civil servant, Sir George, but it happens that I do know something about the House, and I know that if we're in the news, just about the time that Question's asked, the Ministry spokesman can make that M.P., whoever he is, look silly. And of course make us look good. Give me a story that has some size and guts in it, and I'll do the rest.'

'Yes, Miss Walsingham,' said Sir George, regarding her thoughtfully, 'I'm sure you will. A very sound approach too, let me add. But obviously we need a coup of some kind. Now some of you may think my general policy too cautious. And up to now, I'll admit, I've felt we must move slowly, not to risk over-spending as COMSA has done. But any project that has what Miss Walsingham calls "size and guts" in it, I am ready to back to the limit. I believe—and this, I suspect, is the Ministry view—that this Question in the House may be the beginning of a campaign to establish that either DISCUS or COMSA is clearly redundant. Then one of us must go.'

'Or both of us,' said Tim Kemp, still smiling.

'You've heard something, have you, Kemp?'

'A whisper. Saloon Bar stuff. *My spies tell me*—the usual line. May be nothing in it. I might have been dreaming it—but Neil's heard it too.'

'Quite right, Tim. You see, Sir George, the P.M. might have to go over the heads of both the Minister and the Lord President. Too many people may have turned his joke against him. And if both DISCUS and COMSA are comic, then he might prefer to abolish both of them, starting all over again—a little Ministry of Culture perhaps, Continental style. Mind you, this is only vague talk so far.'

'Let's leave it then,' said Sir George sharply. It was intolerable that these fellows should know more than he did. 'The immediate question is—where is our big dramatic project. How do we make news? Well?'

After a few embarrassing moments of silence, Tim Kemp began mildly: 'Well, Mr Chairman, I can't promise anything. But it does seem to me that the transformation of a vast mansion into a place where artists can live and work might be a newsworthy item—'

'I'd buy it,' cried Miss Walsingham.

'Of course. And I do happen to be seeing Lady Bodley-Cobham tomorrow morning, at her house in Berkshire—'

Several voices cried him down. They had all tried. She was quite impossible. It was now really a bad joke, that scheme of hers. Sir George now made himself heard. 'No, no, Kemp, nothing there, I can assure you. Waste of time.'

'Is it? Then why am I going there, Secretary-General?' Tim's tone was rather sharper than usual.

Sir George gave him a bleak look. 'Perhaps so that you can appreciate some of the difficulties DISCUS has to contend with, Kemp. That appreciation might be worth a day of your time to me.'

'It might—yes. But as I shan't come here before I go to Berkshire in the morning—and as I'm told Sir Michael Stratherrick may be calling on her himself later in the day—I'd like one or two things to be made quite clear to me.' He smiled at Sir George, who was still looking bleak. 'First, this scheme has the kind of size and weight you want, eh? Secondly, supposing that to be true, you would be ready to back it to the limit, eh?'

'Knowing the difficulties as I do—and you don't, Kemp—I don't think this is worth our discussion.'

'Why, what else do you propose to discuss, Mr Chairman?'

'Really, Kemp—'

'With all respect, Mr Chairman,' said Kemp firmly, 'as you've arranged for me to see this woman, I'm entitled to have an answer to my two questions.'

'And I must say I agree with him,' cried Miss Walsingham. 'From my angle—'

'You've told us about that, Miss Walsingham. And I've already approved in principle.' Sir George now spoke as from a great height. 'If Mr Kemp can make any sense of that woman's proposals—and I doubt it because I doubt if she's right in the head—I will go a long way to give any practicable scheme the full weight of DISCUS support. And that's all we can do today, I think. Thank you.' Sir George now withdrew, more in a mental and spiritual sense than a physical one, for the meeting had been held in his room and his own desk was only a few feet away; but somehow he withdrew, climbing invisibly to a higher level.

'I shall want five pounds from you, Neil,' Tim Kemp said as they went out. 'Expenses for tomorrow.'

'What you'll get is exactly one pound twelve shillings and ninepence. You're forgetting I've already done this Bodley-Cobham trip myself.'

'I'll bet Sir Michael Stratherrick doesn't do it for one pound, twelve and ninepence tomorrow. I wonder what's happening at COMSA this afternoon.'

At that very moment not only was Sir Michael chairing a staff meeting, he was also regarding his subordinates with haughty disfavour, as if they were the odds and ends of a clan who had just thrown down their claymores. 'My God—I've never seen people so stricken with panic. If one can use that term. It doesn't sound right, but you know what I mean.'

Out of the corner of his left eye he shot a glance at Shirley Essex, who was sitting, away from the table, on his lefthand side. On her knee, no doubt exquisite though so far he was still only guessing, was the shorthand notebook at which she all too often stared in dismay. But who the hell cared? Today she was wearing the pale blue shirt and the dark blue skirt—simple but ravishing. And here she was— with Miss Tilney still toiling remotely in the Bedford and Creative Fellowship field—and she would be here after he had dismissed the meeting, and tomorrow he was taking her with him to Berkshire and Lady Whoosit. Behind his mask of dark and haughty disdain, which was part of his showing-off for her benefit, Sir Michael could feel his spirits rising and expanding.

After glancing round at the faces of his colleagues, Dudley Chapman became their spokesman again. He had just the right face, meaty and slabby, for sound spokesmanship. 'I can't pretend to feel happy about it, Director. And Summers—you know him, I think, sir—in the Lord President's office—'

'I know him, Dudley—an imbecile—'

'He may be, but he knows what a Question in the House could mean.' A murmur of agreement went round the table. They all knew what a Question in the House could mean.

'Have you ever been there and listened to this highly organised twaddle?' Sir Michael produced a snort of contempt, and then turned to Shirley just for the pleasure of looking straight at her. 'Don't put that down, Miss Essex. You didn't hear it.' He hoped she would return his smile, but she didn't. The trouble was, she really thought this meeting a great and terrifying occasion.

'The question is,' Chapman was saying, 'what lies behind it. Is it a move to get rid of one of us? And if so, do we go or DISCUS? I'm certain that financially they're sounder than we are. As you know, Director, I've tried to point out—'

'And I've tried to point out, Dudley, not once but a score of times, that we're on a different financial basis. Whenever George Drake recklessly orders another hundred sheets of blotting paper, he's spending public money. Nearly fifty per cent of our funds come from outside the Treasury. Thanks to me,' he continued, pretending to be very boastful in order that they would think he was not boasting at all when indeed he was, 'and my astonishing powers of persuasion— to say nothing of two of the worst dinners and most boring evenings I have ever had—we enjoy generous grants from two wealthy foundations.' Now he looked round at the others. 'Dudley knows all about them of course. Who better? I'm really making this point for your sakes. I'm trying to give you courage, fortitude, faith and hope. Or am I?'

'I'd say you weren't,' said Edith Frobisher dryly.

'Very well, I'm not. Now I'll tell you what's wrong with us. And it's nothing to do with questions in the House, for which I don't give a damn. We're dull—and getting duller. We yawn at one another over lakes of tepid tea. We ought to be half-plastered, gay and full of devilment. Audacity! *Panache!* We ought to be planning something here and now that would frighten George Drake and his Education backers to death. You'll observe I'm saying *we*—not you. I'm giving myself a share of the blame. I've been dull too. I've been a victim of the English virus too—whatever it is that turns them into mumbling zombies. But if I've been bad lately, you people have been worse. I spent most of this morning—God help me—going through those enlarged memos that I asked Miss Bury to collect, copy, duplicate. It was like walking through glue in a fog. You know your own reports are dreary, but have you tried reading everybody else's? I'd like to make DISCUS a present of them. Now for God's sake, children, forget about this terrible Question in the House, which I don't think even worth discussing, and find me something audacious, gay, dazzling and beautiful for COMSA. And don't imagine I'll be lolling here. I'm making a start by paying a call tomorrow on this daft rich old woman who's already defeated DISCUS. I'll confess that a year ago I wouldn't have gone near her. But now I feel we can't afford to ignore even this dubious chance. And that's what all of you ought to be feeling. Desperate but gay, just as if you were Celts. No, Dudley—no, Jeff— the meeting's over. I like the last word, and you've heard it.'

He got up and moved away, turning his back on them as they filed out. Then he went to his drink cupboard, half filled a glass with the strong malt and added a third as much water, took a good gulp, and then swung round to look at Shirley. He knew she would still be there because he had warned her that she would have to stay on after the meeting.

'Well, Shirley, do you think that did any good?'

'I don't know,' she said softly and slowly. 'But I think you're wonderful when you talk like that, Sir Michael, I really do. I'm sure if anybody talked to me like that—' But there she stopped.

Yes, you little devil, he told her, savagely but silently, it's time I did start talking to you. He had these savage moments, suddenly flaring in the dark of his mind: a wild part of him fought the trap. The old Greeks had had the right idea about this kind of thing; it was an infliction, a dreadful gift from Aphrodite, merciless after being flouted so long. (He could imagine a chorus of his afternoon women imploring the goddess to punish him.) A few hours, at the most, in or on a bed with this girl, and the spell would be broken. Meanwhile, however, it held him, even though he was capable of some rational thought outside it. 'Would you like a drink, Shirley?'

'Do you think I ought?'

'If I didn't, I wouldn't have asked you. But of course you don't have to take one, just as you don't have to refuse one. We're now in Liberty Hall.' He announced this so bitterly that she stared at him in wonder.

'All right,' she said. 'I'll just have a little glass of sherry, thank you, Sir Michael.'

While he went for the sherry, he reflected sombrely on his predicament. He had not asked her yet to meet him out of this building and working hours—her trip to Berkshire with him tomorrow was to break this ice—but already he knew a good deal about her. And all this knowledge was against him. She was hugely and solidly respectable, as if all that journalism and television about her generation had never existed. She was ready to walk out of this job at any moment, which meant that she might vanish as soon as she had really taken offence at anything he might say or do. She was not altogether stupid—she was quick and perceptive about any little sexual move he might try—but there was no real intelligence behind that astonishing face. Her work for him, which made Miss Tilney seem a marvel, was maddeningly slow, almost dim-witted. She lived in some horrible Northern suburb and forest of television aerials; and she was the only child—curse the luck!—of funny sweet old Dad, an assistant cashier at a manufacturing chemist's, and anxious loving Mummie, who had somehow conceived and brought forth—God only knew how or why—this golden scourge of Aphrodite. And here he was, Michael Stratherrick, who after a few swift sure moves had been able to transform so many calm and devoted wives, some of them with *1st Class Hons,* into yielding and gasping creatures, here he was, as bewitched as an eighteen-year-old, not knowing what to do or to say next.

He gave her the sherry, and, just to be touching something, insisted playfully that they touch glasses. He kept their fingers together for a moment, and enjoyed a sense of achievement. Then he could almost see and hear that chorus of women turning to point and giggle at him with broad, coarse and implacable female irony. And he knew he was not merely being fanciful. This monstrous infatuation, from the moment he saw her face looking at him out of mythology, had churned up forgotten depths in him, depths of primeval wonder and ancient superstition: he was entranced, and now more than half out of his mind, because there was revealed to him, across a desk and a shorthand notebook, the face and figure of what Jung had called the *anima,* the soul image.

She rarely broke any silence between them, but now she did. 'Are you really taking me with you tomorrow afternoon? Because if you are, I wish I could get my hair done.'

'Why, what's wrong with it?'

'Oh—I ought to have it done. And I don't see how I could at lunch time.'

'Take the morning off.' He made it an order.

'Oo—could I? But what will Miss Bury say?'

'I'll attend to Miss Bury. I'll tell her you rang me, to say you weren't feeling well. Leave it to me.'

'But she knows I'm going with you tomorrow.'

'Does she? Then I'll tell her you're not. Much better, really.'

'But then on Thursday she'll want to know what was the matter with me. She's terribly nosey, Miss Bury.'

'Well, tell her something—anything.' He was irritable, detesting this miserable office-intrigue stuff. 'Have some more sherry?'

'Oh no, thanks ever so much.'

Taking the very small sherry glass from her, his hand closed over hers. The contact, slight though it was, touched with flame his

71

smouldering senses. He stood over her, not moving though burning. However thick her cocoon of old-fashioned suburban respectability, she was a woman and must know what he was feeling. He said nothing and kept as still as he could, not to break the current.

She looked up at him. It was a look thousands and thousands of years old. 'All right then. Just one. And I mean it—just one.'

'Just one what?' This was so far removed from his experience that he really did not know what she was talking about.

'You want to kiss me, don't you?' She was quite matter-of-fact. 'Well, just one, then. And not one of *those* kisses—a nice one.'

Feeling foolish above the pounding of his heart, he kissed her full on the lips, but delicately. Then, with a great effort of will, he forced himself to move away from her. He drained his whisky before looking at her again. After this matter-of-fact approach, she might now be thumbing through her notebook or powdering her nose, but to his surprise she was sitting exactly as he had left her, staring at him, her eyes bright and large and her mouth perhaps trembling a little. And now what? He really did not know what to make of her. He might never have been near a woman for years.

'All right then, Sir Michael.' There was no change in her tone. 'I'll take the morning off and have my hair done properly. But if I'm supposed to be at home, I can't meet you here, can I? Where do I go? Railway station?'

'No. I'll hire a car. This woman's house is miles from any station, I gather, so we might as well go by car.' Glad to escape feeling foolish, he was now the curt executive. 'I can't pick you up here of course or anywhere too close. Be somewhere on the west side of Berkeley Square at two-fifteen.'

She repeated this, carefully.

'And bring a notebook.'

She nodded. 'But what about the notes of this meeting? Aren't I supposed to be doing them?'

In some ways, he told himself, she learnt fast enough: half-an-hour ago she would not have tossed him this *supposed*. 'Doesn't matter. I don't want my oratory on record, and there wasn't much else. Except *Question in the House.*' He saw she was bewildered. 'All right, Shirley, type out something like this. A meeting held at four-thirty—today's date—with so-and-so-and-so-and-so attending and the Director taking the chair. After some discussion of a possible

Question in the House, the chairman appealed to the meeting to support his belief that COMSA was in need of a more imaginative and audacious policy. Have you got that?'

'No, you were much too quick.'

'I'll repeat it then.' When he saw she had got it down, he went on: 'After the meeting the Director was invited by his temporary secretary, Miss Shirley Essex, to give her one nice kiss. He did this, and then, to her enormous relief, behaved like a perfect gentleman.'

'I don't see why you have to be sarcastic at yourself.'

'Berkeley Square—two-fifteen sharp, please, Shirley. Goodnight.' He went to sit down at his desk. When he looked towards the door, she was standing there, looking across at him. 'That's all, Shirley.'

'I know. Goodnight.' Then, instead of moving, she began crying.

He jumped up. 'Now what's this—?' But by the time he had reached the door, he could hear her running down the corridor. After giving himself one more whisky, he felt he could not endure another evening wriggling inside this trap, so he rang up Clarice. No reply. He tried Mavis, who was reproachful and anyhow had a dinner engagement. Andrea was home and said at once she was longing to see him, but then he knew he did not want to see her, and gabbled some rubbish about suddenly hearing she had been asked to do the sets and costumes for the new play at the Aldwych. After that, reduced to imbecility, he sent his forefinger up and down four Essex columns in the telephone directory, finally peering—his eyes watering a little after so much small print—at *Jevon M. Essex, 5 Winston Avenue, N.16*. And after that, he told himself, he had to go either to the club or clean out of what was left of his mind.

At the club, four men he had been dodging for weeks closed in on him.

9

IT WAS TWO-FIFTEEN exactly when Sir Michael saw Shirley waiting for him in Berkeley Square. She was wearing a suit—cobalt green perhaps—and a rakish little brown hat, and looked not only entrancing but also, to his surprise, very smart. In the pale April sunlight the square suggested a fine watercolour of itself. This was one of those unusual early afternoons when Mayfair seemed to have taken itself out of London into some mysterious foreign capital, belonging perhaps to a wealthier Ruritania. Sir Michael, who had lunched lightly but had awarded himself a bottle of an excellent Traminer, now found his spirits rising on that rare tide of happiness which is controlled by some other moon, not the one the rocket men are aiming at; and he immediately opened the door from the inside and drew her into the car as if she were a wonderful prize, which indeed she seemed to be.

The car he had hired was a landaulette, sufficiently large and luxurious, but its driver was not the type to open doors and fuss with rugs. He was a gloomy youth with longish hair, looking as if at any moment now he might turn into a pop singer, and though he had condescended to listen as Sir Michael had explained how they might find their way to Lady Bodley-Cobham's place, somewhere in the Henley-Wallingford region, he had made it clear that he took no interest in this journey. Most of his days and nights, it appeared, were spent driving what he called 'stars of stage, screen and TV' to studios and night clubs, and obviously he regarded this expedition to Berkshire as so much vague slumming. In three minutes, he and Sir Michael had taken a powerful dislike to each other.

'You're looking exceedingly smart, Shirley,' Sir Michael told her as soon as she was settled by his side. 'I don't know if Lady Bodley-Cobham will be pleased, but I know that I am—indeed, delighted.' He made sure now that the wall of glass between them and the driver was secure, and went on: 'By the way, how are you at reading road maps?'

'Oh—I don't think I'll be any good, Sir Michael, though I'll try.'

'It'll soon be up to us, my dear. Within an hour or so—I prophesy here and now—we'll be lost unless we keep an eye on a road map. This driver's an imbecile. Once outside London, you'll see, he'll behave as if we were trying to find our way in Outer Mongolia. However, it may be an adventure—if you like adventures.'

'I think it's lovely riding in a big car like this.'

'Good! And you have your notebook?'

'Look!' She held it up in a small brown-gloved hand, which he covered with his own, ungloved, whereupon she dropped the notebook in her lap, whipped off her glove, and let her hand rest in his. This split him at once into two warring halves, one of them feeling an ass over this hand-holding nonsense, the other knowing a burning delight.

Later, as they stopped and started and ground their way through some Western suburb, he said: 'Has it ever occurred to you, Shirley, that now we've stopped believing in Hell we are in fact creating it here on earth as fast as we can? The traffic, the noise, the shoddy shops, the idiotic advertisements, the meaningless faces, the whole damnable confusion and chaos—if it isn't Hell—what is it? Or don't you think like that?'

And of course she didn't. And not, he concluded, because she was insensitive and stupid but really because there were twenty-five years between them and she had grown up with everything that filled him with horror. The hand he was holding—now a little sticky, so that he released it, ostensibly to light a cigarette—belonged to another age, in fact *this* age. And it struck him then, rather sickeningly, that if he abandoned all pretence and told her what he felt about that strange beauty of hers, plundering mythology and poetry in praise of it, she would not understand what he was talking about and would stare at him as if he had suddenly gone out of his mind. But then, after all, she was a woman, age or no age; and behind her flat little statements and complacent clichés, there might be a timeless complexity of subtle perceptions and feelings. Could he risk it?

They were now running into rain, the ruined world outside blurring and fading. He felt her move a little closer to him, doing it, he was sure, instinctively. Because he no longer wanted to talk, out of feminine conscientiousness she began to prattle away. Beginning, on common ground, with the type represented by the driver, she told him that what she called 'boys', the young men of her generation, did not attract her at all, although she had had plenty of attention from them, especially at the Swimming Baths dances, which she no longer attended. They were all too young, callow and shallow for her, though one 'boy' had been 'nice', rather 'delicate' but 'artistic', mad about his camera; but he had gone to live with an aunt in Bournemouth. To all of this, and much more, he listened half in a dream from which his earlier rising spirits had fled. The afternoon darkened; the rain was fiercer; the car arrived at nowhere and then stopped; the driver was lost.

The next forty-five minutes were all exasperation and frustration and map-cursing and roads that became lanes and farm tracks and dead ends. The driver was sullenly unco-operative, now wanting nothing but an order to turn back; Shirley remained cheerful, helpful in spirit but utterly unhelpful in fact; and Sir Michael, even his desire defeated by the muddle and rain and the time running away, began to damn under his breath the whole expedition, which seemed idiotic anyhow, nothing like the gay COMSA foray he had first imagined. Even if he found this Bodley-Cobham woman, he felt he would have no patience left for her.

It was well after four when at last they turned into a drive that had been neglected for years, and bounced and bumped their way towards a monstrous folly of a mansion—*circa* 1875 and the creation of an architect who spent his evenings drinking brandy and reading the novels of Scott. If Lady Bodley-Cobham was actually in residence, the mansion offered no outward sign. But undoubtedly this was the place. Sir Michael helped Shirley out and told her to run for cover to the enormous front door, and then he turned to the driver, who had not stirred, and said he would have to wait but might be able to do so inside, over a pot of tea.

'What—in there?' said the driver bitterly. 'It's an 'ouse of the dead, if you ask me. Proper Charlies we're goin' to look, comin' 'ere!'

'All right, sit there and brood,' Sir Michael told him sharply.

When he joined her, Shirley was tugging away at a giant bell-pull. From somewhere inside there came a harsh jangling. But nothing else happened. When she looked up at him, smiling rather uncertainly, he was moved to put a hand to her cheek, cold and damp and exquisite. Then he gave the bell a savage pull, and the jangle within had not stopped when the door was flung open.

'What you want?' The man's tone was as darkly suspicious as his look. He wore a stained white housecoat, baggy flannel trousers, and what appeared to be enormous felt slippers. 'We no buy anyzing.'

'I am Sir Michael Stratherrick.' He made it loud and clear. 'I arranged to call upon Lady Bodley-Cobham this afternoon.'

The man was not impressed. 'She no say to me you come 'ere.' He shook his head, pushing out his underlip. 'She no say anyzing to me. Not anyzing—nozing, nozing!' He was one of those exiles who while being overwhelmingly foreign never suggest any particular country of origin, belonging to some unknown peasantry: a kind of Chico Marx character.

'Now look here, I've come specially from London to see Lady Bodley-Cobham, and I don't propose to stand here arguing with you. Either take me to her or tell me where I can find her. Come along now.'

After nodding dubiously and grunting, the man admitted them and then led the way along a corridor piled high with those tea chests used by furniture removers. He made a turn to the left and indicated a doorway. 'What I say?'

Sir Michael gave him a glare and his card. As the man went in, leaving the door open behind him, they could hear somebody laughing but only distantly, as if the room were enormous.

'It's all a bit peculiar, isn't it, Sir Michael?' Shirley looked at him wide-eyed. 'I'm glad I'm not here by myself. You can't believe anybody's living here, can you?'

'I might have known,' he muttered. 'She'll turn out to be some eccentric old monster. Ten to one this will be a dead loss, Shirley. My fault. I should have let one of the others tackle her first. Stupid.'

'You didn't want them to do what you weren't prepared to do yourself, Sir Michael,' she said proudly. 'Like a true Leader.'

For a moment he thought it was irony—and he would have welcomed it, even if he were the victim—but then her shining gaze told him she was speaking from the depths of a true and loyal heart. Good God—what was he up to, where was he going?

The synthetic foreigner, grinning now, returned to point the way. This was necessary because at first sight the room, lofty and immense, looked like a chaotic furniture warehouse. Couches and sofas, large tables and small tables, armchairs and upright chairs, clocks and cabinets and pictures and marble busts and bronze horses, were all jumbled and piled up to make fantastic and rickety walls between which they passed, like entering a kind of trench of furnishings.

Having pointed the way, the houseman hurried off, leaving them to it. They found themselves in a sort of central clearing in the jungle of walnut and mahogany. There, seated in a chair like a throne was a colossal old woman, her hair dyed a fierce Venetian red, her face painted as thick as a clown's. And perched below her, at ease and smiling, was Tim Kemp. He was smoking his pipe; she had a cigar. Both were holding glasses, and between them were several bottles of gin of various brands, which they had obviously been sampling generously.

'Hello, Stratherrick!' said Kemp. 'Why, it's you, Miss Essex. What a pleasant surprise!' They must have been drinking for hours, Sir Michael concluded. He had seen Kemp like this before, floating as high as a kite.

'Pleasant surprise be damned,' the old woman shouted, pointing her cigar and glaring over it at Shirley. 'Haven't I told you people not to bring gals here?'

'You haven't told *me*,' said Sir Michael firmly. 'And Miss Essex happens to be my secretary.'

'I know what she happens to be,' Lady Bodley-Cobham began.

Kemp stopped her. 'No, you don't, Annabel. This time you don't know. Most other times, but not this one.'

'How the hell do you know, Tim?'

'This child's a friend of mine, Annabel.'

'Well, I can't even see her properly. But then I don't want to. I can see this Sir Michael Thingummy, though. Tall, dark and handsome, and probably no dam' good. Used to be hundreds of 'em round Cannes. Give him a drink, Tim.'

'Thank you,' said Sir Michael. 'I'll have some whisky.'

'Not here you won't,' the old woman shouted at him. 'There isn't any. We drink gin here. That's one reason why Tim and I took to each other at once. But then he's a sweet little man. Knew it at once. A sweet little man.'

'Yes, he is,' said Shirley Essex surprisingly.

'You shut up. Thought you'd sunk through the floor by this time—'

'Annabel—Annabel!' Tim sounded almost severe. 'I'm taking Miss Essex away—'

'To do what?'

'To find her a cup of tea, if I can. And to let you and Sir Michael have a talk—'

'He won't get anything out of me, Tim. I know the type. Used to meet hundreds of 'em—foreigners mostly of course—hand-kissers—professional charmers. Never got round me. Well, off you go, Tim, but don't be too long. And try and make this gal understand—they're all such malicious little bitches—I don't pretend to be living here. I'm just *camping*—that's all;—camping—till I decide what's to be done with my Derbyshire place. Better take a drink with you, Tim. And give me one. What do we have this time?'

'Plymouth,' said Tim, moving towards the bottle. 'Got a suggestion of a fresh morning at sea about it. Remember those fresh mornings at sea, Annabel?'

'No.'

'Neither do I,' said Tim, pouring out the drinks.

Lady Bodley-Cobham cackled, and then looked at Sir Michael. 'See what I mean? He's a sweet little man who doesn't give a damn. All the rest of you come here sweating with anxiety and keep clearing your throats—'

'I don't,' said Sir Michael boldly. 'And I'll take a touch of that gin, thank you, Kemp. Not my idea of a drink, but better than nothing.'

'On the bold tack now, are you?' Lady Bodley-Cobham blew some smoke in his direction. 'But let me tell you. I've never liked good-looking Englishmen—'

'I'm a Scot.'

'Worse, if anything. The point is, you're all petted and spoilt to death before you're out of the nursery. Crammed with conceit Here to be looked at, not to do anything. Vain idle sods. No use to a woman. Might as well keep a stuffed giraffe.'

Glass in hand, Tim Kemp went over to Shirley. 'We'll go this way.' He took her to the other end of the enormous room, this time along a path between precarious walls of bookshelves and piled-up books, cases of butterflies and birds, animals' heads, shields and swords and guns. 'It's just like England, isn't it? Such a clutter of old rubbish, you can hardly move.'

They came out into a bare corridor with a stone floor and damp-stained walls, all unwelcoming and melancholy. 'This won't be as bad as it looks,' he told her, 'so don't start puckering up those wonderful features. To begin with, behind the second door on the left is a lav, which is the first thing you want, isn't it? The next thing is a cup of tea, and while you're in there, I'll get one for you.'

'Oh—thank you, Mr Kemp,' she cried. 'But where do I go when I come out? This place terrifies me.'

'I'll be waiting just round the corner, near the kitchen, and I'll find a place where we can have a cosy little talk. That's what you want, isn't it—a cosy little talk?'

'Yes, I do, Mr Kemp. And I'm so glad you're here.'

There was a bathroom next to the lav—no towels, no soap, though; a disused bathroom it looked—and there she spent some time recovering her face from its bewilderment and distress. Then she found Mr Kemp, smoking his pipe and sipping his gin, just outside the open doorway to the kitchen, noisy with people talking all at once and laughing. He took her into a sad little room that had a table and a few chairs in it and nothing else. But on the table was a tray with tea things on it and the largest teapot she had ever seen.

'Help yourself,' he said. 'And I don't want any. This was probably the housekeeper's sitting room—or something of the sort. Not very cheerful, but we wouldn't be able to talk in the kitchen. Only four of 'em in there—but it's a party. The cook, who's a mad old Irishwoman. A local girl, mentally defective but pleasant and obliging, unlike most of the mentally effective. Antonio the houseman—that isn't his name but that's what Lady Bodley-Cobham calls him. And your driver.'

'Our driver? But he's such a miserable sulky chap.'

'In the car, no doubt. But not in there. He got the party going. Feel better now, Miss Essex? Shirley, isn't it?'

'Yes, it is. And I feel much *much* better, thanks to you, Mr Kemp.'

'Call me Tim, Shirley.'

'Tim. That awful old Lady Bodley-Cobham frightened the life out of me.'

'Just her manner. And anyhow, she's a bit plastered of course. We'd been drinking and talking several hours before you arrived.'

'You must have been, Tim. I nearly died when I heard you call her Annabel.'

'It's her name—and now we're friends. And you and I are friends, aren't we, Shirley? So now you can tell me how you're getting along with Sir Michael.'

'Oh—Tim!' And a golden naiad stared at him above the teacup. 'I love him. I can't help it. I've tried not to—but I love him.'

'Only natural, Shirley. It's what I expected. But you remember

80

what I told you about him, don't you?'

'Of course—every word. And I know it's true what you said.'

'If he simply has another plaything—'

'I know, I know. And it's awful. All the time I want him to touch me—'

'And then what happens? Where are you? Where is he? You have to rescue him from himself.'

'That's what I keep telling myself, Tim. I do understand, I really do. But it isn't easy—when I love him. I'm not one of those cold calculating girls.' She might have been an indignant tea rose.

Tim took another sip of gin and then, not without some effort, looked immensely solemn. 'Now let's examine the situation as it appears today. He's here. He's brought you with him, proof positive he's not in his right mind—'

'What do you mean—?'

'He's in love—or at least infatuated. Now then—this visit will be a dead failure. Take my word for that.'

'I know it.'

'And you're going to feel very very sorry for him—'

'I am now—'

'It'll be worse tonight, when he'll want to give you dinner somewhere and then take you to COMSA or to his flat. You'll want to give in—and if you do—'

'I know, I know.'

'But if you don't, if you hold out, if you tell him you're not that kind of girl, then there he is, already tired and disappointed, and now frustrated again, and there could be an ugly scene—'

'Do you think I haven't thought of all that?'

'I don't know, my dear. But there's only one thing for you to do. Take him home with you. Refuse to dine with him. Tell him dinner or supper is waiting at home for you both. And it's either that—or *Goodnight*. A good test of his feelings. Now, Shirley, there's a telephone on a wall bracket just round to the left. Ring up your mother and prepare her. And when you've done that,' he added, rather sleepily, 'ring up DISCUS and ask for Sir George Drake.'

'Oughtn't I to do that first?'

'Certainly not. Mother first; Drake second. Life first; DISCUS and COMSA second.' He had already closed his eyes.

When she returned, after a mixture of appeals and commands to a bewildered Mummie, to tell Tim she had the DISCUS call for him, he was fast asleep; and for a moment she hesitated to wake him. He looked something between a gnome and a very old baby. However, she gave him a little shake: 'Tim, your call to Sir George Drake.'

He peered at her mistily. 'Good God—why, girl?'

'You said you wanted to talk to him.'

'What about?'

'Oh, don't be silly, Tim. How do I know? Perhaps about Lady Bodley-Cobham.'

'Quite right. Thank you.' He was up now. 'Let me see—which way—?'

She went with him to the telephone, and decided to hang around, partly in case of any accident but also because she was curious.

'Drake,' he began, 'Kemp here. . . . Certainly it's important. Wouldn't be talking to you if it wasn't. Besides, I may not be back for several days. . . . Why? Because tomorrow I go with Lady Bodley-Cobham to Derbyshire. . . . Don't keep saying *why*—it sounds idiotic . . . . I'm going with Lady Bodley-Cobham—by the way, a splendid sensible woman even if a trifle eccentric—to examine and then report on the mansion and extensive grounds, including a small lake, you may remember, that she's prepared to put at the disposal of a combined Creative Arts Centre scheme.' Tim's voice was now reaching an oratorical tone. 'It will be a place where advanced young artists of all kinds can live and work—the novelists writing anti-novels, the playwrights anti-plays, the painters and sculptors creating anti-art. I have persuaded her—and it took some doing—to contribute fifty per cent of the costs of conversion and fifty per cent of the running costs for the first three years.... Incidentally, Stratherrick's here, but making no headway, I imagine. . . . I am not suggesting you can make a move before you have my report. But my report you will have in due course, whatever that means. Meanwhile, I suggest you call a meeting of department heads. . . . No, Drake, you are *not* running DISCUS—you are walking it.' He put down the receiver carefully, saw Shirley and winked at her.

'We ought to join the other two, I think. But where did I leave my glass? Oh—thank you, my dear. Might as well finish this.' Then, taking her arm and moving rather slowly and uncertainly along the corridor, he continued confidentially: 'I didn't tell Drake, who's easily alarmed, but I'm looking forward to this Derbyshire trip. We shall be going in the largest and oldest Rolls-Royce now remaining in Western Europe. I've seen it. Antonio—you've met him, I think—probably a Montenegrin—will be driving us. We're taking the mad Irish cook and the mentally defective girl with us, together with ample supplies of tinned sausages and game pies, that kind of thing, and plenty of gin. The Derbyshire mansion, I gather, is about five times the size of this one, and hasn't had anybody living in it for years. Fortunately I brought a small packed bag with me, foreseeing that something of this sort might happen. Unlike Drake, as I told him not long ago, I'm an intuitive type. What's the matter, my dear?'

'Listen! Oh—gosh—they sound terribly angry.'

'It's about what I expected. I warned you, remember. You'll soon have to use all your tact. Have you any tact, Shirley?'

'Nobody's ever said I had. I'll do what I can, Tim, and thanks ever so much for warning me.'

'And I'll be equally frank with you, madam,' Sir Michael was shouting when they reached the central clearing. 'In my opinion you're a mannerless, feckless, crazy old harridan. Your scheme's as ridiculous as you are, and it gives me enormous pleasure to tell you that COMSA will have nothing whatever to do with it. Shirley, where the devil have you been?'

'I had some tea and then did some telephoning.'

'At my request, Stratherrick,' said Tim. 'My fault entirely. Blame me. And have a drink.'

'Certainly not. We're going. Is that driver anywhere about, Shirley?'

'Yes, I'll tell him.' She hurried off, glad to get away. She could hear the horrible old woman shouting now. What a disaster this had turned out to be! Sir Michael's pride would be hurt. On the way back she would have to draw from somewhere whole buckets of tact.

10

THE GLOOM and the rain outside, the snug intimacy of the car, ought to have encouraged an exchange of confidences, but during the first twenty minutes or so Sir Michael said nothing. Shirley did not try to break the silence but she sat as close to him as she dared, and when the car gave a lurch she did not try to avoid any contact with him but made sure he could feel she was there. The male mind, however, was not functioning in the touching department.

'I feel foolish of course,' Sir Michael announced finally, not so much to Shirley as a person but to Miss Essex there as world delegate, 'as any vain man would. You must have noticed that I'm an extremely vain man. I'm not thinking now of that ghastly old trollop and her impossible scheme, which nobody in his senses could take seriously for a moment.'

'But I heard Mr Kemp telephoning Sir George Drake about it, telling him he was going tomorrow with Lady Bodley-Cobham to look at her house in Derbyshire.'

'I'm delighted to hear it.' And he sounded as if he really was. 'Kemp's off on a vast binge of course, but he'll come back with some notion that'll drive poor George Drake half out of his mind. Incidentally, it's not clear to me, Shirley, how you happen to be so thick with little Kemp.'

'Oh—I'm not—but he's been kind to me—and—'

'He's such a sweet little man,' said Sir Michael rather savagely. 'I know all about that. Don't forget, he used to be with me at COMSA. Now I'll tell you about Tim Kemp.'

'I wish you would,' said Shirley, after waiting a moment or two.

'Nobody can say I take myself and my COMSA responsibilities too seriously,' Sir Michael began slowly. 'But compared with Kemp, I'm just another George Drake. Which is damned irritating of course. It's not that he's simply irresponsible. He's a kind of growing point of anarchy and sheer devilment in any organisation. He's really working for some mysterious other side, some sinister female deity—and this might explain why all you women instinctively approve of him. He's the only genuine subversive type, therefore the last man who ought to be a civil servant. As I told him when I finally got him out of COMSA, he'd come back only over my dead body. People like George Drake or our Dudley Chapman simply see him as boozy, dim and lazy—and he is, undoubtedly—but what they don't see, and I always did, is that he's quite exceptionally perceptive and clever in his own way. And mischievous as the devil.'

'Oh—but there can't be any *harm* in him, I'm sure.'

'Can't there? Don't you believe it, Shirley. Look at this idiotic Bodley-Cobham business. I'm willing to bet a fiver that George Drake put him on to it, after they'd all had a go, simply to involve him in a laborious mess and keep him out of mischief at DISCUS. And what happens? He goes off on some daft boozy saga. He'll entangle Drake in some lunatic scheme. And at the same time he's made me look a fool. And he's so confident, after ginning it up for hours with that old monster, that he can calmly take you off somewhere—'

'But he saw I was nervous and all embarrassed, and that I wanted to—to powder my nose—and then have some tea—'

'You told me when we first met,' Sir Michael cut in, darkly, 'he'd given you lunch and talked about me—'

'I told you. He only said you were very clever but not happy—'

'I know, I know. But is that *all* he said?'

'It's all I can remember.'

'Is it? Is it? Are you sure?' He had twisted round, and now shot out an arm, put a hand on her far cheek and turned and lifted her face towards him. Then he kissed her, and though she tried not to respond, she found she had to, before jerking her face away.

He took out his cigarette case—elegant and apparently made of gold; and she was sure some woman had given it to him, some rich, unimaginably sophisticated, wicked woman—but he did not open it. 'All right. Where shall we dine?' he asked in a rather thick, strange voice.

She felt herself trembling. This was the moment. 'I promised I'd go home. I don't want to leave you, not after it's been such a miserable disappointing day, but you could come and eat with us. I told Mummie you might—Michael.'

'Thank you, Shirley,' he heard himself saying. 'Let me think.'

And he had to think, fast and hard. He knew at once that he would never persuade her to dine with him now, and because that had always been part, indeed the chief part, of his plan for the day, an empty and melancholy evening threatened him. But was that worse than what she had proposed, the dreadful little suburban house, the tinned peaches with Mummie and Daddy, and Shirley herself transformed, perhaps for ever, into a typist at home? On the other hand, perhaps he was being offered a way out of the trap; this might mean the end of this ridiculous infatuation, dwindling at once into an obvious absurdity in this atmosphere of Mummie-and-Dad. Certainly he could look a fool for a couple of hours, but after that he might easily cease being one. She didn't know it, poor child, but she was really inviting him to break the spell. He looked round and down at her upturned face, not clearly seen now in the poor light, and wondered how strong that spell was.

'I told Mummie that anyhow you'd be taking me home in the car,' she said rather apologetically, 'so I ought to ask you if you'd like to have supper with us. They call it supper though it's just the same as dinner really. And my mother's rather good at cooking. Though of course all of it may seem dull and dreary to you.'

'I've never found my club very exciting in the evening.'

She ignored that, busy with her own thoughts. 'Don't think I'm silly enough to believe that when you see me at home with my parents, it's really me. I'm more myself at work than I am there, though that's not really me either. I suppose I'm not me anywhere yet except in my own thoughts. Will you come for supper then?'

'If you really want me to, Shirley. I'm not sure, for various reasons, it's a good idea.' He hurried on, before she could frame a question. 'But then I'm the man who thought visiting that Bodley-Cobham monster might be a good idea. The truth is, as I said earlier, I'm a vain man, no doubt far too pleased with myself, and I've had such stupid people to deal with at COMSA that I've inflated myself almost off the ground. When I was running the Institute, before COMSA, I was mostly concerned with artists, and they can be maddening and damnable, but they're not stupidly thick all the way through like Dudley Chapman, Jim Marlowe, Hawkins and Tarlton and Byrd—or like George Drake and his crew, even though they are a bit better than mine. I suspect there's something fundamentally idiotic about people who want to administer the arts. Together they create an atmosphere that makes me despair and then want to do something reckless and ridiculous. And of course vanity, conceit, pride, all come running to help. By the way, you don't have to listen to this stuff. Think about something else. Perhaps you *are* doing.'

'Usually I am when people talk a lot.' She was thoughtful, solemn. 'But not with you. I love listening to you even when I don't quite understand what you mean.'

This simple confession released so many conflicting feelings in him that he did not know what to say. Then he realised that he was badly in need of a drink. 'Does your father drink whisky?'

'No, he doesn't, I'm afraid. Just beer—cider, sometimes. Mummie has sherry—on special occasions—but not the kind you'd like.'

'I'll tell the driver to stop at a pub. Want to come in with me?'

'I'd rather not, if you're not going to be long.'

'I'm not. I like drinking but not in the average English pub—the half-wits' paradise.'

Ten minutes later he was back beside her with a half-bottle of Scotch, which he opened by unscrewing a little metal cup. 'Want some?'

'No, thanks. Mummie'd smell me at once and have a fit and blame you. I mean, after you'd gone. But the funny thing is that if we weren't going home, I would have some, and I've never wanted to before.'

'It mightn't suit your style.' He was offhand, being busy filling and emptying the little cup. He had a good head and could drink a lot of whisky, far more than most men, without making an ass of himself; but like many seasoned drinkers, not phlegmatic in type, he responded at once to even a small amount. It began immediately, he felt, to change the atmosphere and then the part he had to play in this different ambience. And now they were on the move again, there were more street lights and neon signs slashing at the wet windows, and the whole pitch of things seemed higher, more dramatic. 'Does this fellow know where to go?'

'I told him, when you went to the pub. And then I began to think.' She hesitated.

'Changing your mind about that invitation to supper?'

'No, of course not. But all the same I could see a lot of good reasons why I oughtn't to have done it. It just mightn't work for anybody. And I couldn't find a good reason—not then—why I should ask you, yet I still wanted you to come. That's silly, isn't it?'

'It's not rational, certainly.' He had swallowed the fifth tot and was now screwing on the cup. 'But the rational is a very small part of us, very recent and not the most enjoyable. Now, girl.' And he put an arm round her, drew her closer, and bent his face to hers. But then she became just another woman, so much hair, soft skin, trembling lips; only his blood wanted her; his imagination, in which this senseless infatuation was fixed yet burning, held aloof from this adolescent courtship, waiting for some very different moment when her beauty—hardly hers; a random gift—would be naked and triumphant but then immediately possessed, done with, ready to be forgotten. He was glad now he had accepted her idiotic invitation. Imagination had trapped him; comic reality might soon release him. Meanwhile, he released her, decided he needed at least one more tot of whisky. On, on, then, to 5 Winston Avenue, N.16, to Mummie, to Daddy, to tinned fruit and the Telly, to Michael Stratherrick his sensible self again!

As soon as they were outside No. 5, semi-detached with tiny garden, Shirley vanished indoors, presumably to change and primp, before Sir Michael had signed the driver's chit, reluctantly tipped him ten bob, and told him in effect to get back to his 'stars of stage, screen and TV'. Her parents were waiting at the door to welcome him. He had decided to play safe; he would be the amused, rather whimsical, condescending but kindly great man, the girl's amiable chief, not her friend. He hit what seemed to him the right note at once.

'Mrs Essex, it's extremely kind of you. I felt I had to bring your daughter home, after taking her on a rather long and tedious journey into the wilds of Berkshire, and then she insisted I should stay for supper. I hope I'm not being a nuisance.'

'Of course you aren't, Sir Michael,' she cried, smiling though flustered. 'It's a pleasure, I'm sure. So long as you'll just take us as we are.'

'We don't pretend to be anything but simple people,' said Mr Essex, heavily and rather severely. 'And so long as that's understood, you're welcome, Sir Michael.' But he neither looked nor sounded welcoming; not resentful, but guarded, suspicious, like a police inspector about to receive some dubious evidence.

'I don't know if she's told you,' Sir Michael began hastily, not quite in character, 'but your daughter's been taking over while my own secretary's out of town, doing a little COMSA research for the University of Bedfordshire. And of course I'm very much obliged to her. Not easy to take over at short notice, especially as she's a newcomer. When she's had a little more experience, I'm sure she'll make an excellent secretary for somebody. Not for me, unfortunately. My own secretary, the one who's been out of town, a most capable middle-aged woman, has been with me ever since I became Director of COMSA. But we must try to find a place for—Shirley, isn't it?—on the secretarial level as soon as we can. With rather more responsibility she'll receive rather more money of course—'

As he rattled on in this style, like somebody on an Appointments Board, Mrs Essex smiled and nodded and her husband nodded without smiling; but Sir Michael began to feel, with growing dismay, that just as he was performing, so were they. Whatever Shirley may have told them, whatever they may have deduced from her recent chatter and manner, this official employer's guff did not fool them. They let him run on but *they didn't believe him*. What they did believe, he could not tell as yet. But now he felt damnably uneasy.

The room did not help. It seemed to him uncomfortably bright and hot and shiningly polished and carefully arranged, like a stage set— Act One of a comedy about Winston Avenue, N.16. And now Mrs Essex disappeared to cope with supper; Shirley remained upstairs; and he was left with Mr Essex, who poured out, with more care than Sir Michael had seen taken about anything for weeks, two glasses of pale ale. This would be tough going.

He had been pleasantly surprised by Shirley's mother, very much a suburban housewife no doubt, but, after all, a woman, about his own age, perhaps a year or two younger, and by no means unattractive, still pretty if plumpish, well worth taking to bed. And behind her obvious housewifely anxiety and snobbish fluster there was, he felt, a cool feminine appraisal of him, probably devilishly intuitive. But even coping with her might be agreeable. On the other hand, Shirley's father, Jevon M. Essex, whom he was facing now over the pale ale, was a disaster in slow motion. He was a man in his early fifties, who held himself very stiffly and had a narrow head, an inquisitive nose, a small but bristly moustache, and a long and obstinate and idiotic chin. It was impossible to believe that any part of Shirley had issued from his loins; a young and despairing Mrs Jevon M. must have given herself to another man sometime, probably in the Blitz. And the manner and style of Mr Essex were even worse than his appearance. He spoke slowly, giving intolerable weight and solemnity to any platitudinous trash, the sweepings of mass media, he chose to inflict upon a listener. He was the 'serious reader' that the worst editors in Fleet Street had in mind. He was the man who telephoned to producers of television programmes. Knowing himself to be the backbone of the country, flattered by politicians of all parties, he was enormously conceited, far worse in his ponderous self-approval than the most egocentric artist Sir Michael had ever known. To share a roof with him would be a Chinese torture.

By the time Sir Michael had reached these conclusions, supper was ready. Shirley was wearing a kind of party dress, much too fussy and quite wrong for her; perhaps she read disapproval in the first glance he gave it—he had complimented her several times earlier on her choice of clothes—for throughout supper she said little and seemed downcast. The meal began with grapefruit, a detestable idea, went on to braised beef, not bad, and vegetables, and ended with some sort of trifle nonsense in little glass dishes. Mrs Essex, who might have been lively in other circumstances, was all anxiety and fluster. So Mr Essex took charge of the table talk, when he was not champing his way through the meal, not as if he enjoyed any part of it but rather as if he were consuming on principle his ration of foodstuffs.

'I'm going to be frank with you, Sir Michael,' he said. 'When Shirley got a place at the Ministry of Higher Education, I was pleased—very pleased. But then she's suddenly moved to this DISCUS, as she calls it. And then before she can settle—and with no proper notification—she has to go to this COMSA of yours.' Sounding and looking aggrieved, he demanded some sort of reply.

'I know, Mr Essex. It seems all rather confusing and absurd.'

'Well, I'm glad you think so. I'm also very glad we don't try to run the chemical industry on these lines. But of course, as we're always reading in the paper, when it's a matter of spending public money, nobody cares—why should they?'

'As a matter of fact they do, you know—except perhaps in Defence—'

'That's different, quite different. That has to be a first consideration. It stands to reason that the defence of the country must come first. But that's not what I was going to say. I'm going to be frank with you and tell you, Sir Michael, that I'm not at all pleased, not at all, by what's happened to Shirley lately. I'd hoped in the first place she could have got into something more solid, like the Board of Trade—'

Shirley and her mother looked swiftly and despairingly at each other. Obviously they had heard all this many times before, and always, Sir Michael imagined, at this same maddening pace.

'—And then before she's been able to make me understand what this DISCUS is supposed to do, she's been transferred to this COMSA of yours—'

'Mr Essex,' Sir Michael cut in sharply, 'if you really want to know what COMSA is and does, I'll tell you.'

'Shirley's told him,' said Mrs Essex, smiling but still anxious, 'but he only believes what he reads in his paper.'

'Let's talk about something else, please, Daddy,' said Shirley.

'Oh—it's something else that's wanted now, is it? When we've had nothing from you but COMSA-COMSA for the past week—'

'Now stop teasing her, Father,' cried Mrs Essex, getting up. 'Will you wait for your coffee till afterwards? Because it's nearly time for your old *Rusty and the Rangers.*'

'Oh—gosh—' Shirley muttered—'I'd forgotten that was on tonight.' She looked appealingly at him, the first direct look he had had from her for some time: 'I'm sorry, Sir Michael. Do you mind?'

Unexpectedly, astonishingly, he felt then a great and utterly disarming tenderness for her, quite different from anything he had felt before. He longed to take her away, anywhere out of this room, just to comfort her.

'Why should he mind?' her father asked severely. 'He probably makes a point of watching it himself. Some of the foremost men in the country, I read in the paper—men at the top, it said—never miss *Rusty and the Rangers.* Now you and your mother had better hurry up and clear, otherwise there'll still be a clatter when it starts. Over there, Sir Michael, if you please. Now I'll tell you what we decided, before we bought this house. We decided we'd have a decent-sized kitchen, where we could eat when we're by ourselves, and then no dining room, as you see—but a fine big lounge. Then if we had company for supper, like tonight, then we'd eat in here, as we have done. Why a dining room?' He almost glared, as if Sir Michael was trying to sell him one. 'Sheer waste of space, I call it. All you want is a decent-sized kitchen, then a fine big lounge. Then what have you got?'

'I've no idea.' Sir Michael was now being pushed into a chair facing the television set.

'You've got Successful Modern Living,' Mr Essex announced proudly. He switched on the set and sat down, very close, far too close, to his guest. 'If you want to smoke, do so, Sir Michael. Ashtray here. I don't smoke myself—never seen any point in it—but the wife likes a cigarette now and again—she'll probably have one tonight, after she's brought the coffee in—and I'm not sure that daughter of mine doesn't enjoy a puff or two. I'd rather they didn't, to be frank with you, but I don't insist—no, I don't insist. I believe in a certain amount of liberty for all so long as it doesn't turn out to be licence.'

There he stopped because a pretty and very self-conscious girl appeared on the screen to explain what treats it had in store for them. The first of these was another exciting episode of *Rusty and the Rangers.*

'Never miss it,' Mr Essex shouted above the loud preliminary music. 'Good entertainment . . . relaxation . . . always cleverly done . . . and always Clean, not like some of this Kitchen Sink stuff of ours . . . manly. Do you watch it? No? Well, this chap in the white hat is the retired Sheriff—a droll character, very droll. And he's Rusty's uncle . . .'

It was hard to think in front of all that galloping and shooting, but Sir Michael did his best. Why had the girl inflicted this upon him? Was it in all innocence—and stupidity? Was it a subtle and very feminine kind of revenge? And if so, for what? For churning up her emotions when all he wanted was to get her near a bed? And did she know she was stripping herself of all that magic, without which he would never have given her two minutes of his attention? And why—

'He's a dead shot,' cried Mr Essex. 'You think he's a fool. But watch! He's a dead shot—every time!'

Sir Michael stopped trying to think. There was now a lavish expenditure of blank ammunition, all from rifles and revolvers that never had to be re-loaded. Rusty came through in triumph, ready for the next episode. Shirley and her mother arrived, bringing the coffee.

'All that bang-bang-bang!' cried Mrs Essex. 'Gets on my nerves. And I don't suppose you enjoyed it, did you, Sir Michael?'

'A long way from your COMSA,' said Mr Essex complacently, as if he had just drilled a few rustlers himself.

'Quite,' said Sir Michael dryly. 'And an equally long way from the

Western Desert, where I once spent a couple of years.'

The set was now busy with the news but it was difficult to attend to it because the coffee had to be handed round.

'It's this next programme that these two like,' Mr Essex shouted, easily topping a cabinet minister, who was saying nothing in a manner at once frank and dignified. 'Doctors. That's what they enjoy. And I must say it's well done, very well done indeed. You'd really think you were in a hospital.'

Sir Michael said that he did not want to think he was in a hospital, but nobody heard him. After swallowing the coffee, which was tepid and far too weak, he muttered an excuse, went to the tiny vestibule and found his overcoat, and hurriedly drank some whisky while they were arranging the chairs. He returned to find Mrs Essex sitting next to him and Shirley on her other side. Several times during the programme, which did not hold his attention, he glanced across at the girl and discovered, to his surprise, that her face, innocent and rapt in the flickering light of the screen, had recaptured some of the magic it had lost. Ah—well! What next?

What actually happened, just when he was going to tell them he ought to go, was quite unexpected, astonishing him. While Mrs Essex turned off the set and switched on more lights and Shirley began moving the chairs, Mr Essex hurried to the front door, came back to say it was quite fine, and announced that this was the time when he liked to stretch his legs and get some air and that, if Sir Michael would excuse them for half-an-hour, Shirley would go with him.

'No, Daddy,' Shirley began, obviously dismayed.

'Now, Shirley,' said her mother firmly, 'I'm sure Sir Michael won't mind, and you know how your father likes you to go with him.'

The move was so clumsily contrived that Sir Michael felt that he must be standing there open-mouthed. What could he say or do? Two minutes later, father and daughter had gone, and he was sitting only a few feet away from Mrs Essex, looking enquiringly at her. She was not unlike Shirley, but could never have been more than pretty; their colouring may have been much the same, but a finer bone structure had been added to create Shirley's beauty. Probably by that man in the Blitz.

'Of course you saw through all that, Sir Michael,' she told him, smiling.

'I'm afraid I did, Mrs Essex. And I was about to say it was time I went. But of course if you want to talk—'

'It was either me or my husband—'

'Then I'm glad it's you.' And he smiled this time.

But she regarded him earnestly. 'We argued about it, and I persuaded him it ought to be me. You haven't seen him at his best tonight, Sir Michael. The truth is, he's a bit jealous, after the way Shirley's talked. Though of course she's said a lot more to me. He'd go up in the air if he knew half what I know.'

He frowned at her. 'Why? What is there to know?'

'From something Shirley said, I gathered you'd had a lot to do with women. Affairs, I mean. And as soon as I saw you, I knew it was true. I hope you won't be offended—I don't think you will—if I say that from a woman's point of view, you're a dangerous man, Sir Michael. That's something my husband wouldn't understand. But even he feels he's heard a lot too much this past week about Sir Michael Stratherrick and COMSA. Shirley never talked like that about her other jobs—'

'That's not surprising, is it?' he said rather sharply. 'Your daughter's been a typist, just copying, not coming into contact with anybody or anything interesting. And it happens that this last week she's been acting as my secretary—a very different kind of job—'

'And why has she, when there were others more experienced? And she admits that. And why did you take her with you today?' She looked hard at him. 'Have you ever been to any of the other girls' homes?'

'No. But then they've never asked me.'

'Because they wouldn't dare—wouldn't dream of it. I can tell. You're not being really frank with me, Sir Michael. Well, I'll be really frank with you. And please don't take offence. You've done something to that child—and in many ways she still is a child—you oughtn't to have done. Not unless you're serious yourself, and I don't believe you are. You've made her fall in love with you—'

'Oh—come—come!'

'Yes, you have. It doesn't take long for a girl to fall in love head over heels with a special kind of man. I *know*. And what you probably don't understand is that once it's happened she can stay that way for a long long time, just not caring about other kinds of men, the sort she might marry. Shirley's an attractive girl—very pretty—'

'No.' This would do him no good, but he had to tell her the truth.

'Shirley isn't a pretty girl. There are hundreds of them around. Shirley's something quite different, at least to a man with any imagination. She's a beautiful girl, Mrs Essex. And if you want to know why I've insisted upon having her within sight, it's because I wanted to feast my eyes upon that face of hers. I'm not a mere womaniser. I happen to be a man of taste and with a highly developed visual imagination—'

'But that's nothing to do with love, has it?'

'I don't know, Mrs Essex. Honestly, I don't know.'

'You're not serious. You wouldn't think of marrying her.'

'I wouldn't think of marrying anybody. I'm not a marrying man.'

'I know that, Sir Michael. But Shirley doesn't. Girls her age don't, when they're in love.' She waited a moment, as if trying to decide what she ought to say. 'There's something you ought to understand about Shirley. She may seem an easy gentle sort of girl—and in many ways she is—but she can be very obstinate and nobody can make her do what she doesn't want to do. Do I have to say any more?'

'I don't think so, Mrs Essex.' He stood up. 'It'll be a long way in a taxi, so I'd better go by Underground. Is there a station near here?'

'Turn to the left, and then the second turning to the right. You can't miss it.' She was standing now, very close to him. 'You're not going to wait for them, then?'

'I think I'd better not, don't you?' He said it very gently. 'By the way, the situation's rather more complicated than you imagine it to be. I've not really been making plans to seduce your daughter. Though of course I want to go to bed with her, as any man would, feeling as I do. But I've really been drifting   bewitched—rather than planning. This isn't melodrama, you know, and though I may look it, I'm not the villain of the piece.' He smiled at her.

She astonished him then by smiling back and suddenly putting a hand to his cheek. 'If it was me it wouldn't matter,' she said, as she withdrew her hand. 'Oh—no, I'm not suggesting anything. But girls her age can take things very hard. They can be left in a dream for years. What am I going to tell her when she comes back and finds you've gone?'

'You could tell her I've obeyed parental orders.' He began drifting towards the front door. 'You could also tell her to stop seducing *me*.'

'You know that's silly.' She was following him. 'You're an important person—she's nobody.'

'You're underrating your sex.' He put on his overcoat, then took out the whisky. 'I turn left and then take the second turning to the right, I think you said.' He was now filling the little cup. 'Forgive my doing this but I need a drink.'

'I could do with one myself—'

'Oh—take this—'

'No, I couldn't. Some other time, perhaps, Sir Michael.'

'When perhaps you'd be *entirely* frank with me, Mrs Essex.'

'I don't know what you mean.'

'Neither do I.' He drained the cup and began screwing it on. 'And thank you for my supper—and everything.'

'You devil! Here!' And hastily but very efficiently she kissed him. Women—my God!

It seemed the longest journey he had ever made by Underground; a kind of waking bad dream. And next morning he had not been in his room fifteen seconds before Miss Tilney was standing by his side, looking even older and grimmer after Bedfordshire, almost resembling the Ibsen of *When We Dead Awaken*.

'I told Miss Bury,' she said, 'to let Miss Essex know she would not be needed up here. But it appears Miss Essex isn't here this morning. Her father telephoned to say she isn't feeling very well.'

Sir Michael grunted, stared in disgust at the letters Miss Tilney had placed on his desk, and felt he was about to start crossing the Gobi Desert on foot.

11

SIR GEORGE DRAKE'S time of tribulation may be said to have begun at that meeting. Outside it was a delicious May afternoon, even in Russell Square; but no Maytime of the spirit was flowering in Sir George's room. They had crawled halfway down the agenda when Tim Kemp, who had not been seen or heard from for a week, walked in, still cherubic and yet looking more disreputable than ever. He had obviously been involved in some Derbyshire saga of gin and lunacy.

'Mr Chairman, my apologies,' he said. 'I hoped to have been here earlier.' He spoke gravely and very distinctly, like a man with a good head for liquor who has not been really sober for days. Nicola Pembroke, June Walsingham, Joan Drayton, brightened up at once at the very sight of him. And it may have been this that irritated Sir George.

'Very good of you to pay us a call, Mr Kemp.' Sir George spoke with that heavy ironical tone which has made so many schoolmasters unpopular.

'Not at all.' Kemp smiled at him. 'Would you like my report now, Mr Chairman?'

'Certainly not. It can wait. We're busy with other things. Now, as I was saying—about Ned Greene, the painter—'

'I've just been talking to him,' said Kemp, making use of his superb cutting-in technique. 'I ran into him in *The Plough* and then we went along to another place—the Luxemburg Sports Club, I think.' He looked around as if for some confirmation, but there were no members of the Luxemburg Sports Club present. 'Ned hasn't changed at all—so be careful.' He pointed his pipe at Gerald Spenser and then at Sir George.

'I was about to say, when you interrupted me,' said Sir George, calling down from a considerable height, 'that I have been in touch with Mr Greene, and that my wife and I are giving a dinner party for him tomorrow night. Among the guests will be Philip Bathorig, who, as you all probably know, happens to be Parliamentary Secretary, Ministry of Higher Education.' He stopped dramatically, as if for a round of applause, and was annoyed to notice several of them stealing a look across the table at Kemp.

'So Ned told me.' Kemp shook his head. Then he looked as if he were about to say something, but apparently changed his mind. He shook his head again, infuriatingly.

'I shall of course bring up the subject of a special DISCUS exhibition of Greene's work.' Sir George looked at Gerald Spenser, who writhed a little to show how fascinated he was. 'But as you'll be there too—bring your notes of course—you'll be able to put us right on any technical points.'

Spenser nodded away like an enchanted cobra. And now Kemp began nodding, and then kept on nodding throughout a discussion with Nicola Pembroke about a possible concert of Mountgarret Camden's works, to placate him; and then nodded off to sleep. They had to wake him, when they had arrived at *Any Other Business,* so that he could make his report on the Lady Bodley-Cobham project.

'And I need hardly point out, Mr Kemp,' said Sir George severely, 'that as you have been presumably engaged on this Bodley-Cobham project for a whole week, you must have something of some importance to tell us.'

'Well, yes, I have.' Kemp produced from an inside pocket a number of envelopes and odd bits of paper, and began sorting them out. The women watched with that bright-eyed indulgence which is usually reserved for small boys who are grubby and naughty but still angelic. Sir George noticed this look and it made him all the more impatient with Kemp.

'Oh, come along, man. The rest of us have other things to do, even if you haven't. And this Bodley-Cobham thing is bound to be a lot of nonsense, anyhow.'

Kemp looked at him. 'Why?'

'Because, Tim dear,' said Nicola, 'several of us had a go at her and were utterly defeated—'

'All right, Mrs Pembroke,' said Sir George sharply. 'We needn't go into all that.'

She flashed him one of her gipsy's-warning glances, and was clearly about to lose her temper. 'I'm telling Tim he was never expected to make head-or-tail of that ridiculous old woman—'

'No, no, Nicola.' Kemp was gently reproachful. 'She and I are great friends now. We took to each other at once. She's a trifle eccentric of course—but why not? Did you know that poor Stratherrick came down? They had a slanging match for half-an-hour, and then he quit the field, his sword and lance broken, his armour sorely dented—'

'Mr Kemp,' Sir George began, 'either you have a report or you haven't. If you haven't, then I must ask you to explain your absence from this office. And unless your explanation—'

'Here we are,' cried Kemp, holding up two of the smallest and dirtiest bits of paper. 'But first I must explain that Annabel—Lady Bodley-Cobham—'

'Do you call her Annabel?' June Walsingham gave a little shriek of laughter and then fell to giggling with Nicola Pembroke and Joan Drayton.

'Annabel happens to be her name, and as we're friends, that's what I call her.' Kemp took out his pipe, to look more dignified, then put it back again, to continue his story while puffing away. 'She and I met an architect in a bar at Bakewell. We were on our way to her Derbyshire mansion. A nice fellow, this architect—Ludovic Shotter's his name—'

'Oh that chap!' This was Gerald Spenser. 'I knew him slightly at one time. There was some sort of scandal. And he drinks too much.'

'He's had some bad luck, certainly,' said Kemp. 'But undoubtedly an able pleasant fellow. So we took him along with us. We needed an expert—and there he was.'

'Was anybody sober on this expedition?' Neil Jonson enquired, but with a grin, not offensively.

Kemp gave this question some thought. 'Not completely, no. But I'll give you the details later, Neil. The Secretary-General wants my report on the project, and quite right too.' He smiled at Sir George, who replied with a glare. 'Well now, Shotter's rough estimate for the conversion of the mansion is £185,000—'

'Nonsense!' Sir George shouted.

'And our joint estimate of yearly costs,' Kemp continued, ignoring this interruption, 'once the mansion is properly converted, and on the basis of twenty-five creative artists being in constant residence, and assuming they make a weekly contribution of about eight pounds each, is £19,600. This—and the conversion cost of £185,000—is what would be expected from DISCUS—'

'Balderdash!' Sir George, now arriving at his full purple glaring face, was shouting again. To relieve his feelings he thumped the table.

'I've never heard such damned nonsense. And don't tell me you've left this demented Bodley-Cobham woman and this architect fellow with the impression that DISCUS might be willing to agree to this rubbish.' Then he was visited by a monstrous thought. 'And don't tell me that anything's been said in public. Nobody's spoken to the press, have they?'

Kemp stared at him in mild wonder. 'As a civil servant of considerable experience, Sir George, I always avoid the press. But I am under the impression—it was rather a confused though very entertaining evening—that Lady Bodley-Cobham and Ludovic Shotter *did* make a statement to the girl from the *Buxton Weekly Herald.*'

'Oh—my God!'

'A little premature, you think?'

'Premature? It's all a lot of drunken idiocy.'

Kemp gathered up his bits of paper, stuffed them back into his inside pocket, and then rose in solemn dignity. 'Secretary-General, you sent me to Lady Bodley-Cobham to discuss a project, with which so far you'd made no headway. At the same time you told me that DISCUS was in need of some big dramatic scheme. I discussed the project. I examined the mansion to be placed at our disposal. I obtained the best expert advice that was available. I have given you some rough estimates of cost. What more could I have done?'

'He's quite right,' cried Nicola. 'It's the rest of us who wasted time and trouble on that woman—not Tim.'

'Thank you, Nicola.' He looked at Sir George again. 'The important question is not whether we drink or not, but whether we get anything done. I've done what I was asked to do. I'm sorry you think *it's all a lot of drunken idiocy.* Even if you thought it, you might have stopped yourself saying it. I happen to think,' he continued mildly, 'that you behave too often as if this were a farmyard and you a ridiculous turkey-cock. But I don't say so. Now if you want my report properly set out in writing, you can have it—'

'I don't want either you or your report, Kemp,' Sir George told him angrily. 'I didn't want you back here, as you must know—' He stopped, then noticed that all three women were glaring at him.

'I'll stay until I'm transferred elsewhere,' Kemp told him. 'I could have warned you about Ned Greene, but you won't listen. What's more important—because I ran into a Treasury man I know—I could have

100

warned you against a certain Jones, who's due to make an appearance here soon. But why should I?' He had now moved from his place at the table and was halfway to the door. He stopped, however, and took out his pipe to point it at Sir George, who had turned, like all the others, to watch him go. 'I'm sorry for you, Drake, because you're a man entirely without intuition and insight. By the way,' he looked at Neil Jonson, 'where's your Drama man, Hugo Heywood?'

'On leave, Tim,' replied Jonson. 'He's in Ireland.'

'In Ireland?' Kemp looked at Sir George. 'No good will come of that. You'll see. And don't forget,' he added darkly, 'a certain Jones — of the Treasury. Good afternoon.'

In the silence that followed Kemp's slow exit, it was as if Sir George discovered in himself the intuition and insight that had just been denied him. He could not help feeling that he was being menaced from an unknown direction, that dark forces, to which his rational self could not give a name, were already threatening him, that Kemp and the three women now regarding him with hostility and contempt, like spurned witches, had between them left him vulnerable to some unimaginable malignant power. He told himself how ridiculous it was to feel this, but he went on feeling it.

'Nothing more to be done here this afternoon, I think.' He looked at Gerald Spenser and dropped the dismissing tone. 'I'd like a word or two with you, Gerald, about tomorrow night.'

Spenser could hardly wait until the others had left the room, which they did in a kind of indignant silence, almost as if they had angry eyes at the back of their necks. 'You were so right of course about Kemp,' he began. 'I couldn't have agreed with you more. In my opinion he's absolutely hopeless. I don't think I told you, but just before he went off on this Bodley-Cobham wild goose chase, he began hinting this and that about Ned Greene, and I told him straight that if he imagined you and I would leave Greene to him, he hadn't a hope. That's what he was getting at, of course.'

'Probably.' But Sir George in fact did not agree with this view of Kemp at all. 'Tell me something, Gerald. Why do all the women always take Kemp's side, whatever he says or does?'

'Oh, he flatters them, I suppose. That's the kind of thing they like.' Spenser gave a long wriggle of contempt.

'Possibly.' Again, Sir George found himself disagreeing with this view of Kemp. Was Spenser, away from his visual arts, rather stupid?

Refusing to answer this question, Sir George hurried into cosy chat. 'Now about tomorrow night. We have Greene, Philip Bathorig and his wife, you and your wife—er—'

'Dorothea,' Spenser prompted.

'Dorothea, of course. Then an old friend of Alison's, Muriel Tetter, who's keen on the arts, to make up the eight.'

'Absolutely splendid!'

'Did I tell you we're not dressing? We'd have preferred it of course, but Greene won't hear of it. And Bathorig will be coming straight from the House. We did think of taking you all to a restaurant, but I thought it would be easier to talk at home, so Alison's getting in some caterers. Now we won't say anything during dinner, but as soon as the women have left the dining room, I thought I'd explain to Bathorig, really for Greene's benefit, our plan for the special Greene exhibition. We could then settle the whole thing before we join the women, though of course if you wanted to take Greene aside later, to decide on various details, there's no reason why you shouldn't. Indeed, if that's what you'd like to do, Gerald, I'll warn Alison that she must allow you to take Greene into a corner sometime.'

'Couldn't be better,' cried Spenser, now almost phosphorescent with enthusiasm. 'And I do think the whole thing is absolutely splendid.'

'We ought to have quite a good evening, certainly,' said Sir George. 'Alison's very keen—she's a great admirer of Greene's work—and I must say this. She's not always fully co-operative—you know how women are—but once she's really set her heart on making an evening *go*, she's tremendous.'

'I know. And Dorothea's madly looking forward to meeting her again. Eight o'clock, isn't it? Marvellous!'

'Oh—and by the way—you'll be coming by car, won't you? Alison was wondering if you'd mind picking up Muriel Tetter, who's on your way. It's Mrs Tetter. I have her address here somewhere. Could you make a note of it, Gerald?'

Gerald could, and did, and after making a few more enthusiastic noises he went undulating out, leaving Sir George feeling much better. Yet something remained from that silence after Kemp's departure: a shadow flickering and without shape; the ghost of a warning whisper; a vague unease beyond the control of the most splendid of arrangements.

12

ON THAT SAME afternoon, over at COMSA, Sir Michael was regarding his Drama man, Jeff Byrd, with obvious distaste. 'Ted Mitch, Labour M.P. for Burmanley Central,' said Sir Michael very slowly and distinctly, 'is one of the directors of the Burmanley Repertory Company. He has written to you about a forthcoming production. He has given you a strong hint that unless COMSA is prepared to help finance a London run of this production, he will make sure we get into trouble. That is what you're trying to tell me, isn't it, Jeff?'

'Well, yes, more or less.' Byrd was very nervous. He found Sir Michael difficult at the best of times, and the past week or so had been anything but the best of times. The whole COMSA staff knew that its Director, for some mysterious reason, now seemed to exist in a black rage. 'There are one or two things I haven't explained—'

'Tell Ted Mitch to go to hell,' said Sir Michael. 'That's all, Jeff.'

'No, Director, please—*please*! You must allow me to explain—you really must—'

Sir Michael was about to explode but now controlled himself. Why should he take it out of this poor devil, stammering and sweating there? We were all God's unhappy creatures. Because his imagination was fixed upon a beautiful idiot of a girl who had vanished, did he have to torment Jeff Byrd, who was trying to earn a living for a wife and three children, to preserve his self-respect, to protect his very life-illusion? 'All right, Jeff. If I don't understand, then make me understand. And sit down and take it easy, for God's sake.'

'Yes of course.' Byrd almost collapsed into the chair, wiped his face, closed his eyes and then opened them widely, to achieve a look of entreaty. 'I don't care about Ted Mitch. I met him once up there, that's all. But I'm thinking about COMSA. There's a bus we could miss here, Director, there really is. You see, I happen to know something about this production. It's an avant garde American play called *The Dummies*. And it's been the biggest off-Broadway hit for years. Foreign rights already sold everywhere. And the reason that Burmanley's getting it is that Cayley, who runs the Rep up there, is a cousin of the man who directed it in New York. Now it's opening in Burmanley on Tuesday week, and I happen to know that most of the chief London critics are going.'

'Well, you must go too, Jeff, if that's what's worrying you. No need to ask my permission, my dear fellow. You ought to know that.'

'I do. But—this is the point, Director—I want you to be there too.'

'Oh—come—come! I hate Burmanley. I detest avant garde plays, especially if they're American. I don't even like going to the theatre, as you know very well, Jeff—'

'Yes, yes, I know all that.' Desperation brought Byrd some courage. 'I also know that you don't really trust my judgment. And if COMSA has to act quickly—to announce at once that we'll help to put the play on in London—then it'll be hopeless unless you're there. And I also happen to know that Hugo Heywood, who'd probably snap it up for DISCUS, is away on leave, in Ireland. Now *The Dummies* might be one of these freak successes. So it's not a question of Ted Mitch, though he easily might make trouble for us, but of our getting in first, doing exactly what you said you wanted us to do—'

'You have a point, Jeff,' said Sir Michael wearily. 'I've no right to ask you to be bold and adventurous and do nothing myself. So ask them for another seat and tell Jim Marlowe to book a room for me at that terrible hotel and to arrange transport. Tuesday week, you say? Ask Miss Tilney, as you go out, to make a note of it.'

Byrd was out of his chair. 'That's fine, Director. Just what I wanted.'

'I don't promise to like the play, you know, Jeff—'

'I realise that, though by all accounts it's a most fascinating experiment—'

'I don't want a fascinating experiment, but just—for once—a little intelligent entertainment. Oh—and if you're talking to Burmanley—you might ask them if it's possible yet in that city to ask for a modest hot supper. I feel I've faced for the last time that tough bit of cold chicken, the tasteless wafer of ham, the salad on which the beetroot has been bleeding for three hours.'

Byrd laughed and hurried out. Sir Michael sighed and stayed at his desk. There was a lot of old rubbish that had been there for a couple of weeks, so now he went through it and sorted it out, and then called in Miss Tilney, and together they disposed of the stuff. By the time he was dictating the last letter he was on his way to the little drink cupboard. 'Blah blah blah—that'll do,' he called over his shoulder.

'But he asks you to lunch with him,' said Miss Tilney, glancing at the letter.

'He would. Well, the usual thing—*Yes, we must have that lunch sometime.* Better do these letters tomorrow, Miss Tilney.'

'I could stay and get them done tonight, Sir Michael.'

'You could, but you're not going to. Another day won't hurt them. Off you go, Miss Tilney.'

He had poured out a liberal dose of the old malt before he realised that she had not gone. When he turned, she was standing near the door, red in the face, her spectacles misted, her lower lip trembling. 'Now what's the matter?'

'Oh—Sir Michael—it's not my fault, is it—that I'm not Miss Essex?' As soon as she had said it, she looked so frightened that for the second time that afternoon he damped down an explosion.

'No, it isn't, Miss Tilney. But I don't understand your question.'

'I had to say something, Sir Michael. I couldn't go on any longer. Ever since I came back from Bedford, you've looked and talked as if you found it hard to put up with me, as if everything I did and said was wrong. And I've done my best—as I've always done ever since I came to work for you—'

'I'm sure you have, Miss Tilney. I've never suggested you haven't.'

'And I've asked myself over and over again what could be the matter—'

'So in the end you had to make an impertinent remark,' said Sir Michael, suddenly losing patience.

'I didn't mean it that way. But I asked Miss Bury—'

'I don't want to know anything about Miss Bury,' Sir Michael shouted. 'Don't Miss Bury me. Go home, Miss Tilney, and do those letters tomorrow. Goodnight.'

All that the whisky showed him was the prospect of a long, flat, dead evening. He did not feel sufficiently interested in any of his women to offer one of them dinner. He would dine at the club and then, hazy with drink, descend on one about nine or so and then see how he felt. But it was no use leaving it to chance. Which one should he call—Clarice, Mavis, Andrea, Margaret, Polly, or that little Austrian? But the little Austrian had gone away and Polly was out, and his next choice was Mavis, Mrs Mavis Finch-Dewar, divorced these last five years and an old, steady but by no means devouring flame. Mavis, who seemed excited about something, would be glad to see him about nine-thirty. So that was that. He gave himself another whisky, passed an hour adding a few notes to the pile he had been assembling for the last four years for his book on the *Romantic Movement,* a book he never would write while he felt restless every evening; and then he walked to the club.

He had several whiskies, inferior to his own, in the bar, surrounded by men who mostly behaved like character actors in an American play about London life, English gentlemen saying bad lines at the top of their voices. Wearily contemptuous, the Highlander in him, fortified by the whisky, thanked God he would have a woman for company at the latter end of the evening. The dining room was quiet, most of the men in the bar going to distant suburbs to complain of the hard day they had had, and he sat alone and washed down the indifferent dinner with more whisky. He arrived at Mavis's Chelsea flat in a melancholy haze.

It was an over-crowded little flat, rather like Mavis herself, a small dark woman who had an over-crowded little face. But she also had a remarkably fine figure, together with an ardent and open nature, even though there had been a time when Sir Michael felt sure she had made up her mind to marry him. Hazy he might be, but he noticed at once a difference in her; something had happened that had already announced itself when she had spoken to him earlier on the telephone; but all that could come out later. Now, after she had poured out a drink and before she could sit down again, he quickly embraced her, gave her a kiss, and held on; but, without resisting him, she made him feel he was not making the usual progress.

'No use, Michael,' she told him, twitching herself away. 'Your heart's not in it. And neither is mine. I've news for you, my dear. I'm getting married again.'

The old hunter in him mechanically cursed the luck. 'Congratulations! Anybody I know?'

'Sit down. No, over there—much more comfortable. And I'll tell you all about it.'

Knowing now that he was there to be told all about it, Sir Michael slumped down, glass in hand and the bottle within easy reach. It was a very long and confused story, in which one Jock ('Rather like you, Michael, only more dependable') and a travel agency and a visit to the Costa Brava played intricate parts; and he never even attempted to make any sense out of it; he made vague noises to keep her happily going, not enjoying himself but anxious, as he would not have been on a previous visit, not to spoil her obvious enjoyment. And at last it came to an end and, not without some effort, he pulled himself up to give her the drink she had earned. When he settled again in his chair, he found she was looking at him in that curious, half-searching, half-tender, way that women had when you had often made love with them and now it was all over.

'You know, Michael, you're different, aren't you?'

'In what way?'

'I don't know, but you are. What's been happening?'

Suddenly he felt that either he had to tell her or go straight home. So far he had never said a word to anybody about Shirley Essex, not being a confiding man and anyhow feeling he had made a fool of himself. But he might feel better if he told somebody, so why not Mavis?

'Go on,' she said, while he was still hesitating. 'I've spread myself out—no, shut up, you know what I mean—and now it's your turn. And none of your old Highland pride, Stratherrick! Spill it, darling.'

'Well, my dear, the truth is, I've gone and made a damned ass of myself. I've gone and fallen—oh miles and miles deep—for a little suburban miss not half my age.' And half tight though he was, he explained very carefully about Shirley, not omitting, indeed not sparing any detail, that fatal visit to 5 Winston Avenue, N.16.

'Oh—poor you!' cried Mavis when he suddenly stopped. 'Not that it doesn't serve you right in a way—you wicked old lecher—and I know a lot more about your afternoons and evenings than you think. But go on, go on. What happened after that?'

'I thought I was cured, but not a bit of it. I can't get the girl out of my mind—or at least out of my imagination, where she belongs. What I'd do if I found her, I don't know. But the point is, Mavis, *I can't find her.*'

'Michael, you can't be really trying. You know where she lives—'

'Of course I know where she lives. And I must have telephoned a score of times, both during the day and in the evening. And it's not only that she isn't there. Nobody's there. Her father isn't there, and what's more astonishing—her mother isn't there. The whole family's vanished. Sometimes I feel I must have dreamt them.'

'No, be sensible.' Mavis thought for a moment. 'It's quite simple. They've gone on holiday.'

'I've thought of that. But nothing was said to me about a holiday.'

'No, it was after you ran away like that—and I must say, Michael dear, you were rather cowardly about that—there must have been a family crisis. So her father arranged to take part of his holiday at once, and they took her away. While you've been frantically telephoning,' Mavis continued, not without malice, 'she's been in Eastbourne or Hastings, going to the cinema with a bank clerk whose chest is delicate.' She made a face at him. 'Stop scowling, Michael. Can't you see it's all so absurd? Or are you so infatuated that you haven't any sense of humour left?'

'Possibly. Though I've always mistrusted this English thing about *a sense of humour,* as if it was something separate, like the ability to play tennis or bridge. And if I was scowling, it was because I was trying to concentrate on your holiday theory, which I hadn't considered. I've no rational grounds for saying so—I'm being purely intuitive—but I can't accept your explanation, Mavis. I don't know what's happened to her parents, and I don't care, but my own feeling is that she's got another job and may have left home. She didn't apply to us at COMSA for a reference because, after all, she'd only just started with us. She may have applied to a character called Kemp at DISCUS or used an earlier reference. It was Kemp, a very artful little drunk who doesn't like me, who sent her to us, I believe, and sometimes I've wondered if he didn't warn her against me, telling her I'd try to seduce her—that sort of thing.'

'But isn't that what you wanted to do, Michael?'

'Certainly. Any man with taste and imagination could be half-crazy wanting to have her,' he replied gloomily.

She laughed at him. 'I believe you're caught—at last. My guess is that she's a cool determined young woman who won't go near a bed unless you marry her. So now what do you do?'

'I'd be out of my mind to marry her. Wrong age, wrong type, grotesquely unsuitable, even if I wanted to marry, which I don't.'

'Then all you have to do, Michael dear—' she spoke solemnly but there was bright malice in her look—'is to forget all about her.'

'What the devil do you think I've been trying to do? But all this idiotic telephoning! I've never felt such a fool for years and years.'

'It's done you good—'

'I don't want good done to me. And don't be so damned complacent just because you're in sight of the altar or the registry office again. All this Noah's Ark two-by-two existence! Sickening!' He got up, rather unsteadily.

'Poor Michael!' She took hold of his lapels and looked up at him in mock sympathy. 'After all this time—and all those illicit afternoons and evenings—to go and fall in love with a frigid little blonde!'

'No, no, the whole business may be grotesque and idiotic, but it can't be cheapened like that. Whatever Shirley is, she's not in the frigid little blonde class. The appeal, first of all, is to the imagination. It's the spell cast by the *anima,* the soul image. And the trouble is, it makes everything else seem so unendurably tedious. I've been bored with COMSA for some time, but now that she's been and gone, I have to flog my mind to take the least glimmer of interest in it. And I'm drinking too much, Mavis, turning myself into one of those men— and London's full of 'em—just drearily soaking reality away, blurring all the edges from five-thirty onwards. With self-pity creeping in. You've just heard it beginning to whine.'

'You find her, Michael. Then marry her, never mind how foolish it seems. If you don't, you'll find yourself at a dead end.'

So in the morning, discarding what remained of his pride, he rang up DISCUS and asked for Kemp. While the girl kept him waiting, he was still wondering exactly how he ought to phrase his appeal. But then the girl said: 'I'm sorry, sir, but Mr Kemp doesn't appear to be here this morning, and nobody seems to know where he is or when he will be here.' A blank again! And now he must struggle through another blank day, towards a blanker night.

13

Sir George decided afterwards, when he tried to put together what he remembered of that extraordinary affair, that the evening slipped out of his grasp, taking on an alien and hostile character of its own, during the forty-five minutes that they had had to wait for Ned Greene. At eight o'clock everybody else was there, ready to move into the dining room. The three people sent by the caterers, a cook and a parlourmaid and a butler type, seemed to know their job, even though there was something discouraging and far from festive in their appearance and manner. They looked like members of the same ruined aristocratic family, being all three equally tall, thin, elderly, and having almost identical paperish noses and mouths tight with disapproval of their present lot. Alison, who was unusually nervous, told him that the cook had at once disliked everything she had found in the kitchen; and when Sir George himself, making arrangements about the drink, had tried to be hearty with the parlourmaid and the butler type, they had both closed their eyes as if refusing to recognise another burden they would have to bear.

The butler type, however, was anything but idle. In fact, he overdid it. During the long wait for Greene, he came in again and again with his tray of martinis and sherry, with the result that both Sir George and Alison, in their impatience and anxiety, drank far more than usual. Alison, who was looking her best, still seemed to sparkle away; but an hour's steady drinking on an empty and anxious stomach had an unexpectedly bad effect upon Sir George. He found himself beginning to dislike his guests. He could not help noticing that Philip Bathorig, even though he was Parliamentary Secretary, Ministry of Higher Education, had eyes too close together over his long nose and loose mouth, and really seemed rather a cad. And his wife was dim and sad, saw herself in exile in Hampstead, and drank nothing but tonic water, of all things. Gerald Spenser was Gerald Spenser, and his wife, Dorothea, was an indignant Dutch doll kind of woman, who hardly said a word but always looked as if about to make a loud and angry protest. Muriel Tetter he had never cared for; an argumentative woman who never knew what she was talking about; and twice already she had tried to involve him in some meaningless dispute. Moreover, Bathorig, though drinking everything he was offered, was beginning to look bored. Where the devil was Greene?

He arrived about quarter to nine, and without a word of apology. A shortish but powerfully-built fellow, dark and unshaven, wearing a scruffy coat over an equally scruffy turtle-necked sweater, Greene looked as if he had just been paid off after a long voyage in a tramp steamer. He was not drunk perhaps but he was certainly not quite sober; and he seemed to Sir George, to his dismay, a kind of younger, louder, fiercer Tim Kemp.

'Well, Mr Greene,' said Alison, 'this is a great pleasure. But you mustn't blame me if dinner isn't as good as it ought to be. We *did* say eight o'clock.'

'Couldn't make it. Sorry! Angry with me, are you? Keep it up. Suits you.' He gave her a wide grin, then turned sharply away, nearly knocking down the butler type, who was announcing that dinner was served.

'As you live in France these days, Mr Greene,' Sir George told him across the table, 'I've taken some trouble to find this claret we're having. I hope you'll like it.'

'Never touch it, thanks all the same. Whisky for me.' Greene did not actually shout but he gave the impression that he spent a lot of time in places where people did shout; he never tried to modulate his voice, which was deep and harsh, so that his least remark rang through the rather small dining room. Alison had him on her left, with Bathorig on her right. Sir George was between Mrs Bathorig and Dorothea Spenser, and because they were so hard to entertain and he was feeling uneasy and had had too many martinis, he drank a good deal of wine. And very soon he began to feel he was eating dinner in a vaguely disagreeable dream. Even when Muriel Tetter and Gerald Spenser, who ought to have had more sense, began to pester Greene with art talk and questions and were told by him to turn it up for Christ's sake, though this added to the disagreeableness, it was also rather remote and dreamlike. But Alison, he thought, was really looking splendid.

Alison was feeling splendid. She was in truth, as her husband had declared, a genuine admirer of Greene's work, so rich and evocative in that mysteriously beguiling region between representation and abstraction in painting; but, even so, she had been furious with him for being so late and taking so little trouble with his appearance, after she and George had gone to such trouble and expense. And at a first glance he had looked really awful, like a man coming to attend to the plumbing. But when he had told her that her anger suited her and had given her that grin, she had suddenly felt that he did not look awful at all, and that this truly was the man who could paint those wonderful pictures. He had curious, yellowish eyes, human enough and yet, when compared with the tamed and domesticated look of George and his friends, those of a wild animal. He suggested an explosive force, essentially masculine, that the kind of men she met had lost or never had. Moreover, she knew within a few minutes of their sitting down to dinner that she was the only person there in whom he was prepared to take any interest; indeed, she felt he was definitely attracted to her in his own wild careless fashion.

'Could you try to keep your voice down?' she ventured.

'I could. But what does it matter?'

'Because I want to feel you're talking to me and not to the whole room.'

'Fair enough. What's your name?'

'Alison. Does that mean I call you Ned?'

'That's right, Alison. How's the voice now?'

'Much better, Ned. But if you could manage just a little less—'

'How about some whisky here, one of you two?' he bellowed to the parlourmaid and the butler. Oddly enough, they seemed to be far less contemptuous of this manner of approach than they had been of her and George's rather timid attempts to be friendly. Perhaps it reminded them of aristocratic eccentrics they had known. Anyhow, Ned's glass was soon filled.

'How's this, Alison, for keeping it low?' he rumbled in her ear. And before she could reply he had put his hand on her knee. This was at once both a thrill and a nuisance, making immediate action impossible. However, he moved his hand away while he continued without waiting for a reply: 'Soon as we're through here, we're off to the Green Gong.'

'Who are?' Had she been deceiving herself? Wasn't he attracted?

'Well, you are, for one, Alison ducks. And your husband, if he insists, and anybody else, if they must. And I must. I've a date with some types there. We'll have a ball. Know the Green Gong?'

'I've never even heard of it, Ned.'

'It's a big cellar dive. Lot of coloureds go. Plenty of late night talent. You mightn't like it, but let your hair down and give it a try.'

'I'd love to, but I don't see George enjoying it.'

'If George doesn't like it, George can bloody well lump it, ducks. And, if you ask me, these three sad women had better go home and enjoy a nice headache. Why all these twerps anyhow?'

'Damn it, Ned,' she heard herself saying, not sure whether she was speaking out of a new character or out of her real self, 'because you can paint—and I know you can; I love your work—you don't have to be so intolerant and conceited. We've gone to a lot of trouble. You haven't even bothered to shave and find a shirt. So shut up about twerps.'

'That's the idea, woman.' He squeezed her thigh now. 'Speak up for yourself. Does your eyes good too. Brings a touch of mars violet to the burnt umber. Keep it up.' He removed his hand, though she still seemed to feel its warm powerful clasp.

She laughed. 'I don't propose to stay in a bad temper just to please you.'

'Be happy, then. Let go. All the same.'

Yes, Alison was really looking splendid, Sir George reflected, and appeared to be getting on well with Greene, probably because she was nearly as anxious as he was that DISCUS should clinch that special Ned Greene show. Well, it was up to him. It was tonight or never. And he hoped there would be no difficult and delicate negotiations because the disagreeable dream effect was still with him. And if he felt rather tight, what about Greene, who appeared to have hypnotised the butler type into filling his glass with whisky throughout dinner? He felt relieved, even though it meant that the climax of the evening had arrived, when Alison, flushed and sparkling, took the other women away. Now for it.

'I don't drink port or brandy, don't smoke cigars, and I can't stay long,' Greene announced, lighting a *gauloise*. 'I've a date at the Green Gong. I've already told your wife, George, and she's coming. Who else? It's my party—all on me. Well?'

'I'm game,' said Bathorig, who had helped himself to a very large brandy and seemed well oiled. 'So long as there's transport. My wife'll drive herself home. Hates late nights, and of course I'm always having them in the House.'

Greene stared at him. 'What house?'

'Bathorig is Parliamentary Secretary to the Ministry of Higher Education,' Sir George hastened to explain.

'You don't say! Well, the Green Gong ought to do him a bit of good. Next?'

'Well, Mr Greene, Sir George—' and Gerald Spenser writhed apologetically—'I don't think Dorothea and I—'

'You're out—right,' Greene said brutally. 'And so is that woman who wanted to talk about Art.'

But Spenser was not so easily disposed of. 'Naturally I shall stay here until we've completed the arrangements for the special DISCUS show of Mr Greene's work.' He looked pointedly at Sir George.

The latter accepted his cue. 'Yes, Mr Greene, I think you've already been given to understand that we at DISCUS are anxious to arrange this exhibition of your work—'

'Later, later,' Greene cried irritably. 'One thing at a time for God's sake.'

'You mean you prefer not to discuss it here and now?'

'That's what I'm saying, and that's what I mean.' Greene swallowed most of his whisky. 'There's some people I have to talk to at the Green Gong. And don't let's have too many goddam arrangements. When I'm painting hard, I live like a bleeding monk, and half the time it's torture. When I'm not painting, I like to enjoy myself.' He looked quite sullen now. 'And I don't like to wonder if I *am* enjoying myself. Which is what I'm doing now.'

'I'm sorry you're not enjoying yourself,' said Sir George stiffly. 'I don't know that I'm enjoying myself either. But I did understand that we were meeting tonight to settle the question of this special DISCUS show—'

'Well, we are, aren't we? Man, I keep telling you. First, we go down to the Green Gong.'

'Seems quite reasonable to me, Drake,' said Bathorig, with a wide silly grin.

'Very well, then. We go to the Green Gong, whatever that is.' Sir George, who had decided not to drink any more before they had their discussion, now poured himself a liberal helping of brandy. Avoiding Spenser's reproachful glances, Bathorig's wide silly grin, and Greene's yellow glare, he looked down at the table and proceeded to drink his brandy. With it, merging with the disagreeable dream, came vague but disturbing recollections of things that Kemp had said about Ned Greene. He couldn't say he hadn't been warned.

'Let's go, man, let's go,' Greene shouted, slapping the table and then jumping up. And with the guest of honour in this frame of mind, the party soon disintegrated. Feeling dazed and a little sick, Sir George found himself suffering a peculiarly unpleasant taxi ride with a queerly excited wife, a lip-licking Parliamentary Secretary, and an eminent painter who was either drunk or close to lunacy. And the claret alone—three Chateau bottles of it, and some of it swishing dubiously around his inside as if it were the cheapest muck—had set him back nearly seven pounds. And what those aristocratic caterers would charge (he had left them to Alison, now, for no reason he could discover, giggling like a seventeen-year-old), God only knew!

14

THE GREEN GONG was the kind of place Sir George had read about, always with disapproval, but had never dreamt of visiting before, even though Alison, in one of her moods, had suggested more than once that he ought, as head of DISCUS and patron of contemporary arts, to know more about London's night life. He never did learn exactly where it was, but it seemed to be somewhere in Soho, surrounded by strip-tease clubs. They went down some steep stairs, and civilised London vanished. It was as if they were pushing their way into the tropics. First there was a small cellar, some kind of bar, and then, down a few more steps, there was a much larger cellar, darkish and very crowded, hot and smelly. There were jazz noises, throbbing and stinging. As far as people could be distinguished at all in that crowd and dim lighting, there seemed to be as many coloured people as there were whites. Greene, with an arm round Alison, led the way, cheerfully shouting and pushing, to some far table that must have been reserved for him. By the time Sir George arrived there, after arguing with two girls who told him he must be 'Joyce's friend, Old Pops Pitworth', he found that three small tables had been crammed together, and that there were about ten people between him and the rest of his party.

Unfortunately, what with the heat and the wine and the brandy he had had, he was desperately and unquenchably thirsty, and Greene proved to be a liberal if not attentive host. Various drinks, notably a curiously sour whisky and something with a lot of rum in it, made their appearance before him, arriving out of the dim confusion and soon thickening and fantasticating it. There appeared to be about twenty people now between him and Alison, Greene and Bathorig.

'We're sick, man, sick,' the man was telling him across the table. He was a man with one eye and a reddish beard; a sinister-looking fellow.

'Not enough air, don't you think?' he heard himself saying in reply. 'No proper ventilation.' An obviously sensible remark.

A huge bellow of laughter hit him on the neck, coming from an enormous warm squashiness that had arrived behind him, and with some difficulty he turned to see the largest and fattest coloured woman he had ever noticed anywhere, a kind of soft purple mountain of a woman, wearing, like a spring forest, a bright emerald evening gown. She stopped laughing to say something to him, but he could not catch what it was. And One-eye-red-beard, after shouting down a girl with a deathly white face and smudged eyelashes, was talking to him again. He did not listen because a most amusing thought had crossed his mind, namely, that here in the Green Gong the whites were too white and the blacks too black. This made him laugh.

One-eye-red-beard pointed a long finger at him, only a few inches from his nose. 'Okay, man, okay,' he was shouting, 'laugh, go on, laugh, while there's time.' Clearly not a man with whom a sensible friendly talk was possible. Meanwhile, the warm squashiness at his back had gone, two sharp boninesses taking its place. The enormous coloured woman was in fact standing in front of the piano, moaning in a deep hoarse voice the absence and loss of something she referred to as a sugar stick, which seemed to him absurd though by no means as funny as all the people round him seemed to think. To avoid One-eye-red-beard, he screwed himself round to face the two boninesses, who turned out to be a young man and a girl, a washed-out-looking pair who appeared to stare at him fixedly and had insane pale-blue eyes. And the young man, without saying a word, handed him a large mug of something. The enormous coloured woman announced her final despair over this preposterous sugar stick business, and was deafeningly applauded.

After she had gone, there was something like a lull, during which Sir George, who was now trying to avoid the four pale eyes as well as One-eye-red-beard, stared at the remote wavering end of the three packed tables, and noticed idly that Alison was no longer there and that Greene was on his feet, shouting across at an entwined pair that might be Bathorig and a thin girl with auburn hair and perhaps might not be them at all, because everything was becoming ridiculously confused. Nevertheless, his ears being in better shape than his eyes, he distinctly heard Greene shouting 'Studio Flat, 58b Cromwell Road', and not once but twice. This seemed to him very amusing.

Remembering that he had never thanked the pale-eyed young man for the mug of something, he turned himself round, being careful to ignore One-eye-red-beard on the way, and addressed some words of thanks to one of the pale-eyed washed-out pair—he was not sure which one it was. They were so alike, it was ridiculous. It was not this thought, however, that now made him laugh aloud, as he tried to explain to them. It was the idea that he could ever have consented to come to this place simply in order to negotiate, on behalf of DISCUS, with Ned Greene, eminent painter, an exhibition of his pictures. Explaining the absurdity of this idea became quite a laborious job; the precision he wanted to achieve was difficult; the pale-eyed pair were rather stupid and not as good at listening as they were at staring; and there was the complicated business of buying drinks for them, which he insisted upon doing, even though both waiters within call did not seem to be able to take his order seriously. He did at last pay two pounds for something or other, but by this time One-eye-red-beard, the deathly-white-face girl, the pale-eyed pair, an angry coloured man, were all talking to him at once, and he seemed to be having to defend the organisation, policy and outlook of DISCUS. And then—the thought coming like a thunderbolt—he knew what he must do: *he must go*. This took some doing, but he was a man, always had been, who could command patient endeavour, determination to carry things through, controlled purposeful energy, and he did it.

The young taxi-driver, discovered after many small ludicrous misadventures proving that London's late night transport was almost anarchic, appeared to be a lunatic. 'Now look, chum,' and Sir George heard him quite distinctly, 'you have to make the noises. I'm no lip reader. Now let's have it with the sound turned on, then we know where to go.'

Very well, he was not the only man who could be distinct. 'Studio Flat,' said Sir George, using extreme care and all his patience, '58b. B for Burgundy. Cromwell Road. Crom-well.'

'C for cock-eyed,' said the taxi-driver. 'I've got it. We're communicating.'

The taxi bumped him about a good deal and offered him too many whirling light effects, so that his head ached and he felt rather sick again, but after that nightmare Green Gong, all those unbelievable people and all that shouting and arguing, it was pleasant to have a small cool place of his own in which he had not to answer anybody. Nothing much happened except that at the two last traffic halts there was some funny business with a woman in a small red car who kept hooting at his taxi. 'Either she's benders or a pal of yours, chum,' said the taxi-driver when they stopped and he had accepted a ten-shilling note.

'Nonsense,' said Sir George severely.

'Look out, she's here again.'

But Sir George was already approaching the imposing but hospitably open front door of 58b. He read with great care and some difficulty a notice board that told him he would find *Studio Flat* on the fifth and last floor. The lift was waiting but not happy about working so late; it took him, after stopping twice and apparently shaking with anger, no further than the fourth floor, where, after some confused exploration, he found he would have to climb some steep stairs, unlit and mysterious, up to *Studio Flat*.

If there was a front door to the flat up there, he never noticed it, and he felt no scruples about walking straight in, for after all this was where his party was supposed to be ending and anything called a Studio Flat ought to be a sort of open house. He found himself in a dimly lit corridor with several doors along it. One of them showed a sliver of light, suggesting that the company was assembled behind it. So that was the door he opened. And there, deep in dalliance and as naked and blanched as pieces of tinned asparagus, were the thin girl and Philip Bathorig, Parliamentary Secretary, Ministry of Higher Education. Hastily, before they had time to notice that anybody had looked in, he shut the door. Shocked and more confused than ever, he turned the wrong way and then seemed to be looking down, as if from a little gallery, into what was probably a darkened studio. He saw nothing, but he heard something, and he knew at once that it was Alison who was making those muffled ecstatic noises, even though it was years since he had heard them last. He crept back into the corridor, trembling, then almost tumbled down the stairs, hoping to God he could work the lift and get out into the air before he was sick.

A little red car hooted at him as he reached the pavement. Somebody got out and approached him as he stood there trying to beat back the increasing waves of nausea.

'Sir George, it's me.' It was June Walsingham.

'Excuse me a moment,' he gasped. 'Going to be sick.'

He managed to reach the gutter before spewing out, putting it where it belonged, the whole foul stinking night. He waited a few moments then, using a handkerchief to clean his lips and passing the other hand over his sweaty hair, and suddenly remembering now that he had taken a hat to the Green Gong, a hat it could keep, before he rejoined Miss Walsingham.

'Sorry, Miss Walsingham,' he croaked. 'Disgusting exhibition.'

'You poor man! But it's happened to most of us,' she cried in her usual large, musical comedy manner, cheerfully unruffled. 'And now you'll soon feel better. I caught sight of you in that taxi, and thought you were badly pickled. So I kept in touch, wondering what was going to happen to you. But I live along here anyhow. And I'll tell you what I'm going to do, Sir George. I'm taking you to my place, to make you some coffee, and then when you're fit to travel I'll run you home.'

She seemed so sensible, friendly, warm-hearted, that if Sir George had not just been sick, he felt he would have embraced her. This was the kind of woman, larger and better than life, a man needed. And in the car he remembered asking Joan Drayton about her and then refusing to listen to what he felt would have been some saga of sexual irregularity. And now this same woman had just watched him vomiting into the gutter. And here she was, sitting close and warm — and he was glad of that because now he felt cold — perfumed and painted and undauntedly blonde, with a black cloak worn carelessly over a scarlet dress, and yet deeply and satisfyingly maternal, an Earth Mother hurrying a car along the Cromwell Road.

He was stretched out, at her insistence, on the sofa in what seemed to him a surprisingly large and well-furnished sitting room, when she brought him the coffee. He was not sleepy but he felt deathly tired; no longer drunk, as he realised he had been, but not yet his usual sober self; a weary somebody else perhaps, yet somebody very much George Drake as well.

'This'll do you good,' she told him. 'Very hot, very strong. You're still looking nearly as white as a sheet. The usual pink's gone. Now then, drink this. I'm having some to keep you company. Any brandy in it, d'you think? No, perhaps not.' She sat down in a low chair, close to where his head was resting.

'Thank you, Miss Walsingham—'

'June, for God's sake, or we'll soon be back at a DISCUS meeting. Let's imagine we're a long way from Russell Square.'

'Yes, June.' He tried a sip of the coffee, which was indeed very strong and hot. 'You know, I'm only fifty-two. And I've always thought of myself as a young fifty- two. But just now I suddenly feel like an old man, or at least what I imagine an old man feels like.' His voice trailed off.

'I could tell you some surprising things about some old men I've known,' she said cheerfully. 'One or two of 'em famous too.' She sipped her coffee, then smiled at him. 'I don't think you know about me, do you? I imagine the rest of 'em do, so you might as well know. Then you can talk. For the last ten years I've been the mistress of a very well-known man—never mind who. We couldn't marry, though I always secretly hoped that sooner or later we might. That's what women with lovers always hope, and I don't care what they say. Well, that hope's gone, and now he doesn't need me any longer. He still pretends he does, but he doesn't. So I've walked into a wall, like the big bloody soft fool I am.' And, to his surprise, two tears, not large and welling but small and angry, darted out of her full darkish blue eyes. 'Now you can talk, if you want to. And it might do you good—so long as it's not Secretary-General, Chairman-of-the-board, dusty stuff.'

'All right, June. Well,' he went on slowly, 'I've had one of the most horrible evenings I ever remember. Useless, lunatic! As you know, we arranged a dinner party for Greene. Went to a lot of trouble and expense.' And then he described, as best he could, everything that had happened—except that he said nothing about Alison. She must have noticed this omission but she never mentioned Alison when she asked him a few questions, and he could not help feeling that she had guessed what had happened.

'I know the man who owns that Studio Flat,' she told him, pulling a face. 'He's away and has lent it to Greene. He's a bastard too. They nearly all are, though some of 'em are hellishly attractive.'

'Not to me, they aren't,' cried Sir George. 'They don't like me, and I don't like them. Undependable, irresponsible, madly conceited! I hate 'em all. And I wish to God I'd never set foot in DISCUS and was running some sensible department. Having to kowtow to that unspeakable Greene and go to his Gong!' And now, even more to his astonishment, his own eyes filled with tears. Sheer fatigue of course.

Not apparently noticing his distress, she said reproachfully: 'Tim Kemp did try to warn you. And I know he warned that wet worm, Spenser.'

'Yes, yes, yes, June,' he replied wearily. 'And you probably think I behaved badly to Kemp at the meeting. Perhaps I did.' He put down his coffee cup. 'Perhaps I so resented his being pushed on to us again that I never tried to make any proper use of his peculiar abilities—'

'That's about it, my dear.'

'And that's bad administration.' His voice shook a little. 'I never pretended to know much about the arts—sometimes I think we'd be better off without them—but I've always considered myself a sound administrator. Not like that conceited ass Stratherrick, who's made such a hash of COMSA. He hasn't a clue about decent administration.'

'If what I hear is true, it may be all the same very soon.' She bent forward and pressed his hand. 'So don't be surprised or shocked if any day now I tell you I'm going.'

He looked with childish rather than erotic longing at her generous display of bosom. A fellow could rest there. I'll be surprised, shocked, disappointed, sad, June. You're making me feel it's my fault—'

'Of course it won't be your fault, you silly man.' She put both hands to his cheeks and shook his head a little.

'Don't do that, please. Got a hell of a headache.'

'Oh—how stupid of me! Of course you must have, poor thing.'

'Really feeling pretty rotten and miserable, I must say.'

'I know, I know—and it's awful for you, isn't it?' And, clucking over him, she somehow contrived, without any fuss and acrobatics, to rest his head against that magnificent bosom and then begin stroking his forehead. To this bliss he surrendered, without further movement, for a magical portion of time that he might have been sharing with his nine-year-old self just back from prep school. Then, as he was dropping off, she suddenly became brisk and businesslike. 'You're feeling ever so much better, my dear, so now I'll run you home—yes, I will, I never mind driving as late as this, when the streets are clear— so up we come.'

He heard her go roaring down the hill as he let himself into his house, and thought of her with gratitude and regret. A superb type of woman, really. There was no Alison of course; he had felt sure there wouldn't be. The house had not yet recovered from that dinner party: it whispered, now forlornly, now mockingly, of absent and treacherous wives, impudent and lecherous guests, idiotic anticipations, silly hopes, bitter reality. And in the middle of the dining-room table was a note—and a pretty damned stiff note too— from the aristocratic servitors, contriving to leave behind them a continuing sniff of disapproval. Sir George went to bed, wishing he could sleep undisturbed for about six months.

15

'SIR MICHAEL,' said Miss Tilney, 'Mr Kemp is downstairs and he's asking if he could see you for a few minutes.'

'Yes, he could. Tell him to come up. Oh—and another thing, Miss Tilney. I'm nearly out of my special malt whisky. You're not desperately busy, are you? Would you mind going along to Purvis and Brown—they're in Knightsbridge, but you once went there before, didn't you?—and collecting a couple of bottles for me?'

'I could go during my lunch break—'

'I know you could, but I'd much rather you spent your lunch break lunching, Miss Tilney. So please go now, after telling Kemp to come up.'

'Very well, Sir Michael,' she said, with mournful resignation.

Thus making sure there would be no listening-in to his talk with Kemp, Sir Michael pushed back his chair, stretched out his legs, and lit a cigarette. A few minutes later, Kemp came ambling in. Like the old antagonists they were, the two men eyed each other with undisguised curiosity.

'Good of you to come all the way from DISCUS, Kemp.'

'I'm not there just now,' said Kemp, making himself comfortable and puffing away at his pipe. 'I had a row with Drake—about Lady Bodley-Cobham's project, by the way—so I awarded myself some sick leave. But when I rang up the office yesterday, I was told you'd telephoned several times, asking for me. So here I am.' He smiled that slow, sweet, deceptive smile.

'I'll come to the point then.' Sir Michael stared hard at him. 'Do you happen to know where that girl is? I mean Shirley Essex.'

'I know you do. I also know where she is.' That damned smile again.

'Well?'

'There's no *well* about it, Stratherrick. What do you want with the girl?'

'Oh—come, man!' And Sir Michael's tone was as sharp as his look. 'That's my affair.'

Kemp puffed at him for a few moments. 'If you're not careful, you'll soon be telling me to mind my own business. Well, I am minding it. Young Shirley's a friend of mine. So I know where she is and what she's doing. And if she thought of you as a friend, then you'd know too.'

'It's a damned sight more complicated than that,' said Sir Michael angrily. 'And don't sit there pretending you aren't well aware of that fact, Kemp. I've thought more than once I've you to thank for all this—this—'

'This what?'

'We needn't go into that. But it was you who sent her here from DISCUS, wasn't it?'

'Certainly. Knowing your interest in good-looking girls—'

'She's not just another good-looking girl, Kemp. I thought you had some imagination. She's a ravishing, maddening beauty.'

Kemp gave him a curious, searching look. 'Quite right. There we agree. Where we differ is that you want to get her into bed, and I don't. I simply enjoy looking at that astonishing face while listening—or sometimes pretending to listen—to her ingenuous girlish chatter. And I'm not going to tell you where you can find her.'

Sir Michael hesitated for a moment or two, then changed his tone completely. 'You probably sent that girl here to torment me. If so, you did a neat job. I'll admit that I can't get her out of my mind. I'll also admit that it's playing the devil with me. I must have telephoned the house at least a score of times, without ever having had a reply. What's happened? You can tell me that, can't you?'

Kemp nodded. 'I can and I will. It's an extraordinary situation. Your visit acted as a kind of catalyst. There was a tremendous bust-up immediately afterwards. Shirley went off to stay with a friend. Her parents had a violent quarrel. I think the explosive material had been building up for some time. Unknowingly you—possibly Shirley too—chucked a match into it. So you've been ringing up an empty house. Her mother's staying with a brother, Shirley's uncle, at Hove. And her father has had himself transferred to a new factory his company are opening, somewhere near Newcastle.'

'Permanently, I hope.'

'You look pleased.'

'So would you if you'd met that man. I take it that Shirley's working?'

'Can't afford not to. And temporarily she's landed a rather fascinating job.'

'I'm surprised,' said Sir Michael gloomily. 'She was a dam' bad secretary, Kemp.'

'But it wasn't in that capacity—'

'Oh drop that!' Sir Michael got up, moved away from his desk only to be called back to it by the telephone. 'No, I don't want to talk to him,' he told it sharply. 'And no more interruptions while I have somebody here.' He moved away again, then turned to look at Kemp. 'Now listen. I don't like you very much, and I know that you dislike me. You think I'm an arrogant, conceited womaniser, not good at his job. I think you're terrible at yours, not because you aren't clever, you are, whereas most of the people here and at DISCUS are just stupid, but you've stopped caring, you're lazy, and drink far too much. Um?'

'A fair statement,' said Kemp mildly. 'But now—what?'

'I haven't seduced that girl, but she's bloody well seduced me. In the mind, the imagination, where I really live. And if, like her mother, you ask me in effect what my intentions are, I can't tell you. I haven't any. It sounds ridiculous, I know, but it happens to be true.'

'I believe you, my friend. Indeed, to be frank, I more or less anticipated some such baffling situation.'

'I'll bet you did. Now—have a heart, Kemp! If the girl's bent on marriage, naturally I can't blame her. And the only person I've discussed this situation with—a woman friend—as good as told me, the other night, to get on with it and risk making a fool of myself. But how the hell can I marry a girl not half my age, with whom I've hardly anything in common, a girl with an entirely different sort of background, a girl who behind that incredible appearance is really just a typical little suburban typist—I ask you, Kemp, how can I?'

'I don't know,' said Kemp, rising.

'Well, you might have given it a thought,' cried Sir Michael, 'before you created this situation. Wild irresponsibility—typical! Now then, where do I find her?'

'I'm not going to tell you. And now I'm not being irresponsible, I'm being—for once—responsible. However, I'll tell her I saw you. Any message?'

'Through you? Certainly not.' And as if he had already dismissed his visitor, Sir Michael went to the telephone. 'Ask Mr Marlowe to come up here, please.' And when he put down the receiver, he saw that Kemp had gone. And with him went a certain warmth and hint of magical possibilities, not belonging to Kemp himself of course, for Sir Michael really did dislike him, but arriving and departing with him through his association with Shirley. His mind, Sir Michael told himself gloomily, was now that of a love-sick imbecile.

'Jim,' he began as soon as Marlowe walked in, 'you know about these things—and I don't. Now surely when a girl—I mean any employee—changes his or her employment, there must be some exchange of insurance cards and P.A.Y.E. forms and that sort of thing between the old and the new employer?'

'If you're thinking about Miss Essex—'

'Why should I be?' Sir Michael was lofty.

Marlowe raised his eyebrows. 'Well, she happens to be the only employee who's left us for some time.'

'All right, it was Miss Essex I was thinking about. Kemp's just been in and he told me she'd landed a rather fascinating job but didn't say what it was. And I'm curious. Can't you discover, through these cards and forms, who's employing her?'

'Not now. Miss Bury told me that Miss Essex looked in, some days ago, to collect her insurance card and P.45 form, and that's that. We've no means of knowing who her new employer is.'

'Damn and blast! We imagine all the time we're now all entangled like Kafka characters with a bureaucracy that knows all about us, yet when we need a simple piece of information, we can't obtain it—a girl can just vanish.'

'Well, Miss Bury doesn't know what Miss Essex is doing, because I asked her. By the way, sir, here's your return ticket to Burmanley—and we've booked you a seat in a smoker. You won't be with Jeff Byrd—he has to travel Second now. Oh—and we've booked your room at the Northern and Midland Hotel—'

'A thousand curses on the Northern and Midland Hotel, Burmanley, Repertory and Contemporary Drama! Yes, yes, I said I'd go—and I'm going. But about this girl, Jim. Surely even in these days it's not easy for a girl to walk out of one job and straight into another!'

'No, it isn't. Miss Bury said she's probably working for one of the secretarial agencies, who supply girls for temporary work. We've had to use one of these agencies from time to time.'

'Jim, I want to know what this girl's doing. Could you start somebody ringing up these agencies, asking if she's there?'

Marlowe looked and then sounded dubious. 'I could of course. But there may be dozens of 'em.' He was cut short by the telephone bell.

It was Dudley Chapman, telling Sir Michael that a man called Jones, from the Treasury Statistical Department, was down below, asking to see the Director. 'And I think this is very important, sir,' said Chapman in his best top-secret conspiratorial manner.

'If it'll make you happy, send him up,' Sir Michael said grumpily. 'I have to see a man called Jones, from the Treasury,' he explained to Marlowe.

At once Marlowe looked frightened. 'I've heard rumours about this chap Jones. I don't like the sound of this.'

'He only wants a few statistics, I imagine. You can let him have some, can't you?'

'I suppose so. But if this chap's going to be hanging around, I don't think I can have one of the girls ringing up these secretarial agencies —'

'Yes, you can,' said Sir Michael sharply. 'But of course it's not your responsibility — it's mine. And start now, Jim. That's all.'

Marlowe almost scuttled away, as if this Jones might suddenly appear and bite him. Sir Michael put the Burmanley railway ticket in his wallet, and mentally cursed the place again. Miss Tilney had not yet returned, so Jones had to announce himself. He also handed Sir Michael a card, which read *I. B. C. T. N. Jones, Treasury Statistical Dept.*

I.B.C.T.N. Jones was tallish, greyish, saddish, with a faint false smile and a manner deliberately contrived to frighten types like Jim Marlowe and Dudley Chapman. He was a silent starer, as Sir Michael realised almost immediately: one of those bureaucrats who omit all easy small talk in the hope that the other man, trying to keep the conversation going, will feel a babbling fool. And Sir Michael wasn't having any.

'I may have to spend a day or two here,' said Jones, having accepted a chair. 'I trust you have no objection.'

'None whatever,' Sir Michael told him, saying no more and ready now to stare him out.

'You'll be here tomorrow?' said Jones, having lost the first rally.

'No. Going to Burmanley.'

'May I ask why?'

'My Drama man, Byrd,' said Sir Michael, conceding him this second rally, 'feels I ought to see a new American experimental play opening there tomorrow. He thinks COMSA might want to sponsor a London production.'

'Do you?'

'Depends on the play. I don't believe in sponsorship for the sake of sponsorship. Also, if it's of any interest, I thoroughly dislike Burmanley.' Sir Michael now closed down, as if for the day, not even bothering to stare.

I.B.C.T.N. had now to open the next rally. 'In fairness I must make it clear that some of us in the Statistical Department are permitted a rather wide field of enquiry. I'm not here simply to gather statistics.'

He was trying this on the wrong man. Sir Michael regarded him calmly. 'Indeed.' Love fifteen, Jones serving.

Jones tried his faint false smile, a watery dawn above ship-wrecked sailors. 'Unlike DISCUS, I believe, you are not wholly financed by a Treasury grant.'

'Half, that's all.'

It was at this point that Miss Tilney, either unusually careless or furious at having been sent away, entered carrying two bottles of whisky. 'Oh — I'm so sorry — '

'No, that's all right. My secretary, Miss Tilney — Mr Jones from the Treasury. Put the whisky in the cupboard, please, Miss Tilney.' He looked at Jones. 'It's a special malt whisky — too early to offer you some, I think — that I drink myself and, incidentally, pay for myself. There is in there, however, a bottle of sherry, kept for visitors, in which you have a share — about nine-and-sixpenny-worth, I think, half of nineteen shillings. Our financial man, by the way, is James Marlowe, a nice conscientious fellow. I have in fact an extremely conscientious, hard-working staff here, trying hard to do their duty. But employed by the National Commission for Scholarship and the Arts — COMSA — they often find it difficult to discover what their duty is. They'd be much happier at the Ministry of Agriculture — or Health.'

Jones produced a short barking sound, as if he were a sea-lion looking at somebody about to toss him a fish. Then, having done with laughter, he stared very hard at Sir Michael. 'Do you consider the work of COMSA generally successful?'

'No.'

'Indeed! Might I ask why?'

'We're in the wrong country, Mr Jones.'

'Would you care to expand on that, Sir Michael?'

'Most people here don't give a damn about scholarship and the arts, and they include nearly all the men who are running the country. They may pretend to, but they don't really care.'

'Do you? Or isn't that a fair question?'

'I don't object to it. Within certain limitations, belonging to my particular temperament, I really do. I wouldn't be here if I didn't, though I have to work for a living.'

Jones got up, his smile now not so faint and not entirely false. 'And tomorrow you're going to Burmanley, though you thoroughly dislike the place. As your Drama man—Byrd, is it?—will be away tomorrow too, perhaps I'll begin with him today. To tell you the truth, I'm interested in the Theatre.'

'You are, are you?' Sir Michael went to the door. 'Miss Tilney, call Mr Byrd and tell him that Mr Jones is coming down to see him. Well, there you are, Mr Jones. Help yourself.'

Jones gave him a queerly speculative look. 'Thank you, Sir Michael. You're rather different from what I expected you to be.'

'I'm often different from what I expect myself to be. We shall meet again, I imagine. Goodbye for the present, Mr Jones.'

16

'THIS IS EXCITING,' said Jeff Byrd as soon as they had found and occupied their seats.

'I gather that,' said Sir Michael. 'I overheard about twenty people in the foyer telling one another how exciting it all was.'

'But don't you feel already that there's a *something* —?'

'No, I don't, Jeff. I don't feel a dam' thing.'

'Well, several of the London critics are here.' He mentioned their names, and then began telling Sir Michael where some of them were sitting.

But if Sir Michael looked here and there, it was not in search of dramatic critics, in whom he took no interest whatever. Before they had taken their seats, he thought he had caught a glimpse of Andrea Babington's magnificent dark-red hair. Being a stage designer, Andrea might be attending this first night, possibly in the hope of redesigning the production for London. He had been trying to keep clear of Andrea even before Shirley Essex came along; she was a fine voluptuous creature but physically cloying and incapable of talking about anything outside the Theatre for more than two minutes; but bearing in mind the melancholy end of such evenings as this, the scarcity of late joys in these Burmanleys and Northern and Midland Hotels, he was now looking to make sure she might be available.

'I think that's the *Daily News* man,' said Byrd.

'Then it's all the more exciting, Jeff.' Sir Michael decided to concentrate upon finding Andrea during the interval.

'What do you think of the theatre? They're tremendously proud of it here.'

'You mean about a hundred people are proud of it, and the other six hundred thousand are either hostile or indifferent. For once I join the majority,' Sir Michael continued, with that relish with which we taste our prejudices. 'I'm old-fashioned—very square—about theatres. I really like pretty lights, red velvet, cupids round the dress circle, that kind of thing. These overgrown lecture halls for schools of surgery make me feel bored or depressed, even before their plays have begun. They're so grimly functional that they're like extensions of the new factories round here. This partly explains why most of the people from those factories stay away. But then you know more about that than I do, Jeff. Do you remember how, just before a play began, the footlights magically illuminated the lower folds of the curtain, and how the music from the orchestra below began to fade? Now there's no curtain, no music, and often no play. Well, let's see.'

'Tremendous success off-Broadway,' Byrd muttered as the auditorium darkened.

After twenty minutes of *The Dummies* Sir Michael was so bored that he tried to think about something else, anything that was not supposed to be happening in New York between a young man, who shouted, and a young woman, who whispered, obviously falling in love. There were only these two characters. All the others were dummies. You had to guess what they were saying—and either it was too easy or impossible—by the responses, shouted or whispered, of the young man and the young woman. Once again, he reflected with no particular satisfaction, the avant garde had been trapped into trying to make a full-length play out of an idea for a ten-minute sketch in a highbrow revue. He began to wonder where Shirley was and what she was doing. It was annoying that while he told himself that he thought of her as a marvellous face and not as a person, he could not recall her face and could only remember her as a person. On the other hand, switching to Andrea, who had to be here to rescue him from a Burmanley night, he found it easy to recollect every detail of her, dressed or undressed. Meanwhile, dummies came, dummies went, the young man shouted, the young woman whispered, and the skyscrapers winked above the skeleton sets. And at last, the one interval, thank God!

'You'd like a drink, wouldn't you, Sir Michael?'

'I'd like several.'

'Well, the manager's laying them on up in his office.'

'I'll join you there, Jeff, but first I want to find a woman I know. I'll bring her if I can find her.'

The foyer was packed of course, and it took him several minutes to make certain Andrea wasn't there. Cursing the luck, he made his way up to the manager's office, well-filled with what he believed Americans called 'free-loaders'; but there, talking to Jeff Byrd too, was Andrea, drinking gin and looking wonderful in an emerald silk suit. And Byrd had some whisky for him.

'Darling Michael,' she cried, 'I'd like to think I was the woman you've been looking for.'

'You are, my dear. I thought I saw you earlier, and I've been milling below, trying to find you. The absolute truth.'

'Lovely! Isn't this *exciting?*'

'Isn't it?' He looked about for another whisky, and now he had to meet the manager, then the director of the play, then a mournful American couple, who proved to be the authors. It was several whiskies later, and the bell was ringing to hasten them to their seats, before he had a chance to speak to Andrea again. They left the office together.

'Are you staying at the Northern and Midland, Andrea my love?'

'Yes, my pet. Third floor—316. But I'm going first to some sort of party they're having. They'd adore to see you there, Michael.'

'No, they might draw wrong conclusions. I'll sup quietly at the hotel—if there's anything fit to eat—and then wait for you, my love. Only don't be very late.'

'I won't, darling, I promise.' She squeezed his arm. 'This party's business, not pleasure. I have to find out if somebody's thinking about taking it to town. That's why I'm here, though now I know an even better reason. Midnight at the very latest. 316, don't forget. Now I go this way.'

Back in his seat, Jeff Byrd was flushed with pale ale and excitement. 'I gather it's the last two scenes that made it a smash hit in New York.'

'That's exciting, Jeff. Did you say anything to the head waiter about supper?'

'Yes, for you. It'll be up in your room. *And* some whisky. I thought, if you don't mind, I'd go to this party.'

'You do. But don't make any COMSA promises.'

'Of course not, Sir Michael. But you'll tell me what you think, at the end, won't you?'

Sir Michael said he would; and the play, with a fresh supply of dummies, now mostly in a higher income bracket, went shouting and whispering into Act Two. Hoping that just once the young man might whisper and the young woman shout, Sir Michael did his best to attend to what was happening. The marriage of the lovers was celebrated, with a full range of dummies, some standing, some sitting, and two lying in a corner, having passed out or about to make love. Then, after a tedious monologue from each of them, came the great end scenes, so powerfully disturbing to Greenwich Village. He, the husband, had a scene with her, the wife, but now of course she was a dummy too. And then she had a scene with him, and he had turned into a dummy. Sir Michael did not wish the play a minute longer, but he felt he could have taken a very brief final scene, mercifully silent, in which they were both dummies. The applause was generous, if not unanimous, and the young man and the young woman had to take half-a-dozen curtain calls, but without their large supporting cast. Happier now that it was over, Sir Michael had to suppress a strong desire to shout 'Dummies! Dummies!' so that they could take a bow.

Byrd, who had been standing up to clap all the harder, now began a confused report about the London critics—this one applauding vigorously, that one hurrying out, a smile on his face, the other one looking thoughtful. 'I think I ought to circulate, to try to discover what they feel about it. Are you going up to the manager's office again, Sir Michael?'

'I think not, Jeff. But off you go. We could meet in the foyer before I go back to the hotel.' And off Jeff went, all eagerness, zest, enthusiasm, just the man to run the Drama department of COMSA except that he was stagestruck and without any understanding of the Theatre. Sir Michael loitered on his way out, not wishing to listen to any first-night gabble from anybody he knew. Then he visited the *Gents*, where a fat man, probably a Burmanley alderman, was puffing and wheezing as he buttoned up his fly.

'Now I'll tell you what I think,' he said without being asked for his opinion. And he stared at Sir Michael quite indignantly, as if they had been arguing for the last hour. 'It's original. You can't get away from that. It's original. There's no doubt about that. Highly original. But I doubt if it'll do for Burmanley. I say,' he shouted, as if he thought Sir Michael suffered from deafness, 'I doubt if it'll do for Burmanley. They're very particular here, very particular. If a piece'll go in Burmanley, it'll go anywhere—that's what I always say.'

'That's what they say in every provincial town I've ever visited, my dear sir.' And Sir Michael marched out ahead of him.

He waited a minute or two in the foyer, and then Byrd came hurrying down the stairs from the manager's office, so excited he could hardly speak. Finally he brought out some confused stuff about this one raving about it, that one fairly enthusiastic, and other ones not quite sure or demanding a better production or liking the young man but not the young woman and so on and so forth, while Sir Michael enjoyed the cigarette he had been denied for the last hour and a quarter.

'What do you think, Sir Michael?' Byrd finally enquired anxiously.

'Promise not to tell anybody at the party, Jeff. A solemn promise, please.' He spoke slowly and softly. 'Right. Well, I think it's a bloody great bore.'

'You don't feel COMSA ought to help a London production?'

'Unless I'm dragged handcuffed and screaming out of my room, COMSA doesn't even mention its name. Sorry, Jeff. Enjoy your party.'

He ate a flavourless cold supper off a tray up in his room, drank the whisky that had arrived with it and then some of his own, smoked several cigarettes, and read without much interest the memoirs of a well-known Paris art-dealer. After half-past eleven, he kept on glancing at his watch. He was beginning to lust for the voluptuous and ardent Andrea. Time loitered and sagged. At two minutes past midnight, compelling himself to move slowly, he climbed the stairs from the second to the third floor, made sure nobody was looking, and then after a discreet tap he tried the knob of 316. She wasn't there of course, and he told himself he had been a fool to imagine that she would be. Ten to one she was still at that party, half-plastered by now. Back in his room, he undressed, added slippers and a dressing gown to his pyjamas, and awarded himself another whisky and two more cigarettes. The Paris art-dealer could no longer be read, so now he divided himself between gloating and glooming. It was twelve-thirty when he pushed open the door of 316, which had been left open half-an-inch to receive him.

'Darling, you've been *ages,*' Andrea said, after he had locked the door behind him. She was wearing a light wrap over nothing but that luminous skin of hers, and was not bothering to conceal anything. She was a bit tight, he guessed.

'No, I haven't, my dear. And I came up earlier. How was the party?'

'Horrible food but lots to drink. It didn't make much sense. I was longing to get away. Kiss me, you ravaged, deceitful, selfish old fraud!'

He did, and their long-experienced hands wandered, and for a few minutes it looked as if it were going to be better than ever. But then, fatally, he disengaged himself to take off his dressing gown and shed his slippers.

'There was a vague silly rumour going round that party,' she said, sitting up on the edge of the bed, 'that you don't like this play, Michael.'

'Quite right,' he replied, almost without thinking as he sat down beside her, preparing for more dalliance. 'I don't.'

'Now, Michael darling, I won't be teased—not in this way. You know very well I'm mad to do those sets and those dummies for a real production—not like this tatty Rep thing.'

'As a matter of fact, I didn't know.' He was a little short with her; the last thing he wanted now was theatrical chat.

She frowned at him, took her hand away from his, and quickly drew the wrap round her, hiding everything of immediate interest. 'Why did you come here then?'

'To meet you—like this, Andrea dear.'

'Oh—don't give me that, when all you've got to do, almost every other night, is to pick up the phone. I'm talking about the play now.'

'Jeff Byrd insisted upon my seeing it.' He was brusque, partly because he was now feeling rather cold. 'He doesn't trust his own judgment. And he's quite right, because he hasn't any. So I had to see this play. So I did. And I thought it was tedious drivel.'

'Oh—rubbish! It's original. It's really experimental. It's exciting. It's—'

'One cute little idea flogged to death for two hours,' he told her as he pushed his feet into the slippers and put on his dressing gown. 'And if you hadn't been thinking how to re-design the production, you'd have realised how fundamentally boring the thing was.'

'I've my living to earn, even if you haven't,' she snapped at him. She was now sitting up in bed, glaring. 'Why do you think you know better than anybody else? Wilkins of the *Gazette* is raving about it. That *Daily News* man says it's the most disturbing play of the year. Do you imagine your opinion's more important than theirs?'

'It is to me. And anyhow they're a couple of imbeciles—'

'Oh—shut up, for God's sake,' she shouted. 'You really *are* the most conceited arrogant stinker. I hate you.'

'What a pity! Goodnight, Andrea dear!'

Five Burmanley business men shared the compartment with him, next morning, on the 9.45 to London. They all had brief cases; they all brought out contracts and estimates and gold pens or pencils;

and almost immediately they all fell asleep. Sir Michael considered them with a sour mixture of contempt and envy. He thought about Jim Marlowe and the secretarial agencies, about I.B.C.T.N. Jones the Treasury sleuth, about Shirley. The train went tearing through the May morning and several English counties, mostly ruined.

17

THAT DREADFUL MORNING began by Sir George arriving in Russell Square over an hour late. A conscientious administrator, he demanded punctuality from himself as well as from the people working under him, and so he hurried into his room feeling ashamed of himself. But it was not his fault that he was late. Alison was going to France on the one o'clock plane, and she insisted upon explaining all over again how necessary it was that she should join Marjorie Sidney, now with UNESCO, in Paris for a few days. She even insisted upon showing him Marjorie's letter again, for the fourth time. He knew very well that this was a put-up job, that she was going to stay somewhere with Ned Greene. He had never told her that he too had visited that Studio Flat; he had allowed her to assume that he came straight home after the Green Gong. He had never even asked her why she seemed now so blankly uninterested in Ned Greene, who, he knew, had returned to France. But clearly she felt he knew *something,* and that was why she had to keep on justifying, right to the last minute, her response to Marjorie Sidney's appeal. It was the kind of situation in which a decent sound man hated to find himself. And now he was over an hour late.

No sooner had he bustled in than Joan Drayton, looking rather peculiar, put a card in front of him. 'He's here, Sir George.'

'Who's here?'

'This man. This Jones. And I've just remembered that Tim Kemp said something about a Jones—'

'Never mind about Kemp. He's not come back—by the way—has he?'

'Tim? No, he's still on sick leave. But this man Jones—'

'Is this his card?' He read it out. 'I.B.C.T.N. Jones. Treasury Statistical Department. Good God! I don't like the look of this. What sort of fellow is he?'

'He's just the sort of fellow you wouldn't like the look of, Sir George, I'm afraid. I didn't take to him at all. He came up an hour ago, asking for you. And I told him you were here every morning at ten, regular as clockwork. But after he'd waited about twenty minutes, he didn't seem to believe me. I think he's with Neil Jonson now.'

'Neil *hates* the Treasury and is probably telling him so. This is unfortunate, Joan, most unfortunate. I ought to have been here of course, but my wife was leaving for Paris. It's an extraordinary thing but as soon as one is involved in any way with Paris, all manner of irregularities seem to make their appearance.'

'Well, I must say I could take some.' But then she recognised Sir George's grave concern. 'Shall I ring down to tell him you're here now?'

'No, no, don't rush things. It'll make this fellow suspicious at once.'

'Perhaps he's only collecting statistics,' she suggested hopefully.

'I don't believe that for a moment. He's been sent to prepare a report on DISCUS. You say he looked that kind of man?'

'Well, he was sort of cool, quizzical, superior—'

'Yes, yes—that's the type.' Sir George thought for a moment or two. 'No, Joan, our best plan is simply to carry on, going through an ordinary morning's routine, just as if nothing had happened. If Jones wishes to interrupt our work, well and good. But we carry on. Now then—today's letters.'

As he went through the letters, with Joan Drayton and her notebook waiting across the desk, Sir George began to feel better. This was sensible administrative work, and he enjoyed doing it. No doubt some of the letters would raise later some teasing and perhaps unanswerable questions, just because DISCUS itself rested precariously on some outer edge of governmental responsibility, beyond which was all the dark lunacy of the arts. But while he was going through the morning's mail in this fashion, with Joan in her experience understanding every muttered exclamation or murmur, it was like being at work in a reasonable department, and he found it soothing. Indeed, after twenty minutes he had forgotten that this fellow Jones might be somewhere below and that very soon Alison would be setting out for Paris, where a Marjorie Sidney would turn almost at once into a Ned Greene raging with drink and lust. He spent another quarter of an hour dictating replies to those comparatively few letters that demanded the immediate attention of the Secretary-General of DISCUS. Familiar phrases flowed from him. Joan was filling her notebook. And it was just when he was enjoying all this that the unfamiliar and the ungovernable exploded, filling the room with noisy strangers.

There were in fact only six of them—a middle-aged couple, two young men, two girls. But they all had imposing physical presences; they were all trying to shake his hand; they were all talking at once; so that they seemed to occupy the room. And before Sir George had recovered from the shock of their entrance, the middle-aged man had filled the glass on the desk with whisky, from a bottle he had been brandishing, and had pressed it into Sir George's hand. Gasping in his astonishment, Sir George was trying to ask them what they thought they were doing.

'Silence now,' the middle-aged man shouted. He had a tremendous bass voice. 'We'll have silence while Sir George makes us a little speech of welcome.'

Sir George stared round at them while they waited expectantly. The middle-aged woman looked rather careworn, but the four young people, who seemed to share a family resemblance, were extraordinarily handsome, black-haired and with bright greeny-grey eyes. The middle-aged man had an unusually large head and face, and looked like one of the more disreputable Roman emperors. 'You have the floor, Sir George,' he said encouragingly. 'We are all ears. We are yours to command, sir.'

'Look here,' said Sir George, 'what *is* all this? Who *are* you?'

'Take a pull at the whisky you have there—I brought it for you, sir—and then tell me if you ever tasted a better drop in the whole of your life.'

'Certainly not,' Sir George told him. 'It's much too early in the day to be drinking whisky.' He put down the glass. 'But what I want to know is—who *are* you—and what are you doing here. I mean, whoever you are, I can't have you bursting in like this. It's intolerable, you know, quite intolerable.'

Here Joan Drayton, who ought to have known better, suddenly began a loud giggling. This set off the two young women and, soon after them, even the middle-aged careworn woman, unable to resist this mysterious feminine impulse, which Sir George had often noticed and regretted before, to find amusement in what were essentially serious situations.

'Will you women be quiet now,' the middle-aged man commanded, not asked, 'while I explain to Sir George and put him out of his terrible misery.'

'But Sir George must have had the message about us from Mr Heywood,' one of the young men insisted.

At once the other five began talking; the young man who had spoken began again, much louder; and in two minutes the room was a bedlam. In his despair and seeing a glass in front of him, without remembering what was in it, Sir George swallowed a mouthful of very strong Irish whisky, then gasped and made motions to Joan to bring him some water. The visitors were still shouting at one another when Joan returned with the water and three or four glasses. The middle-aged man poured out some of his whisky, drank it at once, and then bellowed: 'Will you all be quiet now?'

The four young people stopped, but the middle-aged woman went on: 'I say it was well-known to me at the time that Mr Heywood was drunk.'

'Not at all, not at all.'

'And the girls will tell you the same thing.'

'The last thing I would do,' said the middle-aged man with great dignity, 'in a matter of this kind, would be to ask the girls to arbitrate. They would not know the difference between drunkenness and sobriety, unless a man was making up to them. Now, quiet all, while I address myself to Sir George, who is in a terrible state of bewilderment.'

'I most certainly am. I don't understand who you are and why you're here and why you think you can come bursting into my room—'

'It's intolerable, you know, quite intolerable.' This, done in a fair imitation of Sir George's outraged tone, came from one of the girls.

'Sheelah, you'll not do that,' said the middle-aged woman sharply. 'Do you want me to be ashamed of you?' But it seemed as if the giggling might break out again among the females.

'Sir George,' the middle-aged man began, coming closer and staring hard at him, 'do you give me your word of honour you have had no message from Mr Hugo Heywood—the Head, I understand, of your Drama Department? Your solemn word of honour, Sir George?'

'Really, this is quite preposterous. I don't sit here giving solemn words of honour. But I've heard nothing from Mr Heywood since he went on leave—to Ireland, I believe.'

'And where in God's name did you think we were coming from?'

one of the young men asked.

'Rory, hush now—'

'But, Dad, I'm feeling disgusted—'

'Then keep your mouth tight shut, boy. Now, Sir George,' said the middle-aged man grandly, 'I've been remiss—gravely remiss. I apologise. Do you accept my apology?'

'Yes, I suppose so,' Sir George said peevishly, 'though I don't know exactly what you're talking about—'

'But you accept my apology, so all's well. We'll drink to that.'

Sir George did not want to drink to it, but the man was so insistent, holding out his glass to touch Sir George's, that he gave in, clinked glasses, and took a sip. Meanwhile, the two young men had produced a bottle of their own and were filling glasses. The room was beginning to reek of strong whisky.

'I made a mistake,' said the middle-aged man in a tone of huge noble melancholy. 'Not the first, not the last.'

'You can take your oath on that,' the careworn woman told the company.

'The first, the very first, thing I ought to have done, Sir George, was to introduce myself, my wife and family, my company. I am Shawn O'More, director and leading player of the O'More West of Eire Touring Company. This is Mary Sullivan, in private life Mrs O'More. These are our two sons, Hugh and Rory, our daughters, Sheelah and Paddy, all members of my company. And between us, I give you my word, Sir George, maybe at times with some help from two or three slips of girls and three or four male walk-ons, we can play anything ever written for the stage, sir. We have successfully toured the West, Sir George, for many many years, from one-night stands in small halls, barns if necessary, to whole weeks in Galway and Limerick, with a complete change of bill nightly.' He refreshed himself hastily, making a continuing noise even as he drank, so that Sir George was not able to interrupt him. 'Mark that, Sir George, please mark that—*a complete change of bill nightly*. One of the classics—I can get through my version of *Macbeth* or *Othello* in about eighty-five minutes—followed, in the time-honoured tradition, by some musical items—concluded, again traditionally, by one of at least twenty roaring farces we have in our repertoire. In addition to the classics, Sir George, we play the fine old melodramas—*A Royal Divorce, The Face at the Window, The Monk and the Lady*—'

'Mr Heywood came to see us for three successive nights,' Rory cried, when his father stopped to recollect other melodramas. 'And he said we were marvellous. Dad, you have what he wrote for you, that last night—'

'He was very drunk that night, the poor man,' said Mrs O'More. 'And Sheelah—or Paddy—which one of you was it?—had to slap his face—'

'I did, but not too hard.'

'So did I—but just a light tap,' the other girl added, 'to show him I was not in the mood for his attentions—'

'Shut up, the pair of you. I have it here, what he wrote that last night, when we all took a drop together.' And Mr O'More unfolded a sheet of paper and held it about three inches from Sir George's nose. Sir George took it and noticed that the writing, though undoubtedly Heywood's, looked suspiciously irregular; and the paper itself seemed to be stained with wine and gravy. It was not a document that recommended itself to any sound administrator. It said: *O'More Co.— astonishing versatility and power—beaut. girls—virile men—restore traditional simplicity attack appeal Eng. Th.—here at last what been looking for—urgent message Sir G.*

Sir George took advantage of the silence that he knew would soon be broken. 'Joan, you'd better go back to your office and deal with any telephone messages.' And like the good secretary she was, she went, but obviously with some reluctance.

'That's one that has suffered,' Mrs O'More announced. 'It's there to be seen in her eyes.'

'Will you hold your tongue, Mary,' said her husband, 'when Sir George himself is waiting to speak to us about what Mr Heywood wrote. Now then, Sir George?'

'I gather from this—er—document that Mr Heywood was much impressed by your performances. He's by way of being an enthusiast of course, and being on holiday he may have been drinking more than usual. As I told you earlier, I've heard nothing from him. And I really can't understand why you should have descended upon me, without any warning, in this extraordinary manner.'

He was answered at once by the whole O'More Touring Company, and it took O'More himself a minute or two to shout down the others. When there was quiet again, he looked sternly at Sir George.

'It was your own man, Mr Heywood himself, who said to me "Shawn

O'More, here's the chance of a lifetime. Cancel all engagements", he said. "Go straight to London and present yourselves to Sir George Drake, Secretary-General of DISCUS" —'

'Preposterous!'

This enraged O'More. 'What the flaming hell's the use of sitting there throwing your *preposterous* in my face, when I'm telling you — and I have a remarkable memory, quite remarkable—in his exact words what your own decent man, Mr Heywood, said to me? Rory — Hugh—am I or am I not repeating Mr Heywood's very words?'

'You are, Dad.'

'Every syllable you are, Dad.'

'You hear that?' O'More demanded angrily. He tried to use his glass as a kind of pointer, with the result that some whisky slopped on to the desk. 'So will you, for God's sake, stop saying *preposterous* and *intolerable* and the like? We were asked to take the chance of a lifetime, so we took it, at a great cost—'

Here the other five chimed in again, coming closer to do it more effectively. When all six were shouting at him, Sir George, hardly knowing what he was doing, swallowed the rest of the whisky in his glass, gasped and coughed, and groped around for the water. Still bellowing away indignantly, O'More filled both his own glass and Sir George's.

'Will you please listen to me?' Sir George shouted, thumping the desk. 'Thank you. Now then. In the first place—and Heywood should have told you this—DISCUS does not engage in theatrical management. If you wish to appear in London, then you'll have to find a management that will be responsible for you—'

'That's not the way it was told us,' cried Hugh angrily. 'But did I or did I not warn you and your father the poor man was talking out of the drink he'd taken?' This was Mrs O'More, who might look careworn but could raise her voice with the rest of the family.

'He was no more drunk than I was,' said O'More.

'That's saying exactly nothing,' cried his wife.

'Will you please listen to me?' Sir George appealed to them.

Rory O'More, a darkly handsome but rather sinister young man, leant over the desk. 'It's my belief you had the message and you're ratting on us.'

'And that wouldn't surprise me at all,' said his sister, Paddy. 'He's a disgusting type of the English, this one is.'

'Like that one who called himself a brigadier,' said Sheelah, 'and tried to get off with us that time in Sligo.'

Sir George thumped the desk again. 'The policy of DISCUS,' he began at the top of his voice. But two things happened then. First, the O'More Touring Company all talked indignantly at once. Secondly, into this bedlam reeking of whisky, once the Secretary-General's quiet room, there entered, raising his eyebrows, an astonished stranger. And then like a thunderflash came the conviction to Sir George that this must be I.B.C.T.N. Jones of the Treasury.

They had all stopped shouting to take a look at him.

'Oh—do carry on,' said Jones, with a faint smile.

'And if you ask me,' Sheelah could be heard muttering, 'this one's another of 'em.'

'I am Shawn O'More, my dear sir, if you're interested at all, well-known in Irish theatrical circles—'

'You're Mr Jones from the Treasury, I imagine,' Sir George began desperately. 'There seems to have been some sort of misunderstanding with these people—'

But he had no chance against the O'More Touring Company with its long experience of noisy audiences. Sir George gave it up and stared helplessly at I.B.C.T.N. Jones, who made no pretence of trying to listen but stood at ease, still smiling his faint smile, looking from one to the other of them and occasionally giving Sir George an enquiring glance. There were several minutes of this, during which Sir George broke into a sweat, wondering what on earth to do next.

Joan Drayton came in hurriedly and noisily, so that they all turned to stare at her. 'Sir George,' she cried, out of breath but bright-eyed, 'it's all right. Tim Kemp's here.'

'Now did you say Tim Kemp?' O'More demanded, above cries from his womenfolk. 'Because if there aren't two Tim Kemps in the world, then here's a great friend of us all—'

And indeed as soon as Kemp made his appearance, the whole six of them swarmed upon him, the girls kissing him, the men shaking his hand and thumping him on the back.

'Kemp,' Sir George shouted, leaving his desk, 'can you take them somewhere? Anywhere—out of this room.'

The O'Mores were silent now, looking hopefully at Kemp, who replied: 'Certainly. DISCUS doesn't want them?'

'Of course not. Absurd!'

'Then I'll tell you what I'll do. We'll go round to a pub I think they'd like, for a drink or two and something to eat—'

'You're a civilised decent man, Tim,' said O'More.

'And then this afternoon,' Kemp continued, still looking at Sir George, 'I'll take them round to COMSA—um?'

'A wonderful idea, Kemp,' Sir George told him, 'simply wonderful. Off you go, then.'

Left to themselves, in a room restoring itself to order and decency, Sir George and Jones regarded each other in a silence that Sir George soon found intolerable.

'The whole thing was a ridiculous mistake of course,' Sir George heard himself babbling. 'My Drama man, Heywood, is spending his leave somewhere in the West of Ireland, saw these people performing somewhere, must have dined too well, probably drank too much because the food was uneatable—and, well, you can imagine what happened, Mr Jones—'

He waited for an encouraging word or two from Jones, but to his dismay, Jones kept silent, simply regarding him with that faint but disturbing smile.

'This kind of thing is quite unusual here of course,' Sir George went floundering on. 'Though I'll admit that Heywood's not altogether a sound chap. I've been worried about him for some time. Always wanting to send religious plays in verse round the mining towns— that sort of thing. I've been seriously thinking of appointing another head of Drama—'

If Jones had only said 'Have you?', Sir George would have immediately felt much better. But the man just sat there, faintly smiling and not saying a word. He was obviously the Treasury at its worst.

Sir George mopped his face, then dabbed at the whisky on his desk, threw his handkerchief into the wastepaper basket, and tried again. 'You see, Mr Jones, here at DISCUS—'

18

I**T WAS A** week after their last talk when Kemp called on Sir Michael again. Being a cunning old hand, he timed his appearance to coincide with the morning coffee break. Though still disliking him, Sir Michael was glad to see him. This was chiefly because he hoped for news of Shirley, but also because he was feeling bored. He had been staring out of the window just before Kemp was announced — it was a fine May morning — and wishing he was somewhere else. Now that he had cut out his afternoon women, of whom Alison Drake had actually been the last, he was spending far too much time at COMSA. He mentioned this to Kemp when they settled down with their coffee.

'And the irony is,' Sir Michael told him, 'I spend far more time here now than I did when it was alive. And I know very well — I can feel it in the air — that it's disintegrating. Well, this time you can't say I've been telephoning you, Kemp, so what do you want?'

Kemp smiled. 'I want to do a deal with you. If you'll help me, I'll help you. Cutlet for cutlet.'

'I'd like to take a closer look at these cutlets. Does information about Shirley come into the deal?'

'Certainly. Valuable information, Stratherrick.'

Sir Michael regarded the smiling little man darkly. 'I may already have it. After a devil of a lot of telephoning downstairs — and with that Treasury spy, Jones, drifting in and out all the time — I know that Shirley is now employed by the West One Secretarial Agency.'

'Quite right. And?'

'And nothing,' Sir Michael said bitterly. 'I've been there twice, and all I can get out of that woman in charge, who's so refined she doesn't seem to be talking English, is that Shirley is working for them but out doing some confidential job. The second time — yesterday, in fact — I ate so much humble pie the place must be crackling with broken crust. But no go. Now if we do a deal, can you tell me what she's doing and where she is?'

'Certainly. That's the valuable information I have.'

'What do *you* want, then?'

'I've six Irish players, all O'Mores, on my hands. Friends of mine from Western Ireland—'

'I know. Jeff Byrd was saying something about it, yesterday, but I hardly listened.'

'I've never been able to listen to Jeff myself. We can forget him. But I know a theatre man called Blagg—*Totsy* Blagg—'

'I'll bet he's a scoundrel. Totsy!'

'Certainly. But I know how to deal with him. Now he's got the Coronet Theatre for four weeks, on easy sharing terms. He's talked to the O'Mores, and his idea is to put them into the Coronet, just as wild Irish barnstormers, which of course is what they are.'

'I've never seen any Irish barnstormers. Are these O'Mores any good?'

'In one sense, they're terrible. In another, they're wonderful. Doing their own melodramas and farces. Their Shakespeare is murderous. Shawn, the father, is three times lifesize. Mary, his wife, is at least twice lifesize. The two sons are handsome, dashing, and superbly idiotic. The two girls can't act at all but are ravishing dark beauties. The family, plus a few extras, will go on at the Coronet doing exactly the same traditional programmes they've been doing for years in the West of Ireland. They've brought their costumes with them. They don't need any sets. Totsy Blagg says that a thousand pounds will finance the O'More Season at the Coronet. He can raise two hundred and fifty. I'm providing another two hundred and fifty. COMSA can have a half share at five hundred.'

Sir Michael thought a moment. 'It's one of those things that might, as they used to say, take the town. As a huge joke, of course. You realise, Kemp, that if it succeeds, you're putting up your Irish friends to be laughed at.'

'If I thought their feelings would be hurt,' Kemp said, 'I wouldn't look at the scheme. But if it succeeds, then they'll play to roaring full houses, and that'll never hurt the feelings of any O'More. If the audiences laugh *at* them, they'll put it down to the stupidity of the English. Now has COMSA got five hundred to spare?'

'No, it hasn't. But I might have.'

'Can you afford to lose five hundred, Stratherrick?'

'No. And I may find myself unemployed shortly. But even so, I might take a gamble. Five hundred's dull, anyhow. Five thousand isn't. And if this jape doesn't fall flat on the first night, it might run for months, if not at the Coronet then elsewhere. Look here, Kemp, where and when can I meet these roaring O'Mores and this Totsy character?'

'Six-thirty this evening at the *Salisbury*. You know it? Right then. And now I'm going to trust you, though I never thought I should.'

'I've always regarded you, as you must know, Kemp, as one of the most untrustworthy characters I've ever had working with me. But now you're going to tell me about Shirley, aren't you?'

'I had a card from her yesterday. She's at Cannes. She and another girl from the agency are working for an oil multimillionaire, Prince Aghamazar. He took them with him to Cannes—he keeps a yacht in those parts—but he may be bringing them back to London any day. He's an impulsive type, and as he has an income of about a million pounds a week, he can indulge his whims.'

Sir Michael stared at him gloomily. 'She seems to have wandered into the Arabian Nights. I'd much rather she hadn't. Well, we meet at the *Salisbury* round about six-thirty. If we all go broke, we'll have to see what we can do with Prince What's-his-name. That is, if he does come back, and Shirley isn't at this moment on her way to the Persian Gulf. I might as well tell you, Kemp,' he went on as he followed Kemp to the door, keeping his voice low, 'I seem to be in love with that girl. I'm a bloody fool, but there it is. And I'm not sure you didn't work it. I ought to be booting you down the stairs.'

It was one of those days, coming unexpectedly after a blank period, when a new and richer pattern of events seems to emerge, as if, as the Maya believed, a different god were now shouldering the burden of time. Just after three, when Sir Michael was yawning over a scheme of Edith Frobisher's that would empty concert halls only a little slower than bubonic plague, he was told that a Mrs Essex would like to see him, if only for a few minutes. He felt there could be only one Mrs Essex in his life, and he was right. It was Shirley's mother, looking much smarter and gayer than she had done in Winston Avenue. He told her so.

'Trust you! Well, I've been enjoying myself—at the seaside.' She sat down and smiled at him. 'And I'll have a cigarette if you're having one. It's too early for whisky, more's the pity. And do you know who started this off? Well, you did, Sir Michael.'

'I've heard rumours. Not from Shirley. I've never seen her since that night.'

'I'll bet you haven't. Well, I warned you she can be very obstinate, didn't I? But let me tell you what happened. After you'd gone, we had a real old family bust-up, first the three of us, and then Jevon and me, after Shirley had gone to bed. Things came out that had been asking to come out for years and years. And finally—and I couldn't help it the way he'd gone at me—I told him something I'd sworn to myself I never would tell him.' She paused, obeying a sure dramatic instinct.

'I'm a Celt, Mrs Essex, an intuitive man,' he told her softly. 'And I think I know what you told him, poor devil. You told him Shirley isn't his daughter, didn't you?'

She laughed off her embarrassment. 'You're a regular demon, you are. What with that soft obstinacy that Shirley has and what you know about women, there'll be some fine goings-on between you two, if you ever do live together.' She waited a moment. 'It was in the War of course. I'd only been married a couple of years but I knew then I'd made a mistake. Jevon was away for a few weeks, and I went with another girl for a night out in the West End. Two young Air Force officers—fighter pilots—picked us up, in a nice way. I spent the next three days and nights with Simon—that was his name—and then he had to go back—and of course he was killed. I've seen Shirley look so like him sometimes that my heart's turned over.' She waited a moment, again. 'I never meant Jevon to know. He was so proud of her—fond of her too in his way. But that night it just had to come out. And of course that finished it. He got his firm to send him straight up North. I don't know whether there'll be a divorce or not, and just now I don't much care. I'm not asking him to keep me. Why should he? I've a chance of going into a nice little millinery business—through a friend of my sister-in-law in Brighton—I've always been good with hats—so I'll keep myself. *And* do what I like. If it wasn't for Shirley, I'd be after you, Sir Michael.' She laughed, then looked serious. 'But I'm not in the same class, never was, though I was pretty enough at her age.'

'You're pretty enough at your age—'

'Oh—go on. I know you. But how did you guess?'

'I just refused to believe that man had really fathered her. I couldn't see the least possible resemblance.'

'You'd have noticed it at once if you'd seen Simon. Shirley has more of him than she has of me. And it makes a lot of difference.

She's been waiting for somebody like you to fall in love with. I knew what had happened as soon as she started working for you—knew it before she did. She couldn't stop talking about you.'

'Quite possibly, but—'

'No, Sir Michael, you must let me tell you a few things about Shirley that you ought to know. Now she's not clever, in your sense—no more than I am—but she's very adaptable, which I'm not. She's very quick to notice what to wear, what to say, what to do—'

'I've no doubt she is. But can you see her adapting herself to life with a self-indulgent bachelor of forty-eight?'

'Not if he stayed a bachelor—no. But married to him—yes. If you're thinking you're the wrong kind of husband for her, you're miles out. You're exactly what she wants—and what she wanted before she fell in love with you.'

'Probably looking for the father she ought to have had,' Sir Michael muttered rather gloomily. He did not see himself as a father figure.

She must have sensed what he was feeling. 'There could be a bit of that in it,' she observed cheerfully. 'We're all mixed up, aren't we? But don't make any mistake. That girl wants to be somebody's wife not his daughter. And you're the one. She's made up her mind about that.'

'But she's deliberately kept away from me—covered all her tracks—'

'Now come on, you're supposed to know about women. You've been missing her badly, haven't you?'

'I must admit I have—'

'And if you hadn't, if you'd started cooling off, she'd have popped up again in a flash—'

'But how would she *know!*'

'We've all kinds of ways of knowing. Detectives aren't in it compared with us, when we really mean it.'

'Incidentally, this determined daughter of yours may at this very moment be drinking champagne with her employer, Prince Aghamazar—'

'Oh, you know about that, do you?'

'And, for all we know,' he continued darkly, 'may be finding the advances of this fabulously wealthy potentate irresistible.'

She laughed. 'I might. I've read too many women's mags and seen too many films. But not Shirley. I know her. If she's in love with Sir Michael Stratherrick and is going to marry him, they couldn't make her budge if they offered her India. I had a picture postcard from her—'

'Everybody has—except me.'

'Serves you right for running away that night. I hope you've been biting your nails ever since. That was the idea. You'll have to chase her a bit—a tiny bit. Well, I must go and let you get on with your work.'

But there was in fact less and less work that he felt like getting on with, even if his mind had been free and clear. However, he stayed at his desk until about half-past five, and was giving himself a first touch of the old malt when I.B.C.T.N. Jones arrived.

'You can call this after hours, Jones. Sherry or whisky? The sherry's indifferent, the whisky's superb.'

'Then I'll have it with water, thanks, like you,' said Jones coolly.

'And don't let's play the silent staring game,' said Sir Michael, when they had settled down with their drinks. 'It wastes too much time. Let's talk like men and brothers.'

'It's after hours, as you say. We can try.' He tasted his drink carefully. 'You were quite right. It *is* a superb whisky. Can you afford it?'

'Just. Chiefly by doing without things like motorcars.' Jones took another sip. 'This is outside my terms of reference, but I think I told you I'm interested in the Theatre. I've been talking to your Drama man, Byrd. He's distressed because he thinks COMSA has missed a great opportunity in not sponsoring this American play *The Dummies*. Isn't this the kind of thing COMSA is supposed to be doing?'

'Yes, within limits.'

'Why miss this opportunity then, when you ought to be busy justifying your existence?'

'Because I refuse to play that game, my dear Jones. I saw the thing and thought it pretentious tedious bosh.'

'Byrd doesn't.'

'As far as the Theatre is concerned, Byrd doesn't think at all. He's entirely without judgment. He just enjoys sitting in theatres and watching the lights go on and off.'

'Not a good choice then as Drama man.'

'He works hard, and we have to take what we can get. Any man with really good dramatic taste and judgment can make far more than we could afford to pay. If I thought COMSA had a future, I'd try to find somebody to take his place—a woman probably. Women are the playgoers in this country. Yet how many women are there telling other women what to see?'

'It's a point, Stratherrick. But why do you think COMSA hasn't a future?'

'Come off it. Why are you here, Jones? You're the writing on the wall.'

Jones produced his short sea-lion's bark. 'You don't seem much impressed. Unlike poor George Drake, who dithers and blathers, much to my embarrassment.'

'Nonsense! You love it. I ought to be more worried than Drake, who after all is an established civil servant. I'm not, and if COMSA goes, I'm out. True, half our finance comes from private foundations, but if the Treasury grant goes, COMSA isn't viable. And somehow—I can't explain why—I don't seem to care a damn. I ought to, for various good reasons, but somehow I don't. And now, my dear Jones, you might as well tell me what's going to happen. I promise not to faint or scream.'

'You may not believe me,' said Jones, 'but that's what I like about you—that you don't care a damn. It's refreshing.' He tried the whisky again, nodded and smiled. 'In confidence, COMSA and DISCUS are both going,' he said softly. 'That was decided some months ago. I was told to examine the organisational methods, staff and so forth. There'll be a big new department of the arts in the Ministry of Higher Education. The head of it will rank as an under-secretary. Salary about £4500, I imagine. Naturally I haven't the job in my pocket. But I've been told to make a recommendation. What about you?'

Sir Michael finished his whisky, then slowly blew out some breath, with a sighing effect. 'Nice of you, Jones. I ought to jump at it. I've nothing else in view. I shall probably end up lecturing on art history in the new University of Mumbo-Jumbo, 125 miles by jeep from the nearest railhead. Even so, even though there's a lot to be done with the arts I haven't found it possible to begin trying, I just don't want the job. I don't want to rank as an under-secretary. I don't want to be all cosy in the Ministry of Higher Education. I don't want to be where people are wetting their pants because there's going to be a Question in the House. I'm not the man you want, Jones. But as some small return for saving your neck, do me one favour. Try to make sure most of these people here—and at DISCUS too, for that matter—are not just chucked out, along with a wife, three kids and a mortgage. They've done their best in what is bound to be, for most of the time, an idiotic job.'

'Could you put some of this down on paper for me? It'll help me and could help them. Drake can't do it, because he'd never really understand what he was doing. It'll have to be you, Stratherrick.'

'All right—something on paper.' Sir Michael glanced at his watch. 'I've an appointment at half-past six—in a pub. It's theatre business, you'll be interested to know. With a man called Kemp—you may not have met him; he's probably the only troll in the civil service—and some scoundrel of a fly-by-night theatre manager; and, of all things, a family of six called O'More, touring players from the West of Ireland. It's a question of letting these mad Irish loose in the Coronet Theatre. After we've a drop taken.'

At which L.B.C.T.N. Jones contrived something most of his acquaintance would have thought impossible: he suddenly looked wistful. 'No chance of my coming along, is there?'

'I don't see why not so long as you keep a civil tongue in your head, me boy.'

In the taxi, which was waiting more often than it was moving, Jones said: 'Tell me this. Would you take on a private foundation for the arts if it was the right size and offered you a reasonably free hand?'

'Of course I would. It's the only full-sized job I'm fit for—by training, experience, temperament. But if you're thinking about one of the American foundations, it's no go. I don't get along with American tycoons or academics. They think, quite wrongly, I'm too frivolous, and I can't bear their solemn emptiness.'

'No, this would come out of the Middle East, not the Middle West.' Jones hesitated a moment or two. 'This really is in the strictest confidence, Stratherrick. It's one of these oil potentates, fantastically rich. He was educated here—Harrow and King's, I believe—and he wants to do something for Britain. And he's keen on a bloody great foundation for the arts. His lawyers have already seen us, because of the finance involved. I've met him twice myself, and I believe he'd take any recommendation of mine quite seriously. You may have heard of him—Prince Aghamazar—'

'My God—the Arabian Nights again. What's he like?'

'Oh—a nice fellow. Young, about thirty; charming manners; very good-looking in a dark flashing style; most generous, unlike so many very rich men; the women rave over him, of course—'

'Of course, of course, of course! A seventy-inch diamond of a man—my God! *All* the women rave, do they?'

'All those I know do. My wife—'

'I don't count your wife. No, no, I didn't mean it rudely. He probably gave you fellows and your wives dinner—Beluga caviare by the tablespoonful—Bollinger poured out as if it were lemon squash—wonderful manners, mysterious background, millions to spend—' Sir Michael relapsed into a brooding silence. The taxi was waiting to enter Piccadilly Circus. They were out of it before anything more was said.

'Prince Aghamazar isn't in London,' said Jones, 'but he'll be back any day, I'm told. Suppose I rang him or asked my chief to send him a note—both, perhaps—would you pop across to Claridge's and talk to him about his foundation?'

'I would indeed.' Sir Michael paused. 'Though we mightn't get on, you know, Jones.'

'I think you would.'

'It all depends. No, never mind on what. Let's consider the new primitive movement in the Theatre, which we're about to baptise with Guinness and Jameson.'

As soon as they had entered the big bar and Sir Michael had spotted Tim Kemp, he took him away from the others. 'This will only take two minutes, Kemp. Shirley's mother came to see me this afternoon, but we've no time for that. Now you've been in touch with Shirley since she started working for this Prince Aghamazar, who seems to be somebody any nice English girl, especially if she had a slight temperature, would dream about. But Mrs Essex is ready to swear that Shirley's feelings are just as they were—that she's in love with me. What do you say, Kemp?'

'I say so too.'

Sir Michael smiled at him. 'You administrative-grade troll, you malicious brownie, you cut-down, gin-soaked sorcerer, you wicked little sod, you deliberately sent that innocent girl, after telling her God knows what, to COMSA to plague me, to torment me, to madden me, didn't you? Of course you did. Sheer mischief. But now, my friend,

154

it's beginning to look as if you could have done me a shatteringly good turn, as if I may win and you lose.'

'I don't mind losing,' said Kemp. He gave Sir Michael a long look. 'There's something you're forgetting. Now you may not be quite the same man as the one I was plotting against. In fact, you aren't. Look at the O'Mores, having a hell of a time. Come and talk to them.'

19

ON MANY EVENINGS lately, Sir George, to cheer himself up, had turned his face away from Hampstead, on leaving DISCUS, and had looked in at the club, sometimes still looking in there after several hours. But on this evening, as luck would have it, he had gone straight home, after stopping work unusually early, and had arrived there just before six, wondering what to do with himself. With some vague notion of having a bath almost at once—it was warmish and he had walked quickly from the Underground—he had climbed the curiously melancholy stairs, without looking about him below, and entered the bedroom. And there was Alison, sitting on her bed beside a half-unpacked case, looking weary, drawn, sad.

'Why, this is a nice surprise, my dear. Didn't expect to see you here.'

She said nothing, only shook her head in a meaningless fashion.

'Tiring journey?'

She nodded.

He went closer. 'I take it, things didn't turn out so well over there. Never mind, Alison.' He put a hand on her shoulder and instead of shaking it off as she often did, to his surprise she seized it fiercely, pressed it against her cheek, and then burst into tears.

After he had held her for a minute or two and kissed her gently several times, all affection and comfort, not sex, she pulled herself away, shook her head violently as if angry with herself not with him, and stared rather wildly at him. He knew then she was about to start talking, and he stopped her.

'No, don't, Alison, please. You'll only wish you hadn't afterwards. We'll begin saying things we don't mean. I don't expect you to say anything. I don't want you to say anything. No point in it. Probably far too complicated. You went away. You've come back. Let's leave it at that. Why don't we both tidy up and then have a drink? After that, we'll eat out—somewhere good. We can't afford it, but we deserve it.'

He did not wait for any reply but went straight to the bathroom.

He thought he heard her crying again, but it did not sound the same sort of crying. He went downstairs from the bathroom and mixed the proportions of gin and vermouth that he knew she liked. In about ten minutes she came down in a dressing gown, with her face freshly powdered, and seemed her usual self.

'Thank you, darling,' she said as he handed over the drink. Then, after a sip, she glanced round the room in disgust. 'Really, that woman is a wretch. Look at it.'

'Sorry, my dear, but of course I haven't seen much of her, don't really know whether she's doing her job or not.'

'Well, she isn't. I'll get after her in the morning. I think I'd like a little more booze please, George. And thank God we're going out to dinner! That was a sweet thought. Where shall we go? Oh—yes—and before I forget—what did you mean when you said we couldn't afford it? Nothing terrible has happened, has it?'

Sir George had now re-filled her glass. He took his own and sat down rather heavily.

'And don't for heaven's sake look at me like that, George. It can't be so bad, whatever it is. Your face is a mile long.'

This was pretty cool, coming from a woman who had been weeping wildly not quarter of an hour ago. But he let it pass. 'You may have other views, my dear, but I think it's damned bad. We're not quite out in the street, but we're halfway.'

'What do you mean?'

'We've had a fellow from the Treasury nosing around for the past week or so. I don't like him. And he doesn't like me. We just don't get on. And there's a strong rumour going around that both DISCUS and COMSA are finished, and that the Ministry of Higher Education will set up its own department of arts.'

'Well, they could give it to you.'

'That's out. Not a hope.'

'How can you say that, George?'

'Because I've had to deal with I.B.C.T.N. Jones—all those confounded initials annoy me—and you haven't. You haven't had to look at that smile of his—very faint, very superior, and a death warrant.'

'You're surely not going to let Michael Stratherrick stroll into the Ministry and take over their new department? My God—I'd be furious.'

'Don't worry about that.' Sir George's chuckle was not without malice. 'The one bit of comfort I've had lately is the thought of the report that Jones must be making on that COMSA shambles. I'll bet that by this time he and Stratherrick, who's always as arrogant as the devil, aren't on speaking terms. But you can start worrying about the Drakes, Alison. We could be in for a dreary time.'

'We're not going to be.' She jumped up, all fiery purpose now, hardly to be recognised as the same woman he had found sitting on her bed. 'The Ministry must be expanding like mad. And that's where you belong, and that's where you're going.'

'They wouldn't look at me for their arts department—'

'Oh—damn the arts department! Something quite different—sensible. You can't be sicker of the arts and the artists than I am.' She thought for a moment. 'I know what I'm going to do. I'm going to ring up Molly Avon. He's still an under-secretary there, isn't he?'

'Yes, but I hardly know him—'

'Molly and I used to be great friends. It's terribly short notice—and of course they may not be free—but I'm going to ask if they'll dine with us. I don't know about him, but Molly's fearfully mean, always was, and a free dinner at a good restaurant will bring her out even if she's just put something for tonight in the oven.' She hurried away to telephone, the door banging to behind her.

Now that his wife was all energy, fire and purpose, Sir George felt his end of the conjugal seesaw go down and down. Trying to keep DISCUS going now was like sitting in a chair that was falling apart. Not long ago he had prided himself upon the loyalty of his staff, but now he felt they might be saying anything to Jones, just pumping poison into the Treasury report. It was after the return of that little monster, Kemp, that the rot had set in. Moreover, just as he had come to know and to value June Walsingham, she was leaving to do publicity for one of those fashion magazines that Alison sometimes bought, full of thin girls staring insanely at nothing and of travel advertisements. What was wrong with the English now was that they were suffering from being told all the time that they ought to be lying on a beach in the Caribbean. And if you saved up and went there, Sir George reflected mournfully, you would probably be surrounded by posters telling you to see Windsor Castle and the Yeomen of the Guard and Anne Hathaway's Cottage.

'They're coming,' Alison cried as she returned. 'And I've told them

The Musketeer — '

'Fiendishly expensive and we may not get a table.'

'We'll have to book one of course. Eight o'clock. You do it while I'm running a bath. No, I'll do it — I'll sound like a secretary — and you run my bath, darling. And we'll just not have to *think* about the expense.' And off she went again, obviously in high spirits.

Sir George added a little more gin to his drink, took a sip of it, went rather heavily upstairs to start Alison's bath, then came back to look through the evening paper. And as usual it annoyed him. While he agreed with it in holding that bricklayers ought to be able to rub along for at least another six months on £36 a week, he could not share its pleasure, its delight, at the way in which various bright chaps had made another million or two, all off tax. Then a name in an item of theatre news caught his eye — O'More. No, it couldn't be. But it was, for the news was that the O'More Touring Company, from the West of Ireland, was about to begin a season at the Coronet Theatre, London. Good God! With bewilderment added to his basic feeling of depression, he climbed upstairs again, this time to change his clothes.

There were occasions, when they were about to entertain or be entertained, when Alison insisted upon turning into her company self before there was any company, while she had only him to entertain. It was as if she was holding a dress rehearsal of herself as hostess or guest. And this was one of those occasions. From the moment she left the bathroom, she kept up a bright, brittle chatter, not expecting any support from him; indeed, he always felt she was talking to somebody else, not the man she had been married to for so many years, not the man whose hand she had clutched before she had burst into tears. Moreover, he did not care much for this woman she impersonated, who was much better off than the real Alison Drake, far more sophisticated, cynically in the know about everything, as if she had come out of the gossip columns of the paper or one of those fashion magazines. And tonight this dubious character powdered and painted and dressed herself in the modest Drake bedroom, and then sat by his side in the taxi, chattering all the way, until they had nearly reached *The Musketeer,* which was just off Berkeley Square.

Then his Alison took over for a few dramatic moments. She squeezed his hand hard, and whispered fiercely: 'George, do back me up. I'm sure a lot depends on this. You be nice to Molly while I attend to him. But if I appeal to you, whatever I say, back me up. Promise, darling—*please!*' But it was the other woman, armoured for company, who alighted with him at the door of the restaurant, guarded rather sheepishly by a man who had some of the costume but little of the bearing of a Dumas character.

They were ahead of the Avons, and Sir George was able to make sure that a table was waiting for them. Alison must have been impressive on the telephone, because it was a good table too, in a corner overhung, in a romantic 17th Century French manner, with plaster beams and plastic foliage. *The Musketeer,* the joint creation of a Greek ex-head-waiter, a wholesale butcher from Huddersfield, and two winsomely boyish interior decorators almost out of their tiny minds with excitement, had brought to Mayfair what was undoubtedly a Dumas *père* ambience. And, perhaps to suggest the musketeers in action as well as to add to gracious living, almost everything there except soup and ice cream was brought to the tables in sheets of flame. Dishes that had never been set alight before were *flambé* at *The Musketeer.* The waiters, both the young Cypriots and the ancient, padding Alsatians, had a wonderful time, constantly arriving with flaming swords or sloshing bad brandy about and putting a match to it. And guests who were not too nervous and were determined food-and-wine types enjoyed themselves too, especially if they were not wondering how much this fire service would cost. And the Avons were in this happy position.

Sir Finlay Avon, whom Sir George hardly knew, was an extremely thin fellow, who looked down his nose as if he felt that at any moment the bone there would break through the tightly-stretched skin. His wife, Alison's friend Molly, was really thin and anxious too but was somehow able to pretend, in a dashing illusionist's way, that she was a plump, jolly, Molly-kind of woman. They had heard about *The Musketeer* but had never been there before—indeed, Sir George felt almost at once that Alison had been right and that they were a scraping, saving pair—and now were determined to make the most of this first visit and the Drake's rash invitation. Avon himself, who probably hardly ate at all as a rule, was fairly moderate, but his wife, to Sir George's horror, promptly ordered several of the most expensive items on the menu. If she had been offered two pins, he felt, she would not have stopped short at fresh Beluga caviare—32/6 per portion.

They were well-seated for Alison's tactics. The table was

rectangular, its longer side running across the corner. The Avons, with some space between them, faced the other diners and the vista of flames, and Sir George shared one end of the table with Molly, while Alison more or less monopolised Sir Finlay at the other end. The space between each married pair was not such as to make general talk impossible, but it did encourage Sir Finlay to listen to Alison, who set to work on him from the moment they sat down, while Sir George kept Molly entertained by listening to her. This was easy but dullish duty. He soon understood why the Avons were ready to scrape and save, for they had two sons and a daughter who were still being expensively educated. And very soon he learnt a great deal, more than enough to know they all needed a hell of a rocket, about this intolerable trio.

When the waiter was not fussing between them, probably wanting to set fire to everything, Sir George could overhear enough of Alison's talk to understand the line she was taking with Avon. Her husband, she was maintaining, had never wanted DISCUS, had always considered it unsound, had been compelled to accept some extraordinary types on his staff, and in view of the appalling difficulties he had to contend with, he had really worked wonders. That was the line, and a very good line too, so long as Alison, who didn't always know when to stop, took care not to overdo it.

The most expensive *entremet* on the menu was *Crêpes Mousquetaires* and that of course was what Molly had ordered. The waiter seemed to imagine she ought to have them concocted almost under her nose, so Sir George moved away to his left. He was not having anything himself; there was a limit to what he could afford; and Alison, in her grand company mood, had ordered recklessly herself. This move brought Sir George to the edge of the Sir Finlay-Alison duologue, and he was in time to hear Alison's account of himself.

'The point is,' she was saying, 'George is dying to take charge of something solid and worthwhile. He doesn't like the contemporary arts—or most of the artists.'

'Don't blame him,' Sir Finlay said. 'Don't like 'em myself.'

'George wouldn't admit this—he's fantastically loyal to whatever department he's in—but I know he believes, just as I do, that what the country needs now is more scientific and technological education.'

'He's quite right. What we all feel.'

'When we've achieved that—and not before—we can begin leading people to the arts, really doing what DISCUS—and I suppose COMSA, in its own rather silly way—has tried to do. But the other should come *first*. Don't you agree?'

'Between ourselves, I do,' Sir Finlay told her. His manner of speech was just as thin and jerky as he was. 'Don't admit it in public, of course. Arts people come down like ton of bricks. Fire off letters to *Times* and *Guardian*.'

'Oh—of course they love writing those letters. Long-winded idiots, most of them. You can imagine what George has had to cope with. And he's always so madly conscientious.'

'Who's this? Me?' Sir George felt it was time he joined in. 'Well, any administrator who knows his job can't ignore correspondence, public or private. Can he, Avon?'

'No, he can't, Drake. Must have had an amazing load of rubbish to sort out, past two years. Haven't envied you, must say.'

'Though I know I shouldn't say it,' Alison said, 'George has been heroic—simply heroic. Never even giving a hint that he was dying to do something more solid and worthwhile, the kind of thing most of you must be doing now at the Ministry.'

'Got tremendous job on hand. Higher education. Further education. Science. Technology.' Sir Finlay drank some wine, allowed his nose to quiver a little, dabbed at his mouth with his napkin. 'Really tremendous.'

'Of course, it must be.' Alison smiled quickly at him and then put on her most serious expression, pushing her face forward and narrowing her eyes. 'But George and I feel you're doing the thing really worth doing, whereas with DISCUS—well, you can imagine!'

'Glad to be done with that kind of thing, Drake, eh?'

'Avon, as you must know, I never wanted it, never asked for it, and now I'll be glad to see the last of it.'

'Point taken, old man.' Sir Finlay did his wine act again, while Alison glanced swiftly, brilliantly, triumphantly, at her husband. He in his turn glanced at Molly, who was now greedily gobbling her *crêpes* and preferred not to talk. And then he had just time, before Avon spoke again, to give Alison a grateful look. Certainly she had made her point.

Sir Finlay now lowered his head, looked solemnly at Sir George and then at Alison, and said: 'Sorry in a way. Quite understand of course. Agree with everything you say. But—very much between ourselves—we're having to organise big new cultural department in the Ministry. Take the place of both DISCUS and COMSA of course. Had an idea you might be the man for it, Drake. Sound administrator, I know. So sorry in a way, this is how you feel. Quite understand, though, quite understand. Sensible view. Have to have this culture thing, though. Big department actually. Much more money allotted than you ever saw, Drake. However, there it is. Find a good man somehow.'

Both Drakes stared at him out of the ruins in which they now found themselves. Alison had done her work only too well. Whoever took over that big new cultural department, bursting with finance, possibly glittering with prestige, it would not be Sir George Drake.

'Damned hot in here, don't you think?' said Sir George, running a finger under his collar. And already those kidneys, with their wine-and-brandy sauce, were making him feel uncomfortable. 18/6 too, without vegetables.

But Sir Finlay and the fates had not done with them. He stared down the room, then smiled and lifted a hand. 'Thought I knew that face. Treasury chap with all the initials.'

'Not I.B.C.T.N. Jones?' Sir George turned round at once, in time to see Jones about to claim a table. With him were a dark smart woman and another man. It was Michael Stratherrick.

'Well, you know who *that* is, don't you?' Alison demanded, rather indignantly, as if Sir Finlay might somehow have worked it. 'And if you don't I'll tell you.'

'I wish you would,' said Molly, who had emerged from her *crêpes*. 'He looks terribly attractive.'

'My dear, too many women have thought that, and then wished they hadn't. *That,* Molly darling, is Sir Michael Stratherrick—'

'Oh—of course it is—'

'Who's made such a howling mess of COMSA. And of course it's quite obvious what's going on there,' she continued with mounting indignation. 'He's about to fill the Joneses—because that woman *must* be Mrs Jones—with expensive food and drink, probably paid for by COMSA, so that the Treasury will tell you to put him at the head of your precious big new department.' She almost glared at Sir Finlay. 'And—my God—I must say it's all a bit much.'

'Now, Alison,' Sir George began, for he could see that Avon was rather resenting her tone and manner, 'you don't know—'

'Of course I know,' she snapped. 'And so do you. So don't pretend.' She looked at Sir Finlay Avon again. 'I call it absolutely sickening and disgusting. Don't you?'

'Can't say I do,' Sir Finlay told her. 'Must correct you on one or two points. I can see these chaps, you can't. Jones is dealing with the waiter. Means it's his dinner.'

'Oh—that's nothing, I can assure you. Michael Stratherrick's clever and caddish enough to ask people to dine, and then let the other man order and pay. I know him,' she added, and then immediately wished she hadn't.

'Do you, darling?' Molly was all eyes and ears. 'Tell me.'

'No, no,' Sir George said hastily. 'Alison's only met him on a few semi-official occasions.'

'Next point.' Obviously bent on correcting Alison, Sir Finlay ignored what had been said since he last spoke. 'Know very well Stratherrick isn't trying to wine-and-dine into our new department. Doesn't want the job.'

'You mean he's actually been *offered* it?' cried Alison, almost a *femme flambée* now.

'Naturally not. Province of Minister. Talked to a Treasury man, though, lunch time at the club. Understood that Stratherrick told Jones not interested in the job.'

'Yet it's never even been *mentioned* to George,' Alison said accusingly.

'These men and their club!' But this cry of Molly's settled nothing.

'Gossip of course,' Sir Finlay announced. 'Nothing to do with Ministry. Disproves your second point, though.'

The *sommelier*, who wore a dark blouse and a chain that might have come from the Bastille, was now at Sir George's elbow. A few moments later, after a question to the ladies, Sir George rose nobly above the ruin of his hopes, above all threats of penury, above bewilderment, disappointment, disillusion, and showed the sterling stuff of which he was made: 'Avon, what about a cigar and some brandy?' In other words, what about another 30/– on the bill?

'No thanks, Drake. Don't smoke. Rather finish this wine.'

As it was, the bill came to £16.12.0, and after Sir George had written a cheque and had added two pound notes to it as a tip, indignant queries assaulted his inward ear. How could Jones afford to do his entertaining here? (Unless of course those five initials meant private means.) How could the Avons take this lavish hospitality so coolly? And who could afford to eat here all the time except chaps in industry, the property racket, and advertising? And why in the name of thunder did Alison insist upon coming here, when a fifteen-bob *table d'hôte* would have been a treat to the scraping and saving Avons?

On their way out, Sir Finlay stopped at the Jones-Stratherrick table and Molly was introduced and Sir George met Mrs Jones, but Alison had refused to stop and went off to the women's cloakroom as erect and stiff-backed as her husband ever remembered seeing her. She would be difficult, he felt, after they had dropped the Avons at St. John's Wood and were alone in what would prove to be a pretty damned expensive taxi.

Yet again, however, she surprised him by her mysteriously feminine change of mood. 'No, George darling, don't say it. I will. It was all a horrible flop and a hell of a waste of money—and I'm sorry. But what I'm wondering is why we go on and on, planning and contriving and intriguing, worrying our lives away, when it's all so meaningless. We think we're so grand when all the time we're just like little animals scratching and biting and running round a cake. Why? What's it all for? What's the *point* of it? I can't see any. But I don't suppose you ever feel like this, do you, George?'

'Of course I do, my dear. Most of the time indeed. And that means at least that there are two of us, out in the same boat. You're not alone, Alison. I'm with you. Not very exciting perhaps—'

'I don't want anybody exciting. Besides, you've been very sweet—'

'No, not that, if you don't mind, old girl. Remember, I'm sure I told you, that's what they all say about that mischievous little devil—Kemp. Call me reliable.'

'And so you are, darling. But—and it's all my fault,' she added unhappily, 'I'll bet at this very moment Molly Avon and her grim Finlay are telling each other you're probably not very reliable. Chucking money away like that in a horribly expensive restaurant! God—I'm so tired. Had to be up at the crack of dawn. You see, Marjorie Sidney's mother—'

But he cut her short. 'You don't have to tell me about Marjorie Sidney's mother. Let's forget the whole thing.'

20

BROOK STREET, Mayfair, on a fine morning in late May, and Claridge's Hotel do not immediately suggest a belated back entrance into the world of the Thousand and One Nights, and a London transformed into the magical Baghdad of Caliph Haroun-al-Raschid. But on that morning—and indeed for ever afterwards—Sir Michael tasted in the street and the hotel a flavour of the Arabian Nights. And it was not simply because he had an appointment with the fabulously wealthy Prince Aghamazar. That played its part of course, but there was also the feeling, of which Sir Michael could not rid himself, that now the brutal laws we know only too well, the dreary sequences of cause and effect, could be suspended at any moment, as they are in the immortal Eastern tales.

In the entrance to the Prince's suite, he was received by a kind of Savile-Row Grand Vizier, who had a square-cut beard and a face the colour of a well-cherished brown shoe. From behind a closed door along the corridor came the sound of typewriters. Was Shirley there or, in spite of what he had been told, was she now lolling in satin pyjamas and drinking champagne elevenses on that yacht in the Mediterranean, thoroughly enjoying the aftermath of a fate worse than death? He felt tempted to stop the Grand Vizier and put that question to him, but kept going to the end of the corridor.

What was certain, as he saw at once, was that Prince Aghamazar, who was dressed in a Cambridge blue linen jacket and charcoal grey trousers, was an unusually handsome and attractive young man. His face was lighter in tone than the Grand Vizier's and clean-shaven; but his hair, brows, eyes, seemed almost blue-black. He was drinking coffee and insisted upon Sir Michael having some. It might have been his superbly good manners, but he gave his visitor the impression that he was genuinely glad to see him; almost as if—though this seemed absurd—he was feeling rather lonely or had something weighing on his mind that he was anxious to describe and discuss.

'I've brought a rough scheme for your foundation,' Sir Michael told him when they had settled down with their coffee. 'Shall I run through it quickly for you or shall I leave it for you to read after I've gone?'

'Run through it quickly, please, Sir Michael. And may I say I like that *quickly* very much? Tell me, are you easily bored?'

'Yes, I am. It's been one of my troubles, dealing with officials.'

'One of mine too. I have died of boredom ten thousand times. Now please, Sir Michael, your idea of what my cultural foundation would be and what it could do.' And Prince Aghamazar put his slippered feet on another chair, lit some kind of cheroot, sprawled and slipped down so that he was resting on his shoulders, and closed his eyes. He seemed an odd mixture of a Middle Eastern potentate and a permanent Cambridge undergraduate.

Sir Michael went through his notes at a brisk pace, occasionally looking up either to add a few explanatory remarks or to make sure Prince Aghamazar was not asleep. But the cheroot was still burning, and in fact the young man's eyes were only half-closed.

'I'll make a final point,' he said when he came to the end of his notes. 'It's this, Prince Aghamazar—'

'No, please. I call you Michael. You call me Bojo.'

'Bojo?'

'It's not my real name of course, Michael. But that is what I was called at school—Bojo. And among Western friends, it is what I prefer. Now please make your final point.'

'Here it is, Bojo. If you're looking for an administrator, I'm not your man. And in my opinion, no enterprises, cultural or otherwise, should have administrators at the top, that is, right at the top. This explains why so many things here bog down, arrive at stalemates. The administrators trying to run them slow them up. They can't energise them. They aren't creative. They kill not create enthusiasm. You have to have administration, naturally, but not right at the top. That's my belief, Bojo. So if it's a solid British administrator you want, we're both wasting our time.'

'It's a good point. I appreciate it, Michael old chap. We aren't wasting time at all.' And now he stopped sprawling, sat up, and stared hard at Sir Michael. 'I think all you have told me is very good. I am very keen on all that. But tell me this—are you honest?'

'I don't steal money, if that's what you mean,' Sir Michael replied, rather sharply. 'And I think I'm reasonably honest—perhaps unusually honest, for a culture-vulture—in my tastes, judgments, opinions. I don't climb on any fashionable waggons. I admire talent, any kind, not smart impudence—'

'Yes, yes, the man at the Treasury told me this, and I can see that it is true. But I'm not thinking about my foundation now, Michael old chap. I'm sure we'll agree about that. If you want to take charge of it, then it is yours. But I'm thinking now about something else. It weighs terribly on my mind. I need advice badly and I can't get what I need from any of my own people. I need it from one of you, Michael, one of you English.'

'I'm not English, Bojo. I'm a Highland Scot. Come—you're forgetting our local differences. They're still important.'

'You would not object to a talk about sex?'

'Certainly not. I'm ready to talk about anything except the economics of the European Common Market and Oxford linguistic philosophy. But try me on sex, Bojo, if you want to.'

'You've had plenty of experience with women—Scots and English women?'

'Any amount. Too much, in fact. Perhaps at the moment I don't think I know as much about them as I thought I did. But try me.'

Prince Aghamazar was apparently now feeling so much disturbed that he jumped out of his chair, jabbed the remains of his cheroot into an ashtray, and then paced the length of the sitting room. Finally, he turned to face Sir Michael. 'I have a difficult personal problem. I think it is destroying me, Michael. You see me. I am fairly strong, healthy, virile—a real man. Not, would you say, an altogether unattractive chap?'

'On the contrary, I'd say, Bojo. Most Englishwomen I know would find you very attractive. Quite apart, I mean, from all the money and power you might have—just as a chap.'

'How very kind of you, Michael. I appreciate it very much.' But now the agitated Prince Aghamazar forgot his training as a decent sound chap. His eyes seemed to glitter with tears. He drummed on his chest with both fists. 'I ask you then—what is wrong? I offer everything—yes, everything—even Western marriage—toppers, morning coats, veils, orange blossom—whatever they must have. But it is no use. Is there something wrong with me that nobody will tell me? Let me have the truth, Michael old chap. If it is terrible, then it is terrible. But now I do not know myself,' he shouted. 'Am I a tragic figure for poets or a bloody damned ass?'

'That's what many of us wonder, Bojo. You're not alone. But if I can help you, I will. So now—what happens?'

'You will see.' Still agitated, Prince Aghamazar struck a large loud bell, probably supplied by Claridge's only to potentates from East of Suez. The Grand Vizier appeared, listened to a command in his native language, then disappeared. Sir Michael got up, feeling short of breath, and stared at the door. And then of course Shirley walked in. She was wearing a pale-green linen dress, had an unfamiliar hair-do, was brown and perhaps a shade thinner; but was also herself and—by Heaven—the wonder of the world.

She tried to keep on with the job and look enquiringly at her employer, but it was no use. She stared at Sir Michael, her eyes large and brilliant above a rising crimson tide. He stared at her, muttering something but he never knew what, and moved towards her. She made a funny little helpless gesture. At the sight of it, a long line of Stratherricks, the dark and passionate men who still lived in his face, swept aside the Director of the National Commission for Scholarship and the Arts, and took charge, opening his arms. She flew into them like a great golden bird.

'No, no, no! What *is* this?' Prince Aghamazar was dancing round them in a rage. 'My God—it's too much. You take her at once. You insult me.'

'No, please!' Shirley had now disengaged herself. 'Don't you see? I love him.'

'She's mine, Bojo. We're to be married soon.'

'Oh—Michael! Are we? When?'

Prince Aghamazar, in a most unprincely fashion, looked from one to the other of them, his mouth still wide-open. 'You know each other—?'

'We've been in love for weeks and weeks,' Shirley declared proudly.

'I'm sorry, Bojo, but if *she* was the problem,' Sir Michael told him, 'there's nothing I can do about it—except take her away.'

'This is the girl of course. I began with small things—clothes, jewels, the usual things. No, no, no. Then in the end I offered her everything, as I told you—*everything*. No, no, no, no, no. So I am going barmy. What is the matter with me? Why has nobody told me? Why am I so unattractive?'

'I thought you were terribly attractive, Prince Aghamazar. But you weren't Michael, that's all.' Shirley regarded him earnestly. 'Don't you understand?'

'*Now* I understand.' Delighted, he began shaking hands with both of them. 'Now there is no problem—except of course I am not the lucky chap. You were in love with him, so how could you listen to me? And it might have been a frightful chap—an absolute rotter. But no, it is Sir Michael Stratherrick—a fine chap—who has such clever ideas for my foundation—'

'Oh—Michael, have you? I hoped you might.'

'This is wonderful. You two are happy because you are reunited lovers and are going to marry. And I am happy because you are happy and now I see I have no problem. There is nothing the matter with me. You said *No* to me because you already wanted him. A weight has gone. I feel light and expanding again. It is wonderful. Michael, you must stay to lunch, and before that we will all drink champagne and talk about the Aghamazar Foundation. Miss Essex—as secretary you are now fired—please tell the agency to send another girl to help Miss Farrer—there will be a lot of work to do now that Michael is almost on the job—and now you are no longer secretary but my guest, my friend, and my director's fiancée. I give you my last order—ask for champagne. Oh—and later—a whacking great lunch.' Out of breath, he collapsed and sprawled across the two chairs again.

If Sindbad the Sailor or the Barber's Fifth Brother had walked into the room, Sir Michael would hardly have been surprised.

21

IT WAS ALISON who said there ought to be A DISCUS Farewell Party. This was just after Sir George had been told he was to be given a small new department on the scientific side, which of course the Ministry of Higher Education was expanding at a furious rate. This new department would be concerned with Organic Molecular Chemistry, whatever that might be. What the Drakes could not decide was whether he landed the job because (George's opinion) of Sir Finlay Avon or (Alison's opinion) in spite of him. But there it was, starting almost immediately. And of course Alison felt immensely relieved, and that may have been why she suggested a DISCUS Farewell Party. Moreover, as Sir George knew, there were times when Alison liked to buy a rather large new hat and then play the smiling Gracious Lady.

The affair was soon laid on: 6-8 on Thursday, 30th May, in the Secretary-General's room. All the staff, plus husbands and wives, were invited, except T. Kemp, who had not been seen at DISCUS since the day he returned to lead away the O'Mores. Nearly all accepted — there were of course the usual disagreeable or unlucky types who would not or could not come to any party — and by 6.30 Sir George's room was comfortably full and some of the lowlier guests had overflowed into Joan Drayton's office. There, as so often happens, they appeared to be having a better time than the more important people in the main room.

Here, the party was not going as well as the Drakes had hoped it would. Alison had arrived in her Gracious Lady role, well prepared to enjoy playing it, but after half-an-hour of nodding and smiling and crying 'But you haven't got a drink' and asking people what they were going to do now there was no more DISCUS, she began to feel ill-at-ease. And Sir George, who had seen himself receiving some rather touching tributes from a loyal staff, was rather disappointed by the way the thing seemed to be going. Both of them felt that too many people there, especially the very people who ought to have known how to behave at a Farewell Party, did not seem to be entering into the spirit of the thing.

Nicola Pembroke, whose flashing gipsy good looks had never endeared her to Alison, had brought her husband, the frail musical scholar, a twisted and sardonic man, whose expression suggested that he had just tasted life and found it was simply one gigantic lemon. 'And now there's no more DISCUS, dear Mrs Pembroke,' Alison said to her, 'what are *you* going to do?'

Before his wife could reply, Dr Pembroke came in gratingly: 'She's been asked to look after the music for this new Aghamazar Foundation. It can't be more idiotic than what she's tried to do here, and it might be considerably better.'

'Really!' Alison surveyed them both from a height of Gracious Ladydom. 'That's Sir Michael Stratherrick, isn't it? I can't imagine he knows or cares much about music.'

'Of course not. Who does, anyhow? But at least he's promised Nicola a free hand.'

'And I must say,' Nicola said boldly, 'he's a terrific charmer, isn't he?'

'Nicola has a weakness for charmers.' Dr Pembroke achieved a lemon-tasting grin. 'And I don't blame her, after years of me.'

Alison didn't either, but all she said was, rather coldly: 'He's not my idea of a charmer. And I've always heard he's extremely difficult to work with. Look at COMSA.'

'We can't,' Dr Pembroke told her. 'It's gone. Like DISCUS. Like Tweedledum and Tweedledee.'

'I always understood,' said Alison, dropping the Gracious Lady with some spirit, 'that originally *they* were quarrelsome musicians.'

Meanwhile, Sir George had come face-to-face with June Walsingham, who had looked in from her smart fashion-magazine world and might have just stepped out of one of its glossier pages. 'My dear,' she began, 'you'll really have to do something about these waiters and their so-called martinis. Vermouth and ice-water. They're probably doing you out of a bottle of gin every ten minutes. Well, my dear, how are you?'

Afterwards, thinking it over, he decided he ought to have responded to her intimate approach, making it clear he was not pretending to have forgotten what had happened on that dreadful Green Gong night. As it was, however, rejecting this response, he went too far the other way, and replied rather stiffly that he was quite well and hoped that she was too.

'I feel ten years younger now that I'm out of this place, Sir George. By the way, I see that Lady Drake is with us. Got back from France all right, did she?' There was wicked secret knowledge in her tone, her eye. She probably knew all about Alison and Ned Greene.

'Yes, only a short visit. The mother of an old college friend was ill—something of a crisis—so Alison rushed off to Paris and coped. She's rather good at that sort of thing.'

'Is she? Well, I'm often surprised at the way some women— sometimes the last you'd expect—*can* cope. There are one or two good copers among my new workmates. And some of the hardest bitches I've ever met.'

'I hope that doesn't mean you're not enjoying your new job, Miss Walsingham.' And then he asked himself why he had to talk to her like that. What was the matter with him?

'It does not, Sir George, quite definitely not.' There was a touch of burlesque in her tone and manner. 'Indeed, to be quite frank with you, Sir George, though the going's harder over there, it's a welcome change after trying every day here to run a sack race over quarter-of-a-mile of marshmallows. And *do* tell them to stop watering the martinis. 'Bye now!'

And that might easily be the last of her he would ever see. Annoyed with himself as he watched her push her way towards the door, he felt no relief when a touch turned him round to face Hugo Heywood. He knew that Heywood had been back from leave for almost a week, but they had not met, having indeed been avoiding each other. And now, yellow and baggy-eyed, looking thoroughly dissipated, here Heywood was. He had brought with him—rather cheek, really—a haggard woman, probably an actress, who was wearing too much green eye-shadow and a dress like an oatmeal sack. Heywood's speech was not clear even as early as this, and he introduced the woman with a blur of syllables that sounded like Margo Fallaro. And party or no party, Sir George took a poor view of the pair of them.

'Darling, there must be a *real* drink somewhere.' This to Heywood, of course. Then she looked at Sir George: 'What do *you* say?'

He was rather stiff with her: 'I say there are any amount of real drinks everywhere. But then it happens to be my party.'

'Is that so?' said Margo Fallaro or whatever her name was. 'Well, well, well, well! Tell him what you told me, Hugo darling. Or even half of it. While I dance on that table, maddened by glass after glass of strong liquor.'

'Brilliant actress,' Heywood said as she left them, 'and now she'll only play Becket, Ionesco and Genet. Terrific integrity.'

'And what about those mad Irish—the O'Mores—you told to come and see me?' Sir George made no pretence of talking like a genial host; after all, Heywood had been a damned nuisance. 'I suppose they have terrific integrity too.'

'In their own way they have,' Heywood said aggressively. I'll admit I was plastered, if that makes you happy. But you may be interested to know that those mad Irish are now selling out the Coronet every night. And I heard today that two men you know and dislike are making a packet out of them—Tim Kemp and Sir Michael Stratherrick—'

'Nonsense!'

'No, it's not. They each put a few hundred in, with Totsy Blagg, and now they must be making about fifteen hundred a week between them. Talk about luck! And it was my idea originally. But then you went and bitched it up. I get nothing—the O'Mores won't even see me—DISCUS is down the drain—I can't get a look in at the Ministry, for their new cultural department—Stratherrick doesn't want me for his Who's-it Foundation—and I'm left writing for possible jobs to the better Reps—'

'If anybody cares to apply to me for a reference, I'll do what I can for you, Heywood—'

'Many, ever so many, thanks,' Heywood muttered sourly, and went in search of Margo Fallaro or whatever her name was.

Alison's Gracious Lady manner, now thin and wearing fast, was being tested by Gerald Spenser and Dorothea, the indignant Dutch doll wife. She had never cared for either of them, and had hoped to avoid them. The very sight of them, she knew, would remind her of that Ned Greene dinner party, which in turn would remind her of many other things she was anxious now to forget. But the wretched Spensers had found her, and were obviously not going to be dismissed with a few Gracious Lady platitudes and smiles.

'You must see that it's all frightfully unfair.' Spenser was hissing and writhing like an outraged serpent. 'Here am I, and all I can find at the moment is something rather shaky and quite shockingly underpaid at Baro's gallery. Nothing else, not a single thing!'

'I'm sorry,' said Alison, retreating as far as she could, about nine inches, because Spenser splashed so. 'What about a provincial art gallery or museum? I'm sure if there's anything George can do to help—'

'But there isn't, you see.' Spenser advanced about six inches, and splashed away. 'I don't happen to have any of the quite ridiculous qualifications they ask for. I was only the art critic of one of our best weeklies for years and years. And now the Ministry isn't interested, because I'm not the civil service type. And Michael Stratherrick isn't, because he's a visual arts man himself. So very soon I'll be selling half-crown catalogues at Baro's, when I'm not licking stamps or sweeping the floor. Simply splendid, isn't it?' he added bitterly, staring accusingly at Alison. 'A wonderful prospect.'

'I've said I'm sorry,' Alison told him. 'You don't have to look at me like that, Mr Spenser.'

Dorothea had always looked as if she were about to make an indignant protest, and now she actually did make one. Fixing a round Dutch doll eye on Alison, she began in a high trembling voice: 'Gerald believes—and so do I—that it might have made all the difference if he'd been able to go on with the Ned Greene exhibition. It would have attracted a lot of attention, as we all knew. And it wasn't Gerald's fault—he begged Sir George to settle it with Ned Greene after dinner at your house—'

'My husband did everything he could. But Greene was quite impossible, and insisted upon our going to that ridiculous night club. He's an impossible creature anyhow, as you must have seen—'

'I thought he was awful,' Dorothea declared, and with a firm voice now. 'Keeping us all waiting like that! And then arriving more than half-drunk and all scruffy!'

'I know, I know,' said Alison with some irritation. 'I ought to. It was *my* dinner party he ruined. Have you forgotten?'

'What I haven't forgotten, if you want to know,' cried Dorothea, who once she had found a voice for her indignation was clearly ready to make good use of it, 'is the fuss you made over him, not talking or listening to anybody else, almost sitting in his lap and holding hands.'

'Oh—don't be stupid, Mrs Spenser—'

'Come on, Dorothea, we ought to go.'

'All right, Gerald, I'm coming.' But she had a last shot to fire. 'I don't know what happened afterwards—though I might guess—but you didn't seem to be finding him so impossible while I was there,

Lady Drake.'

Alison turned away, only to discover that about half-a-dozen people, including two giggling typists, had stopped their own talk to listen to this fascinating exchange. She was furious, and turned round again to make her way towards Sir George, who was in a corner apparently arguing with a waiter. She took him away—the room was not so crowded now—and found a space where they could talk.

'I don't know about you, George, but I'm beginning to feel I've had about as much of this as I can take.'

'Why—what's wrong, my dear?'

'Oh—it was those ridiculous Spensers. Raging mad because he can't get a decent job. I told them how sorry I was—though really I can't bear them—and then the silly little woman flew at me—talking all kinds of rubbish. I'd like to go.'

'Can't say I'm enjoying it much myself. Thing's gone wrong somehow. People not in the right mood. And I'd prepared rather a good little speech—thanking them all for their loyalty—making a few little jokes about DISCUS—you know the kind of thing—always done—'

'If you try it here, George, I simply won't stay and listen. Nearly all the responsible people have left already. Just a lot of silly little girls—half-tight. Look at those two. And who's that dreadful man with Joan Drayton?'

'That's her Wally. They've just joined up again, I'm glad to say, though of course it's all very irregular and messy. But as I told you, I'm taking her with me to the Ministry—and she may have to work very hard the next week or two—and if Wally's back and acting somewhere, as I believe he is, she's much happier.'

'With that dreadful man?'

'My dear, when I complained once, you were quite hot in defence of this absurd Wally affair—'

'Oh—do be quiet. Look—Neil Jonson wants to talk to us.'

She summoned a smile for his approach. He had always been her favourite among George's staff, partly because he had always been attentive to her in a rather special way, vaguely romantic, but also because, when she was tired of George's schoolboy conformity, Neil Jonson's general air of rebelliousness and his anti-Establishment prejudices were a refreshing change. 'Well, Neil, are you having a good party?'

'Only just arrived. Sorry to have missed anything.' He raised his whisky-and-soda as if drinking a toast. 'Fact is, I've been seeing Michael Stratherrick.' He smiled at them both and apparently did not notice they had no smiles for him.

'Why on earth were you doing that, Neil?' Alison's tone had now lost most of its warmth.

Sir George had lifted his eyebrows and was keeping them up. 'Not the What's-it Foundation, surely?'

'That's it. The Aghamazar Foundation. Stratherrick didn't want Jim Marlowe to look after the finance. Too timid. And anyhow Marlowe had already decided to go into business—insurance. So he offered me the job and I've taken it. We really begin getting down to it in about a month. And he's really keen this time—not as he was with COMSA. Also, he's getting married.'

'Michael Stratherrick? I don't believe you,' Alison declared with some emphasis.

'Fact, though. The girl came in just before I left. And what's more,' Jonson continued, enjoying himself and not bothering about his audience, 'I know her.' He looked at Sir George. 'And so do you.'

'Why should I know her? Who is she?'

'God help her, whoever she is!' Alison exclaimed with some bitterness.

'Perhaps you never noticed her, though,' Jonson told Sir George. 'She was only one of the typists and wasn't with us long. When we had to let a typist go to COMSA, Tim Kemp fixed it so that she should go. I knew he was up to something though I never knew exactly what.'

'A typist—really!' Alison gave an imitation of a woman laughing in contemptuous disgust. 'And about half his age, I suppose?'

'Hardly that, I imagine. But—my God—what a smasher! I thought so when she was here, when she was just tiptoeing around, shy as a mouse, but now that she's blossomed out and is going to marry Stratherrick and they're both having champagne lunches every day at Claridge's with this Prince Aghamazar, she knocks your eye out. She's—'

But Alison had had enough. 'Neil, you're talking nonsense and you know it, and I've got a blinding headache, and you can stay and make a speech if you like, George, though I think you'll be very silly if you do, but *I must go.*'

So after some argument, from which Neil Jonson withdrew, Alison left for the women's room downstairs, and Sir George went round, shaking hands in a rather abstracted fashion, and then they met below and instead of gaily adjourning to a restaurant (not *The Musketeer*) to round off the evening, they went home, even though Alison declared—and it was about all she did say—there was nothing to eat there.

Waiting for the eggs and bacon Alison was cooking, Sir George remembered the rather good little speech he had prepared, plucked it out of his pocket and tore it up with unnecessary violence. 'Well, we've had our little jokes,' he could hear a ghostly Secretary-General of DISCUS saying to an audience that never came into existence, all looking at him with admiration and affection, 'and after all what would life be without a sense of humour—but now I want to be serious for a moment. I want to express my deep, my warm, my grateful appreciation of your loyalty—a loyalty both to DISCUS and to me personally—' And as they applauded, smiles came through their tears or tears through their smiles, whichever it ought to be—

'George, do come along. We're eating here.' Alison was calling from the kitchen, better than the dining room for this picnic sort of meal. He went along. She was wearing her old housecoat and looking hot and cross.

'Sorry the party didn't work out, my dear.'

'It was a bad idea, I suppose.' She said nothing else for several minutes, while they ate their eggs and bacon, and then she startled him by suddenly exclaiming: 'Michael Stratherrick—my God!'

'What about him?'

'Nothing—nothing—nothing! Do you want some cheese?'

'I don't think so, thanks. By the way, did you run into Hugo Heywood? No? Behaved rather badly, I thought. When I mentioned those O'Mores he'd let loose on me—you remember my telling you— he said they were now filling the Coronet Theatre—'

'I know they are. It's one of those silly crazes.'

'No doubt. But what you don't know, I imagine, is that Stratherrick and Kemp are part-owners of the production, and, Heywood says, between them are making about fifteen hundred pounds a week out of it.'

Keeping her eyes fixed on him, Alison put down her knife and fork and pushed back her chair. 'Oh—no. Not that on top of everything else. *Why*—just tell me why?'

'Why what, my dear?'

'Why *everything?*' she demanded quite unreasonably, and went on, rapidly and angrily, and glaring at him as if somehow it was all his fault: 'Why should it all be so damned unfair? Why does nothing like that happen to *us*? Why has everything to go wrong for *me*? Why Kemp and Michael Stratherrick when you've told me they dislike each other just as much as you and Kemp do? What happens that we don't understand? Why is there no sense or fairness in anything?'

'Well, of course it's hard to say.' Sir George spoke slowly to give his wife time to cool down. 'But there never is any sense in anything when that wretched little Kemp is mixed up in it. And that's one thing about my new job at the Ministry. I've seen the last of Kemp—thank God!'

22

SIR MICHAEL MOVED stealthily, peered at his watch and learnt that it was nearly eight o'clock, slipped out of bed and into his dressing gown, then crept across the room and went out on the balcony. He was anxious not to disturb Shirley, who needed more sleep than he did, but now he was wide awake and wanted a cigarette. The fine June morning was windless and already fairly warm.

This had been their first night in the *Pavilion Henri Quatre,* at St. Germain-en-Laye, where they had a truly splendid bedroom, probably appallingly expensive, but to be paid for out of his Coronet Theatre profits. It was not the first night of their honeymoon; they had spent five days in Paris, at the Ritz, as Bojo's guests; and it had been Shirley who had most firmly declared that they must get out of Paris, much as she was ready to love it, get away from Bojo, sweet though he was, and be by themselves somewhere quiet. Then Sir Michael had remembered St. Germain, perched on its bluff, with its terrace and sweep of forest. He had rung up the *Pavilion* and demanded a truly splendid room with its balcony hanging over the Seine valley. He had not asked what it would cost because Shirley would have wanted to know and might then have said at once that the Stratherricks, whatever the Coronet might be doing, did not throw money away as if they were Aghamazars. (It was her belief—and she never lost it—that in this respect Bojo, Prince Aghamazar, had a bad influence on Michael, who was careless enough about money without trying to compete with an income of millions.) He had now discovered—not at all to his regret; it amused him and added a spice to their relations— that behind Shirley's still incredible naiad or heroine-of-mythology appearance was a formidable armoury of sharp feminine common sense.

Sir Michael began to think about his wife, though still staring down appreciatively at the wide scene below, now emerging from the haze of a fine June morning into the miraculous light of the *Ile de France*: the winding Seine divided by the long railway viaduct, the woods way over on the left, the red-roofed villas in the middle distance, the nearer suburbs of Paris rising smokily on the hill, the city itself etched along the Eastern horizon. Alone for once, feeling detached, almost poised in mid-air facing the capital city of the amorous and the erotic, he thought of Shirley now, and really for the first time, in terms of making love. In this matter he had thought himself beyond surprise, but she had surprised him. Whatever might happen in their bed encounters, her hold on his imagination would remain, and over and above that, or below it, he loved the girl, as he knew when he had asked her to marry him. But he had assumed, not too happily, that either she would be shy, awkward, difficult, possibly frigid, or she would be, on this level of encounter, exactly like most of the others, whose names and faces he was beginning to forget, just another babbling, moaning, scratching, biting, hot and suddenly tiresome victim and prisoner of feminine sexuality. And she had been neither, would always, he was ready to swear, be neither. It might be something in her, it might be some unexpected change in him, but though she was responsive and ardent, eager to learn, refusing nothing, he knew already that somehow she could not be taken finally, would not surrender utterly, rejected any transformation into yet another impersonal victim and prisoner, no matter how often and with what passion he made love to her. It was as if he went further and further into an enchanting country that could never be conquered, never know a contemptuous army of occupation. He suspected already that during the day she would take firmer and firmer lines, start bossing him about, keep such a sharp eye on what they spent that soon he would have to begin lying and cheating a little, and by the time he wanted a quiet life he would probably be trying to share a house with three or four crazy adolescents; but he knew that whenever they met nakedly as man and woman, she would remain this magically desirable and tantalising being. It had taken him forty-eight years to discover that a lot of old platitudes were startlingly true.

Having finished his cigarette, he slipped back through the drawn curtains, saw that Shirley was awake, and pulled them a little apart to see her all the better.

She smiled at him. 'Hello, darling. What's it like out there?'

'Wonderful. Just as good as that walk along the terrace last night. We could have breakfast out here.'

'What time is breakfast?'

'Whenever we telephone to say we want it.'

She sat up, did something to her hair, immediately removed the crumpled sleepiness from her face, and looked beautiful, out of mythology again. She smiled and opened her arms. 'Then there's no hurry, is there? Come here.'

Sir Michael went there.

23

THE ROOM WAS new of course, in fact still reeked of paint; and Sir George noticed, not for the first time, that building and decorating in London were now merely a rough sketch of what they had been in his youth. (When he had looked in a few days earlier, he had found two youths, sadly in need of a haircut, languidly painting bookshelves to the accompaniment of a transistor set.) But everything was in its place, and of the right size and quality—the carpet, the desk, the three chairs, the two telephones. Joan Drayton had her little room outside, guarding him, just as she had done at DISCUS. He was about to call her in, not for any particular purpose but just to see if everything worked all right, when she forestalled him by announcing that he had a visitor—Sir Finlay Avon.

'Morning, Drake. Looked in make sure everything in order.' Sir Finlay seemed thinner, sharper, more staccato, than ever, now that he was at work, not at play. 'Let's see—what are you?'

'I'm Organic Molecular Chemistry,' Sir George told him. 'New to me, of course, but I'm hoping to read it up so that I can understand what these scientific fellows will be talking about.'

'Not possible. Time we understand it, all out of date. Sound administration same everywhere, though.'

'I entirely agree, Avon. But I don't mind telling you I'm very glad to get away from all that DISCUS stuff—music and painting and drama and God knows what. Never knew where I was, and neither did most of my staff. It was like trying to administer a lot of moonshine, with more than half the people you had to deal with more than half out of their minds. Now I'm looking forward to running a sound sensible department bringing me into touch with sound sensible people.'

'Not so sure,' said Sir Finlay. 'Scientists queer customers. Out of their labs, apt to intrigue, pull and push, jockey for power. Keep eye on them, Drake—sharp eye.'

'I will, Avon, and thanks for warning me. I must read What's-his-name—Snow.' Now he went closer—they were both standing up—and lowered his voice. 'I don't know if I have you to thank for my getting this new department—'

'Not specially, no, Drake. Opinion asked, though, when name came up. Said I thought sound administrator. DISCUS impossible job.'

'I'm very grateful. I was worried for a time. To be frank, Avon, I thought my wife had offended you when we were dining at *The Musketeer.*'

'Glad to have been there. Know now—too expensive, too hot, too much food on fire. Your wife did you no harm. Outside domestic affairs, never take least notice what any woman says. Good rule— recommend it, Drake. Always assume they talk like imbeciles in company. Don't know what they're saying. Don't care. Now what about staff? You complete here?'

'Clerical and executive grades—yes. But I'm still short of an assistant I was promised.'

'Let me think.' Sir Finlay closed his eyes, thought, then opened them. 'Quite right, Drake. One Principal, allotted to department as your assistant. Ought to be here now. Must run along. Don't complain about room. All the same. Poor workmanship. Bad materials—muck. Some woodwork cracking already. Gone beyond end real civilisation. Higher Education for what? Lunch sometime, Drake. 'Bye!'

Sir George followed him to the door and, when he had gone, said to Joan: 'I gather from Sir Finlay Avon that I have an assistant— probably a Principal. He might be wanting to report any time now. I'll be here until it's time for lunch.'

'Have you anything to do, Sir George, because I haven't? And I don't like it.'

'Don't worry, Joan. You'll be working your head off again, quite soon. When I've made sure I've got everything I need in my room, I'll probably dictate a preliminary staff memo—loyalty to the department, everybody on their toes, that sort of thing. New urgently important work we'll be doing—and so forth. Try to make everybody feel keen as mustard. That's how I feel, after that nonsense and shambles at DISCUS—'

'Oh, Sir George, I'm missing it, I really am.'

'You wait, Joan. Different thing altogether.' He produced a short but triumphant laugh. 'Now—as some of you people like to say— we're *with it*. Ha ha!'

Remembering first how helpful and friendly Sir Finlay had been, he spent a happy half-hour pottering around his new room and going through all the drawers in his desk. Now and again he thought about Alison, who had been moody ever since that fiasco of a Farewell Party, but he felt he would be able to reassure her, bring her into line with him again, now that he had settled in here. And he was wondering, still happily, if he might safely ask her to call for him here, perhaps to add a few feminine touches to this room, when Joan rang through. 'He's here—your assistant—rank of Principal—'

Frowning, unable to imagine why Joan should sound so bubbling and giggly, he replaced his receiver slowly and carefully.

And then Sir George heard somebody saying: 'Well, we don't know much about this either, do we? But it'll be a change.'

It was Kemp.

Also available from Great Northern Books:

Low Notes on a High Level
A Frolic
by J.B. Priestley

The world's greatest composer, Stannsen of Norroland has completed his Tenth Symphony and to coincide with the official visit of Norroland's President to Britain he has offered the honour of its world premiere to the English Broadcasting Company Symphony Orchestra, and its outlandish and moderately-talented principal conductor, Sir Lancelot Telly. The Royal Festival Hall is booked, Royalty is invited, there is a heatwave of publicity, but there is a huge problem: Stannsen's score includes a part for a seven-foot-high instrument called the Dobbophone, invented and played by his former best friend Dobb. The two men have fallen out and Stannsen hopes his symphony will reconcile them. Dobb refuses to participate and without him there can be no performance. There is panic and dismay at the E.B.C., not least for Sir Lancelot who sees his chance of fame slipping away from him. Enter the beautiful Inga Dobb, niece of the instrument's inventor and goddaughter of Stannsen who will attempt to break the deadlock between the two men and reunite them as friends. Will she succeed? Will the performance go ahead? Will Sir Lancelot conduct this great symphony?

Demonstrating Priestley's love of music along with his playfulness and versatility as a writer, this zany and at times anarchic romp satirises the contemporary world of broadcast media, its avant-garde playwrights and poets, its philistine administrators and its inane panel games and their too receptive audiences.

As our national broadcaster comes in for ever increasing scrutiny, this is very much a novel for today.

'*Fun ... written in the old comic spirit.*' **Glasgow Herald**

'*A highly spiced extravaganza ... Sheer rollicking entertainment.*'
Evening Herald (Dublin)

J. B. Priestley titles from Great Northern Books:

Novels

Angel Pavement
Bright Day
Lost Empires
The Good Companions
Low Notes on a High Level
Sir Michael and Sir George

Non-fiction

English Journey
Delight

Biography

Priestley at Kissing Tree House: A Memoir
by Rosalie Batten
J. B. Priestley's Personal Secretary 1968-1984

Britain Speaks
J.B. Priestley broadcasts to the World
by Austin Mitchell

www.greatnorthernbooks.co.uk